I0672823

THE MOHICANS OF PARIS

MONSIEUR JACKAL

*

Novels You Must Not Miss

Crown 8vo.   Cloth.   7s. 6d. net.

At all Libraries

Jacob's Well   PIERRE BENOIT

Considered by the French critics as the most virile book
yet written by the author of " The Queen of Atlantis," this
novel has sold in France to the tune of three hundred
thousand copies.

Eros   J. A. T. LLOYD

A powerful novel by the author of " Prestige," which was
described by *The Times* as " a ' New Grub Street ' up-to-
date, written with a greater vivacity than George Gissing."

The Shooting Party   ANTON CHEKHOV

This is the only long story that Chekhov wrote, and it is
now given to English readers for the first time. To those
who have seen " The Cherry Orchard," and read his short
stories, the publication of this book will be a literary event.
It is translated and has an Introduction by A. E. Chamot.

According to Jill   NORA K. STRANGE

The fourth novel by the author of " An Outpost Wooing "
and " A Wife in Kenya." It is in a somewhat different
vein to her previous work, and will certainly be pronounced
her best book.

John's Penelope   BARONESS ALBERT D'ANETHAN

An absorbingly human story set in Japan. It could only
have been written by one who has lived in intimate relation
with the Japanese for many years. The description of the
earthquake is masterly.

Summer Bachelors   WARNER FABIAN

Another daring book by the author of " Flaming Youth "
(240th thousand) and " Sailors' Wives." The naked truth
about the American " smart set."

A Riff Bride   L. NOEL

A romance of the Riffs, by the author of " The Caid."
Owing to the great interest focussed on Morocco at the
moment, this story of love and adventure is going to be
very popular.

Trample the Lilies   CHARLOTTE MANSFIELD

A modern romance of England and Spain written as the
result of a year's sojourn in unknown Galacia, the most
beautiful of Spanish provinces.

London : Stanley Paul & Co., Ltd., 8 Endsleigh Gardens

The Mohicans of Paris

Monsieur Jackal

by
ALEXANDRE DUMAS
Author of " The Neapolitan Lovers," " Love and Liberty,"
" A Life's Ambition," etc.

A NEW TRANSLATION.
EDITED, WITH AN INTRODUCTION
by
R. S. GARNETT

WILDSIDE PRESS

CONTENTS

EDITOR'S INTRODUCTION

WHEN my publishers lately asked me for " a new Dumas —a long one, please," I thought naturally of "Les Mohicans de Paris." At the same time I remembered how the sight of the book had stupefied my friend Joseph Conrad, who, just then, was trying to complete a novel in one volume.

I was then living in a house in the quadrangle of the British Museum, Bloomsbury. The rules of that Institution then allowed anyone so resident to send to the Library for books. These having been searched out, were carried round to the house. On one occasion I felt moved to ask for " Les Mohicans de Paris " in the first edition. Conrad and I happened to be standing talking at a front window, when a man clad in a very short alpaca jacket which threatened at each step to fly into fragments—a man with his chin on the top of a pile of volumes and his clasped hands at the bottom of the same—slowly approached in our direction.

" My dear fellow, what is that? " asked Conrad.

" A man with a book for me," I replied.

" *A* book? "

" ' Les Mohicans de Paris,' by Dumas."

" Excuse me, my dear Garnett," said Conrad, " it is not ONE book of Dumas, but his *Oeuvres Complètes* that are being carried here."

" What do you bet? " asked I.

" Anything you like. I am sure of winning."

" And so am I."

We went round to the hall door, where presently the man arrived. Conrad's stupefaction was comic to witness as he saw, when we had completely unloaded the unhappy official, that the cover of each volume bore the title

" Les Mohicans de Paris."

He never forgot this " adventure," as he called it, and would occasionally ask me :

" How far have you read now? "

Had Conrad opened the book he would have found a vast margin and many blank pages. Still, making due allowances, the romance is sufficiently lengthy even for Dumas and my publishers.

But if my publishers want a lengthy romance they must, of course, have it. The only stipulation I make is that they cannot have it in one volume.

This version of " Les Mohicans " will, in fact, be in several volumes, but as the romance is what is known in France as " un roman aux tiroirs," the reader will, it is hoped, proceed from volume to volume like a bee flying from flower to flower and like the bee sipping honey all the time.

How did Dumas come to write it? Well, I have made some researches and I have convinced myself that it was in this way. Having founded his journal, " Le Mousquetaire," he had to make an announcement of forthcoming stories wherewith to attract subscribers. Alexandre had the proof before him when, as I have brought myself to believe, a caller with an idea for a romance was announced. After the usual exchange of compliments, I think they must have conversed as follows :

" Let us see your idea, *Monsieur*," said Dumas to the caller.

" It is a magnificent one, M. Dumas. Has it ever occurred to you in what manner cats disappear in Paris? "

" Cats? "

" Yes, cats."

" *Diable!* " exclaimed Dumas. " It is true! A friend of mine lost a favourite one . . . an Angora . . . as lately as last Thursday."

" Exactly."

" Did you st—that is, do you know what became of it? "

" I can guess, M. Dumas. It was the victim, no doubt, of my killer of cats."

" Of your killer of cats? "

" Certainly. Of the gentleman who is to be, under your favour, the hero of your new romance."

Dumas became intrigued. He reflected that no other novelist, either ancient or modern, had had such a hero.

" This is very interesting to me," he exclaimed. " Develop your killer of cats. What kind of man is he? "

" He smells very strong of Valerian."

" Of Valérien? "

" Exactly. It is the same thing."

" But Valérien was a Roman Emperor who reigned between 252 and 260 B.C. and was made prisoner by the Persians."

" I know nothing of him, M. Dumas. I am not a *savant* like you. The valerian I mean is a herb, the root of which has a strong smell beloved of cats."

" The best proof that you are not a *savant*," replied Dumas, " is that you have just taught me something I did not know. Proceed. You can't imagine how much you interest me."

" Well, M. Dumas, I have little more to say. The hero of your romance . . . a man of the people—his pockets full of valerian, spends his nights in Paris killing cats. This is my idea for your next romance."

" And an excellent one," declared Dumas benevolently. " I will consider it. *Au revoir mon cher confrère.*"

But the " Confrère " was not to be so easily disposed of.

" Pardon me, M. Dumas," persisted he, " but when will the romance appear? "

" When it is written, Parbleu ! "

" But when will that be? "

" My dear *Monsieur,* you must know one thing and that is my romances are never written until they have been announced."

" Then the announcement? . . ."

" Will appear to-morrow," promised Dumas, who was overdue at a rehearsal, and taking his pen, he added to the announcement proof which lay on the table :

" *Les Nuits de Paris par un tueur des Chats.*"

On seeing this done, the " confrère " of Alexandre Dumas took his leave, enchanted.

As witness, if I err, a full copy of the announcement as it appeared on the fourth page of " Le Mousquetaire " :—

L E   M O U S Q U E T A I R E
PAR ALEXANDRE DUMAS
JOURNAL ARTISTIQUE QUOTIDIEN LITTÉRAIRE

Contenant en Causeries, Romans, Nouvelles du Monde et du Théâtre la matière d'un tiers de volume par jour.

Esprit de d'Artagnan, loyauté d'Athos, vigueur de

Porthos, finesse d'Aramis, le Mousquetaire réunit qui s'éparpille d'ordinaire dans les autres feuilles.

ENGAGEMENTS LITTÉRAIRES
PUBLICATIONS NOUVELLES

POUR COMMENCER DEC. 25 AU 30 JANVIER 1854

EL SALTÉADOR, Roman de Cape et d'Epée du temps
de *Charles-Quint* - - - - quatre volumes
PAR ALEXANDRE DUMAS

LE MARÉCHAL FERRANT, Roman historique du
temps Louis XIV faisant suite à la série des
*Mousquetaires, de Vingt ans après et du Vicomte de
Bragelonne* - - - - quatre volumes
D'ALEXANDRE DUMAS.

POUR PARAÎTRE SUCCESSIVEMENT

LES CRIMES INVISIBLES - - - - par *Mèry*
LES ROSES BLEUES - - - - par *Alph. Karr*
LE CHEMIN LE PLUS LONG - par *Alex. Dumas Fils*
PLACIDE LE FILIBUSTIER - - par *Paul Bccage*
UN ROMAN - - - - - par *George Sand*
L'ILLUSTRE BRISACIER - - par *Gerard de Nerval*
LA DUCHESSE DE KINGSTON - par *la Csse D'Ash*
PORTRAITS DRAMATIQUES ET FOYERS
DE THÉATRE - - - - - par *Lockroy*
LES NUITS DE PARIS - par un Tueur des Chats

CRITIQUE ET REVUE des THÉATRES, paraissant
le lendemain des représentations, par Alfred Asseline
EN COURS DE PUBLICATION
LES MÉMOIRES DE M. ALEXANDRE DUMAS
20 *VOLUMES*
LA VIE ET LES AVENTURES DE LA PRINCESSE
DE MONACO. 4 VOLUMES

Most of Dumas's author friends failed him, and to our
loss he failed to continue the " Vicomte de Bragelonne,"
but had he not always the famous idea about the killer
of cats to fall back on ! Now Dumas justly prided himself on his talent for making a silk purse from a sow's
ear. He had found the idea for his " Count of Monte-
Cristo " in an incoherent short story called " The

Diamond and the Vengeance," and one of his most suc-
cessful comedies was the outcome of his sitting through
the first and only performance of a tragedy by a rival
dramatist. I think that the apparent impossibility of
making anything out of the killer of cats must have provoked him to try; probably he reasoned in this way :

If such a stupid fellow as my " confrère " appears to
be, could find in Paris such a singular character as a man
who makes his living by enticing cats with valerian,
killing them and selling their fur to furriers and their
bodies to restauranteurs, who serve them up as hares,
why should not I, Alexandre Dumas, find a host of
equally queer people and write a romance of the under-
world? Fenimore Cooper's " The Last of the Mohicans "
so enthralled the public in the days of my youth that the
name " Mohicans " was given to a class in Paris difficult
to describe but perfectly well known. I will write a
romance of Paris as it was when I was five-and-twenty.
And to interest myself the more, and by way of contrast
to the killers of cats and the like personages, I will introduce myself and certain of my old friends as characters.
After all, Paris is the most wonderful city in the
world. . . .

Dumas found ample material, and the announcement
" LES NUITS DE PARIS PAR UN TUEUR DES
CHATS, 2 volumes,"
actually gave place to that of
" LES MOHICANS DE PARIS, 32 volumes."

Naturally, Dumas's " confrère " was much astonished
to find his killer of cats introduced into the opening
chapters of " Les Mohicans " (where you will find him
and his valerian, dear reader), and it is the fact that later
on he was heard to declare that his magnificent idea had
been spoilt by the great romancer.

I think that this proprietor of an idea must have been
the only person in Paris disappointed in " Les Mohicans "
as it appeared day by day in the *feuilleton* of " Le Mousquetaire." No other writer in those days, or it may be
conjectured in any, so enchained the interest of the public
as did Dumas—*" le roi de feuilleton."* Read what de
Villemessant, the editor of the " Figaro," wrote of him
in 1872 :—

" What was remarkable above all in Dumas, and it
explains his long *vogue* and his great popularity, is this :

he addressed himself to every intellect and knew how to set every string in vibration under his pen; bursts of laughter alternated with tears; the author of the " Impressions de Voyage," that *chef d' œuvre* of wit and humour, has also signed one of the most moving pages of modern literature :—I speak of the article that he published on the death of the Duke of Orleans in which he recalls his own mother's death; he was kneeling at her bedside when suddenly he felt a hand on his shoulder, and looking up saw the pale and agitated countenance of the Duke who had come to grasp his hand.

" The recollection of this article impresses me even now; I recall that I read it while in my bath, and my emotion was such—I cried to such an extent that I feared I should make the bath overflow.

" In those days we all impatiently watched at the window for the arrival of the porter with the newspaper —we wanted to learn as soon as possible how the author would extricate himself from such and such an incident interrupted on the previous day by these words : ' La suite à demain '; in family circles nothing but the romance of the moment was talked of, and they discussed from morning to night the fate reserved by the writer for such and such a personage.

" I myself had the habit of reading my *feuilleton* in my bed ; and if it had failed me on any occasion I should have got up in the middle of the night to procure it at any price."

This testimony to the popularity of Dumas from the man who so frequently disbursed tenpence a line for the serial rights of his romances is overwhelming. And it is delightful, too, for Dumas never wrote a story the influence of which was not a healthy one.

" Les Mohicans " has had many editions—one beautifully illustrated by Phillipoteaux. And the critics? They had nothing to urge against the new romance which they had not urged against its predecessors, in allusion to which their chief, Sainte-Beuve, wrote :

" As for Dumas, all the world knows his prodigious *verve,* his easy *entrain,* his happy *mise en scène,* his witty overflowing dialogue, his light narration which runs without pausing and which knows how to clear obstacles and annihilate space without ever failing. He covers immense canvasses without ever fatiguing either his pen or his reader." Another great critic, Jules Lemaître, endorsed this when he said that Dumas possessed the wonderful quality of stringing out his narrative to the crack of doom, and at the same time making it appear to move with headlong rapidity.

"Les Mohicans," begun just ten years after "Les Trois Mousquetaires" and "Monte-Cristo," seems with its vigour, ease and freshness to have charmed its readers just as did those epics. Dumas, of course, in writing of Paris in 1827, was on very secure ground. This time he needed to consult no historical documents, to study no manners of a past age—he had only to consult his memory. With the bold astuteness that characterised him by inviting his readers to follow him into a *tapis-franc,* or low cabaret, where he was hardly treated "like a young prince come to visit his father's subjects," as Thackeray says, he challenged comparison with Sue's "Mystères de Paris." Sue's readers, taking him seriously, had trooped off to HIS *tapis-franc,*[1] "Le Lapin Blanc," in search of La Gouailleuse, Chourineur, Maitre d'École and the rest of the characters, only to find that they never existed. Dumas's characters, on the contrary, modelled on types in every section of Society, could perfectly well have been found each in the right quarter of Paris. Sue's facts and figures may have been carefully got together, but as he could do nothing with human beings, he invented inhuman ones.

Here, I have no doubt, some of my readers will be thinking that I am overlooking Dumas's gift of imagination, but this is not so. "Les Mohicans" abounds with imaginative touches, usually of a dramatic kind—every work of Dumas does—but they are perfectly in accord with human nature. And his *mise-en-scène* is always simple and taken from the next street. Unlike Victor Hugo, he needed no Notre-Dame or tomb of Charlemagne to set off his characters. Does he need an ecclesiastic, he gives us a simple Abbé, not a Bishop Myriel. Nevertheless, he did invent a character then new to French fiction—a detective. Yes, his M. Jackal, whose advice "en tout, cherchez la femme" was caught up over all Paris, to be quoted all the world over, was the fore-

---

[1] *Tapis* is an abbreviation of the old word *tapinet,* a hiding or hidden place. *Franc* is an allusion to the guests who were *affranchis,* that is liberated thieves.

runner of the M. Lecoq of Gaboriau, of the Sherlock Holmes of Conan Doyle *et hoc genus omne.*

Cherchez la femme! " The women all the time ! One cannot take a step without meeting them on one's road," wrote Denis Diderot. Says a misanthropic French writer, Alfred Delvau, who was applauded by all women haters, " ' The women all the time.' They are entangled with everything in life. They interfere in everything. They are in everything. They are the eternal subjects of discussion and of dispute. When two mountains give battle to each other it is because of them. When two friends quarrel it is because of them again. When two men cut each other's throat, it is still because of them. When a revolution takes places in any part of the world, whatsoever, it is they who have caused it. There have been three or four hundred Trojan wars since the first, and there will yet be some thousands of others. All the women are Helens and all the men are Greeks, without playing with words. Handsome Paris was an invention of old Homer. Helen would have had herself carried off by Menelaus himself rather than not be carried off at all."

Dumas knew better ! . Women to him were ever charming and by him were ever charmed. To attempt to analyse or generalise about the sex seemed to him supremely absurd. Life to him was full of good things and he grasped them with both hands. . . . To him, then, M. Jackal was something of a monstrosity and his eternal pursuit of the woman as the wanted criminal an obsession.

I have touched on Dumas's popularity in his own time. This was incontestable; what was contested was his future. It was insisted that books so numerous and apparently written so easily and certainly so brilliantly, could not *live*—certain critics compared the stories to fruits which having ripened quickly as quickly decayed. And, indeed, I doubt whether anyone, except indeed Dumas himself, would have predicted with any confidence that many of his tales would be read by generations in the next century. That this would be the case, not merely in France but all the world over, possibly Dumas himself failed to imagine. It was forgotten that when a character becomes alive, death cannot clutch him. Becky Sharp cannot die, Mr. Samuel Pickwick cannot die, Jane Eyre cannot die, Mrs. Proudie cannot die, the four Musketeers cannot die, Chicot cannot die, the Count of Monte-Cristo cannot die.   The Count, indeed, is the only deceased person whose former existence really interests in the South of France.   Napoleon I may not have existed—*possible*—but the Count of Monte-Cristo! The first person met with in the *Midi* will tell you the least fact about him with the greatest detail.   How Dumas contrived to create so many real people is a mystery which will never be solved.   It was one of the sorrows of his critics that not only could they not do the like, but they could not explain how it was done.   I do not know either, but let us notice Dumas's procedure in the present romance and we may learn something.

He takes a simply enormous canvas—32 volumes.   And with the firmest of handling he begins by painting a tiny bit of Paris on a carnival night, placing three characters in the foreground.   He uses each character to explain the other by contrast.   Directly we know them—but not an instant before—he moves them into action.   But what action!   He knows exactly to a hair's breadth where they stood, how they looked, how they behaved, of what they thought.   And he convinces the reader—*how* is the mystery—of the truth of his every word.   Why?   Because he has convinced himself before beginning to write.   But reality is not enough for Dumas; he must have romance and poetry as well, and at the instant that reality is choking the reader, presto! romance and poetry enter and charm him.   In place of the suffocating atmosphere of a cabaret, the degrading episodes of a fight, we have air, space, moonlight, the peculiar, enchanting atmosphere of Paris pervading all—then mystery, beauty, love—the unknown, the unattainable, for which every created being at times long.   Dumas, the Wizard of the South, leads his readers from wonder to wonder—and observe that each succeeds the other inevitably—but the reader is unconscious of being led—it is he who, as Jean Davy or as Ludovic, or as Pétrus, is leading; Dumas has contrived by a species of hypnotic suggestion to transform each of the intelligent and deserving among his readers into the skin of one or other of his characters.   I remember a family who, when "The Three Musketeers" was being read aloud to it, chose which character he or she was—before the reading could far proceed each had to ! Until it was established for all time that Mr. Sam Johnson was D'Artagnan, that his three younger brothers, Henry, Peter and Reginald, were Athos, Porthos and Aramis respectively, that his sister Alice was Miladi and his sister Eveline, Mme Bonacieux, that house was a house of discord. In like manner it will not be Salvator who will be living in the little white house in the rue St. André-des-Arcs, but you, Mr. Jones, my reader, who are so doing, and are in love with Fragola; it will not be Fragola who has golden hair and cherry lips, it will be you, my dear Miss Smith, another esteemed reader, who possesses those beauties and who, very creditably and entirely naturally, are in love with Salvator.

During the Great War a stranger—a military celebrity of somewhat awful dignity—condescended to visit the ancestral home of a Baronet. He arrived very late at night, apparently in a very bad humour, and asked to be shown to his room at once. There the trembling menial who had conducted him ventured to tell him that another guest, a certain distinguished officer, had sat up to see him.

" Say I am much obliged but he had better go to bed," vociferated the celebrity. " Here ! Bring me ' The Three Musketeers ' at once ! "

The affrighted menial managed to leave the room and to falter down the staircase into the smoking-room, where awaited him the Baronet his master.

" Well? " asked he.

" He wants three mosquitos brought him immediate," answered the menial.

" Three mosquitos? In his bedroom ! "

" Yes, Sir Charles ; that's what he said."

" You are an idiot. Take him this book from me and say that I am in the middle of the second volume."

At breakfast the next morning a gratified guest greeted his host genially and showed him, with the aid of the slop bowl, sugar tongs and salt cellar, how the Musketeers had held the bastion of Saint-Gervais.

To hold the attention of English military potentates and Baronets, of whom it may be observed Dumas knew nothing, his romances must have some special quality, and if I am asked to say what it is, I must reply that it is " Charm." And I think that our author charms partly because he saw, knew and loved his creations from the first to the last. Never does one of them say a word or take a step that is not his own word or step, the reason being that to his creator he is a real person who can by no possibility do otherwise, any more than can Mr. Lloyd George talk like Mr. George Robey or Miss Rebecca West swing a racket like Mlle Lenglen. For this reason Dumas's characters are individuals who interest. It is humiliating, when we come to think of it, how few novelists can create many really different characters—a dozen or so and they are at an end—the rest have a family resemblance to each other or to the author. Dumas created hundreds of characters who are all different and who resemble him in no sort of way.

Need I add that Dumas's enchanting art of narrative and his brilliant dialogue are unsurpassed by any more modern writer? Dante Gabriel Rossetti wrote of him as "the sole descendant of Shakespear." Probably Rossetti did not know it, but, as a matter of fact, "Hamlet" captured Dumas when he was a young man, and all his life through he was a devotee of the Swan of Avon. Hence, the Shakespearian infusion in Dumas's works—realism intermingled with romance—hardly to be so largely found in any other writer.

I should explain that, to assist the reader's comprehension of the complications of the story, the interpolated episodes will each be contained in a single chapter, and that in this adaptation rather than translation I have altered the name of one of the characters from " Jean Robert " to " Jean Davy "; Robert being a Christian name in this country and Davy being one of Dumas's own names and one under which he occasionally wrote, it seemed to me reasonable to give it to the character who is Dumas himself thinly disguised. In giving us the character of Jean Davy, did Dumas describe himself as he really was? On the evidence of a friend of his, he did. Let the reader compare his description of Jean Davy in Chapter I of " Les Mohicans " with the following portrait from the graphic pen of the novelist known as the " Comtesse Dash " :

" Alexandre Dumas was superbly built—a finer figure and a more gracious presence it would have been difficult to meet with. Everyone knows his great height—his hand and foot were extraordinarily small. In those days,

2

at certain balls, kneebreeches were still worn. Dumas willingly donned them and showed a pair of legs which would have gained him many ' Bonnes fortunes ' in the 18th century. He had very beautiful blue eyes of the colour of a sapphire and the radiance also. His expression was mobility itself." And she adds : " He loved the weak. He supported tiresome friends for years because he was necessary to them. He ran all over Paris to help them, passed his nights by their bedsides, watched over them, changed their linen, lifted them, worked near them—worked above all. It was not seldom that he passed forty-eight hours without sleep. He was a Titan."

As, thanks to the popularity of our author, this book will be read in China and Peru, I must add a few words to Chinese and Peruvians about the cabarets of Paris, in one of which the reader, in company with Dumas, will shortly find himself. Readers of '' Le Mousquetaire '' did not need to be told why Bordier's was full to overflowing, and why Jean Davy and his friends went much as a matter of course to a cabaret after their evening's amusement. A Parisian feels the need to do so. Why? Because he is a Parisian, of course. But why? . . . Well, I don't know of any other reason unless it is necessary that the waiters, who largely compose the population of the City of Paris, should earn their livelihood, and how could they do so if the cafés were empty of customers? If that reason is not convincing, I must add, although loath to do so, that a Parisian " salon," or sitting-room, is the last place in the world where anyone sits. It usually contains a bust of an ancestor, a hard sofa, two rows of chairs and a marble clock, with no hope of any food or drink. It is the salon, and rather than sit in it, the Parisian hies to his café, where, in the open air if he pleases, he eats, drinks, smokes, chats, reads, writes, plays dominoes and does everything, in short, except go to bed. Were all the cafés to close their doors simultaneously, the people would at once open as many new ones.

Bordier's was one of those *tapis-francs* which from its situation hard by the Markets was permitted to be open all night, the idea in the minds of the guileless authorities being that, otherwise, the six thousand country people arriving in the small hours with their produce, and the market porters, would perish of hunger and thirst. As a matter of fact, the thrifty country folk brought their own provender with them and drank at the pump. I say nothing of the porters—and Bordier's, Barattés, Paul Niquet's and other like establishments were thronged by revellers who had done the theatres or were doing the town. It was not until 1860 that the authorities woke up to this notorious fact, and closed these night haunts at the moment they used to open to be opened at the moment they used to close.

In 1827 there was no gaslight in the streets of Paris, so I beg my readers in China and Peru to imagine when reading Dumas's first chapter a big city full of shadows cast by occasional oil lamps, hanging on strings, and torches carried by more or less fearful pedestrians.[1]

R. S. GARNETT.

[1] My Publishers ask me to add that the next volume of " The Mohicans of Paris," entitled " The Carbonari," is in active preparation.

MONSIEUR JACKAL

CHAPTER I

THE GENTLEMEN OF THE MARKET

THE *mardi gras*[1] of 1827—a miserably gloomy, foggy day—was nearly over. In fact, midnight was about to overtake the three young men who were afoot arm-in-arm in that unsavoury spot, the rue St. Denis. Two of them were singing the most popular of the ditties they had heard at the Coliseum that evening; the third contented himself with sucking the gold knob of his cane.

The two singers were attired in the then favourite Carnival disguise of market porters.

I have a certain reason for remembering the dress of the third man, though five and twenty years have passed since I last saw it. Taller by a head than his companions and seemingly older, certainly graver than they, he was wrapped in one of those large brown cloaks with velvet collar which were then fashionable, but are now only to be seen on the frontispieces of Chateaubriand's or Byron's works. Under his cloak he wore black trousers, tight enough to set off his shapely leg and fine ankle; his small foot was neatly arrayed in silk sock and varnished pump; though it was obvious that he had no connection with the

---

[1] Shrove Tuesday.

Army his black coat was buttoned in military style, showing an edge of white piqué waistcoat above and below; round his neck he wore a black satin cravat and on his head of curly hair a crush hat, to be shut up and carried flat under the arm at a ball or expanded to its full height and worn like a " topper."

Everything was of superfine elegance and could only have been made by one of the tailors of the boulevard du Gand accustomed to satisfy the exacting demands of the young " dandies " as they were then called, or, to use to-day's expression, young " lions." Yet, strangely enough, their wearer was no dandy: his bearing was too independent, his movements too free to suggest a mere slave to his clothes. He had torn off his gloves on leaving artist friends in the rue Ste. Appoline as if the restraint were irksome. On his first finger was a large seal ring.

His companions' dress strikingly contrasted with his own Byronic attire. Their idea of a market porter's habiliments was carnivalesque—satin trousers with blue and white stripes, plush waistcoats with cerise collars, one wearing a red scarf round his waist and the other a yellow; silk stockings with gold clocks and shoes with diamond buckles. They were be-ribboned from head to foot and on their hats were wreaths of red and white camellias, the smallest of which at this time of year must have cost at least a crown. With flushed cheeks and laughing eyes they seemed the joyous spirit of the past, while their companion, in his black clothes, might have been taken to personify the sombre future attending the funeral of the passing hour.

Now what had brought these three oddly assorted young men together, and why were they traversing at midnight one of those fifty muddy streets which cross Paris like a great black furrow from the boulevard St. Denis to the quai de Gèvres? The two "porters," already somewhat heated by their potations, were on their way to a feast of oysters in the Market. The young man in the cloak, having drunk nothing more intoxicating than barley-water and gooseberry wine, was on the way to his home in the rue de l'Université when the masqueraders happened to run into him.

"Why, it's Jean Davy!" cried they in spite of the darkness.

"Ludovic! Pétrus!" replied the man in the cloak, for in 1827 Louis and Pierre, as names, were out of date, and had to be disguised as Ludovic and Pétrus.

All three had then shaken hands; after which Pétrus, who was a painter and Ludovic, who was a doctor, had insisted that Jean Davy, dramatist, should come and sup with them at Bordier's in the Market.

"Bordier's?" I can hear my readers cry. "Bordier's is a confectioner's!"

So it is, but it was not so in 1827, that is in the second year of the reign of Charles X. It was not even a cabaret. It was simply a Thieves' Den.

There were seven such in Paris:—

The *Chat-Noir*, rue de la Vieille Draperie in the city.

The *Lapin-Blanc*, facing the Gymnase.

The *Sept-Billards*, rue de Bondy.

The *Hotel d' Angleterre*, rue St. Honoré, facing the Civette.

Paul Niquet's, rue aux Fers.

Baratte's, in the same street.

And finally, *Bordier's*, at the corner of the rue Aubry-le-Boucher, and the rue St. Denis.

Two of these places had their speciality.

The Chat Noir specialized in burglars and pickpockets while the Lapin Blanc, facing the Gymnase, catered preferably for shoplifters and garrotters. Bordier's, however, opened its hospitable arms to any and every variety of malefactor who could pay for a drink. That these were numerous may be attributed partly to the fact that the *sergents de ville* as known to us had not yet been created, the safety of the city reposing in the hands of five or six inspectors and one officer to each district . . . say, seven men to watch over a whole population of " voleurs à la carouble,"[2] " voleurs à la fourline,"[3] " charrieurs,"[4] " scionneurs," " vantarniers,"[5] to say nothing of released convicts, prostitutes and " bandits " innumerable.

The six inspectors went about their business in civilian clothes and when they made an arrest lodged their prize to start with at the Depôt, where for the sum of sevenpence the first night and fivepence for each succeeding night he could have a room to himself. Inadequate as were these six inspectors, they knew where members of the criminal classes were usually to be found, as do the police of our own day, but they could only make arrests when they caught

---

[2] Thieves with false keys.
[3] Pickpockets.
[4] Sharpers, especially at bureaux for the exchange of coin.
[5] Footpads and garotters.

their criminals " in the act." The law is clear on
this point as thieves realize and they knew they could
enjoy themselves at their houses of call in comfort.
Yet to-day all seven of these places have disappeared.

Bordier's alone has survived; but the Thieves' Den
of 1827 is now an elegant confectioner's, where they
sell sweets and pastries and delicate liqueurs; nothing
whatever remaining of the low cabaret to which we
are forced very apologetically to conduct our readers.

At twenty paces from the rue de Batave, however,
Jean Davy stopped.

" Where did you say we are going to sup?" he
asked.

" At Bordier's," cried Pétrus and Ludovic together.

" At Bordier's?"

" Of course. Why not?"

" Why not? Because there is always time to
change your mind when you are about to do a stupid
thing."

" Stupid?"

" Isn't it stupid to eat cat and drink logwood at a
lowdown place when you might feast like a king at
Véry's or Phillippe's or the Frères Provenceaux!"

" Why are you so contemptuous of cats and logwood, my dear poet?" asked Ludovic.

" You forget, my friend," remonstrated Pétrus.
"Jean Davy has just had a big success at the Théatre-
Français. Why, he is making 500 francs a performance. His pockets are bulging with gold and he has
turned aristocrat."

" Are you pretending that you are going to
Bordier's for economy's sake?"

" No," replied Ludovic. " We want to see a bit of life, old man."

" Where's the necessity ? "

" I donned the guise of a Coster-King to go and have supper in the Market. I've got to within a hundred paces of the place and I mean to sup there or not at all ! "

" Listen to the sawbones ! " said Pétrus. " The hospital and operating table have prepared him for every sort of horror; as a philosopher and materialist he's proof against any surprise. But as a painter I have not invariably supped even off cats and logwood. I'm used to living skeletons, with less brains than your ghastly 'specimens,' old man, and when I haven't had a sou to call my own I've descended to the lion's den and the bearpit for my amusements. So I'm not easily disgusted, thank God ! But our young exquisite here "—he pointed to his tall companion—" our sensitive young genius, our new Byron, our heir to all the Goethes, our Jean Davy here— what's he going to do in that den of thieves ? Look at his little hands and feet, listen to his charming creole accent. Can you see him in that resort of infamy ? Why, he never knew his right foot from his left when drilling ! He won't have the least idea what footing to stand on in our Burglars' Paradise ! And think ! Are his chaste ears, familiar with the lisping lays of Millevoye and Chénier, to be assaulted by the brutalities of pads and prostitutes ? NO ! We will go no further with him. Who is this stranger within our gates ? Get thee behind me, Jean Davy ! "

" My dear Pétrus," replied Davy, smiling at this

diatribe, characteristic of the studios of the time, "my dear chap, you're only half-seas over . . . but you're pure Gascon!"

"Me? I'm from St-Lô! If there are Gascons at St-Lô, then there must be Normands at Tarbes!"

"Well, my Gascon of St-Lô, I tell you you're not so black as you paint yourself! You're ashamed of your own virtues, that's all! You've never been down into the lion's den or the bearpit, and you know nothing whatever about these filthy drinking places in the Market. Neither does Ludovic. Neither do I or any other self-respecting man, be he gentleman or bricklayer."

"Amen!" yawned Pétrus.

"Oh, yawn if you want to! Boast of your imaginary vices! And why? Because you've heard that all great men have them—that André del Sarto was a thief, and Rembrandt a drunkard. Oh, pose if you want to! It's your business to pose. But before us who love you like a brother be and remain yourself, Pétrus."

"Finished, O blackcoat?" asked Pétrus.

"Almost."

"Then on we go!"

Pétrus started off again singing a ribald refrain as if he wanted to prove that Jean Davy's good-natured remonstrances had had no effect on him.

As he reached the last line they entered the Market and half past twelve sounded from the clock tower of St. Eustache.

"Well, where's it to be?" asked Ludovic, who so far had said little. He was a quiet, thoughtful fellow and let himself be led by his friends, sure of finding something to observe wherever he might be. "Where are we going to sup? At Paul Niquet's, Baratte's or Bordier's?"

"At Bordier's," cried Pétrus. "Bordier's was recommended to me and Bordier's it shall be!"

"All right. Let us go to Bordier's," said Jean Davy.

"Unless you have a preference for some other Temple, O chaste nursling of the Muses!"

"You know I have never been here before. Besides, it is only a choice of evils."

"Here we are, then. Is it sufficiently vile to please you?"

"Vile? It is unbelievable!"

"Good! Then let us go in!"

Cocking his hat over one ear, Pétrus swaggered into the place with all the nonchalance of a hardened habitué. His two friends followed him.

CHAPTER II
BORDIER'S AND JOHN BULL

THE cabaret was full and more than full: it was overflowing.

The ground floor—which one would have difficulty in recognising if one saw the charming little shop which stands in its place to-day—the ground floor consisted of a sunken room, smoky, damp, and dirty, where a crowd of men and women in divers costumes swarmed pell-mell. Costers and fishwives predominated. Some of the women, the prettiest and most coquettish, wore their fishwoman's bodices décollettée, and their sleeves turned up above the elbow. They were rouged and patched and by the use of a strong oath or two rather gave the lie to their silk petticoats and caps of lace. Their disguise was double, both of dress and sex, for their voices were deep and bass; yet, oddly enough, they received as much attention as any from the mob of men in carnival mood who made up so great a part of the mob.

They were all shouting, laughing, singing in so much confusion that description is impossible except of such few details as stood out from the mass.

The noisy crowd looked impenetrable. The men's muscular arms seemed to belong to the women's slender bodies, so closely were they crushed together; a bearded head seemed to spring from a voluptuous throat and a coarse, hairy chest to belong to a delicate young Jewess barely fifteen years old! Even Pétrus, had he tried to paint the scene, would have found it impossible to apportion the various arms, legs and feet to the mass of heads and bodies.

The groups that did stand out were a Pierrot who seemed to sleep as he stood against the wall, a little Pierrette sitting astride his shoulders; so that his own head being hidden by the girl's stockings, he seemed to have a tiny one, two short arms and the stature of a giant: a Punchinello who was trying to walk round the room with a child supported on each of his humps; a Turk who was hopping on one leg to prove he was not drunk; a youth dressed as a monkey, bounding from chair to chair; thereby causing the goddess of Folly and the god of Carnival, most lugubrious of all the Heavenly deities, to emit little squeaks of astonishment.

On the three friends entering the room they were greeted with noisy cheers.

The Pierrot stuck out his head from the billowing skirts of his Pierrette. The Punchinello suddenly stopped, like a star that encounters a comet. The Turk tried to lift both legs at the same time, which brought about his downfall and the annihilation of a table that received his weight.

To crown all, the monkey leaped on Pétrus's shoulders and began to pull his costly camellias to pieces.

" Let us go ! " said Jean Davy. " I don't like this place."

" Go? Before we've really got here ? " replied Pétrus. " What are you thinking of ? They'd suppose we were afraid and would chase us through the streets of Paris as His Majesty Charles X chases boars in the forest of Compiègne."

" What do you think ? " asked Jean.

" As we are here, we may as well stay," replied Ludovic.

" Oh, as you please. . . ."

" Attention ! " cried Pétrus. " They have their eyes on us. As a dramatist you know the value of a good entrance ! "

He went to the sort of crater that had opened beneath the unfortunate Turk, of whom nothing could now be seen except his boots and the tip of his aigrette.

" Mr. Mussulman," said he, the monkey still sitting

on his head, "you remember the words of the
Prophet, Mahommed ben Abdallah, nephew of the
great Abou Thaleb, Prince of Mecca?"

"Can't—shay—'do!" hiccoughed a voice from
the depths of the broken table.

"If the mountain won't come to the Prophet, the
Prophet must go to the mountain!"

Seizing the monkey by the scruff of its neck,
Pétrus lifted it from his head as if it had been a hat
and holding it at arm's length, he added:

"Accept, my good Mussulman, my sincere good
wishes."

He then put the child back on his shoulders but it
scurried promptly away, sliding down like a real
monkey from a coco-nut palm and disappearing into
a dark corner. Pétrus' courtesy was greeted with
enthusiastic applause by all but the Turk who was
sparing of words. He seized the hand Pétrus held
out to him as a drowning man might seize a straw
and the painter hauled him onto his feet though they
proved an unstable support. The good Mussulman
was tottering in his faith!

"There are too many people here," said Pétrus.
"Let us go upstairs."

"If you like," said Ludovic, "though for my part,
I find this crowd interesting."

A waiter had been hovering round them ever since
they entered and he now interposed.

"You wish to go upstairs, gentlemen?"

"We may as well."

"The stairs are here, monsieur." He showed
them a ladder that snails might comfortably have

slid up and down but was somewhat inadequate for human beings. However, our three friends essayed the ascent to the accompaniment of jeers and sallies. Not that the company knew why they laughed. Their object was simply to make as much noise as possible for noise to them was almost as intoxicating as liquor.

On the first floor as on the ground floor, the place was full. There was the same mass of people in a smoky room, with torn, greasy paper on the walls and red curtains at the windows. A Greek key pattern straggled across the curtains, picked out in green and yellow.

Viewed from the threshold, this crowd seemed even a degree below even the one downstairs. In the dim light of three or four lamps, it looked like the jumble of horrors haunting the brain of a drunkard.

" Bordier's Hell seems the reverse of Dante's," remarked Jean Davy who was the first to enter. " The higher you go the worse you get."

" Well, what do you think ? " asked Pétrus.

" I think it is horrible—but interesting ! "

" Let us go higher still," suggested Pétrus and Ludovic approved. So the three young men started climbing the ladder once more, finding it narrower and more slippery the further they ascended. On the second floor they found much the same scene, but the ceiling being lower the air was even more nauseating.

" Well ? " asked Ludovic.

" What do you think, Jean Davy ? " demanded Pétrus.

" Let us go higher still," said the poet.

On the third floor, it was even worse. Both on and under the tables and benches were some fifty human beings—if Man still deserves that name when he has descended to the level of the beasts. These fifty creatures, men, women and children, were lying asleep by their broken plates and bottles, all messed with sauce and splashed with wine. The room was exceptionally dark for it was lit by but one lamp resembling, it might have been thought, the solitary lamp left burning in a sepulchre if the hoarse snoring of the sleeping wretches had not shown the topers to be alive, even though their brains were dead.

Jean Davy felt sick; but he controlled himself. His heart might break but his will would not bend. Pétrus and Ludovic exchanged glances. Both were now ready to leave. But Jean Davy, seeing that the ladder, though now straight against the wall, led upward, started to climb again, seeming more at ease than he felt.

"Come along!" he cried. "You wanted to come! Come up higher still!"

They opened the door of the fourth floor room. It looked much the same as the others but the people in it did not. They consisted of five men wearing blouses and smocks seated at a table on which were the remains of a dish of pork and eight or ten bottles, bristling like quills but less symmetrically arranged.

The three friends entered, the waiter who had followed them from floor to floor still hovering behind them. They stopped just inside the door, glancing round the room, and Jean Davy made a sign as if to say:

3

" This is the place for us."

His pantomime was so expressive that Pétrus replied:

" Oh, we shall be housed like princes here ! "

" We shall want for nothing," said Ludovic, " except air to breathe ! "

" Good," replied Pétrus.   "We can get that by opening the window."

" Where would you like the table set, sirs ?" asked the waiter.

" Over there," said Jean Davy pointing to the corner opposite to that which held the five men already sitting in the room.

The ceiling was so low that they had been obliged to take off their hats and even then the head of Jean Davy, as the tallest, touched the ceiling.

" What would you like, sirs ? " asked the waiter.

" Six dozen oysters, six mutton cutlets and an omelette," replied Pétrus.

" Wine, sir ? "

" Three bottles of good Chablis and some seltzer water if you have any."

At this order so typically aristocratic, one of the five other guests turned to stare.

" Oh," said he, " good Chablis and seltzer water, eh ? So we're being honoured by the visit of young lordlings, are we ? "

" Nobs," cried the second.

" Cracksmen at the very least," jeered the third.

All five burst out into a loud laugh. As detective stories and the Memoirs of Vidocq had not as yet familiarized well-bred people with thieves' slang, our

three adventurers did not understand that they were
being taken for the aristocracy of the criminal classes,
so they paid little attention to the laughter that followed these insults. Jean Davy had laid aside his
coat and cane, and the waiter was about to run off to
execute his orders when the man who had called our
friends "lordlings" caught him by the apron.

" We asked for a pack of cards, my friend. Why
have you not brought them ? "

" You know I cannot let you have cards at this
hour."

" Why not, pray ? "

" Ask M. Delavau, the Minister."

" What has he to do with us ? "

" Nothing with you, perhaps, but a lot with us."

" What can he do to you ? "

" Close our establishment; which would mean that
we should not have the pleasure of seeing you here
any more."

" But if we cannot play, what do you expect us to
do here ? "

" You are not bound to remain ! "

" You are not polite. And I shall complain to
the landlord ! "

" Complain to the Pope if you like ! "

" You dare to laugh at me, you——" The man
sprang up, bringing his fist down on the table with
a bang that made the bottles jump, but the waiter had
already flown downstairs and the roysterer sank back
into his seat, waiting for someone else on whom to
wreak his rage.

" He has forgotten I'm John Bull," he murmured,

" and that I could kill an ox with a blow of my fist. I shall have to remind him ! " Seizing a half empty bottle of wine he applied his mouth to the neck and disposed of the contents at one gulp.

" John Bull has a grievance," murmured one of the other four to his neighbour, " and, if I know anything about him, someone will have to pay for it ! "

" If he is in that sort of humour," whispered back his confidant, " those sham aristocrats over there had better look to themselves."

Meanwhile our three friends, with one accord, had made their way to the window. The combined odours of food, wine and tobacco, to say nothing of the more human emanations, made the air of the room almost impossible of respiration by people accustomed to a purer atmosphere. Probably the window had not been opened since the last day of the preceding summer. Pétrus, who was the first to reach it, raised the lower sash and fastened the hook that seemed the only means of keeping it open.

This simple action gave John Bull the excuse he wanted and he now rose from his stool. Planting his fists on the table, he addressed our young friends.

" You have opened that window, monsieur ? "

" As you see, my friend," replied Pétrus.

" I am not your friend ! " roared John Bull. " Shut that window again ! "

" My dear M. Bull," replied Pétrus with ironic courtesy, " my friend Ludovic here, who is a doctor, will tell you in two seconds what elements are indispensable to a hygienic atmosphere."

" Elements ? Hygienic ? " growled John Bull, nonplussed.

" Air, monsieur," explained Ludovic in the same tone of ironic courtesy adopted by Pétrus, " if it is not to be injurious to the lungs of man, should be composed of seventy-five to seventy-six per cent of nitrogen, twenty-two or three per cent of oxygen and two of nitrogen.   A little more or less, that is to say."

" Is he talking Latin? " asked one of John Bull's companions.

" I will talk to him in good round French," cried John Bull.

" Suppose he doesn't understand? "

" Then we will talk in action! "

He clenched his fists, each the size of a baby's head, and in a voice that with men of his own class would have silenced all further opposition, he roared:

" Shut that window!   And make haste about it! "

" Oh, you want that window shut, do you, M. Bull? " said Pétrus, leaning against the sill with his arms crossed.   " Well, as it happens, we do not! "

" So you think you have a right to a voice in the matter, do you? "

" Why not? Every man has a right to his opinion. You seem to think the privilege should be extended to the brute beasts."

" Croc-en-Jambe! "[1] thundered John Bull, addressing one of his cronies who looked like a rag-picker, " I believe that lousy lordling meant to call me a brute!   What shall I do to him? "

" Make him shut the window first—and then knock him on the head."

" I will! "   Turning to our friends he roared: " Shut that window! "

[1] Crook-leg.

" Why ? " asked Pétrus calmly.   " It isn't rain-
ing ! ".

John Bull filled his huge lungs with the air that
seemed unbreathable to our young friends, and did it
with such sudden force that the inhalation sounded
like the snort of the savage animal from whom he took
his name.   Davy, feeling that a brawl was imminent,
tried to avert it, though he feared it was nearly impossible; yet if anyone could bring about peace it
should be he for he was easily the coolest person
present.   He therefore quietly approached John Bull
and used the voice of persuasion.

" I am sorry, sir, but we came in here from the
open and really felt suffocated."

" Of course," said Ludovic.   " There is nothing
to breathe in this room except carbonic acid."

" Please let us have the window open for a few
minutes, just to renew the air.   We will shut it again
after."

" You opened it without my leave."

" What if we did ? " cried Pétrus.

" If you had asked permission I might have allowed
you to open it."

" I opened it to please myself," said Pétrus, " and
I shall keep it open to please myself."

" Be quiet, Pétrus ! " whispered Jean Davy.

" I will not !   Do you think I will be ordered about
by objects of that sort ? "

At the word " objects " John Bull's cronies rose
as one man and approached the window with the
obvious intention of aiding their bull-like friend.
Judging by their bullet heads and savage expressions

they were four rough customers and like their com-
rade, were only awaiting a chance to break the
monotony of their carnival night with an exhilarating
fight.

It was easy to guess each man's trade. The one
John Bull had called Croc-en-Jambe was more than
a mere rag-picker, though the lantern standing by the
table with the forked stick from which he took his
nickname proclaimed him scavenger. He not only
bought and sold old rubbish but he helped himself
to all he could collect from dustbins and gutters,
thrusting the crooked prongs of his stick into the
very interstices of the stones. This class of industry
was suppressed by the police some eight or ten years
ago and indeed had sunk into decay through the
decent paving of the streets, but in the old days the
filthy stream that coursed along the gutter sometimes
proved a very Pactolus to the Croc-en-Jambes, because
of the rings and precious stones so often found there,
dropped by passers-by or even shaken out of window
by a too zealous maid, shaking a mat.

The second man was known by the punning
sobriquet of Sac-à-Plàtre in allusion to his trade, that
of a plasterer, as the stains of lime and whitewash on
his person sufficiently indicated both to friends and
enemies. John Bull was one of his best friends and
the way in which this relation was formed deserves
to be told, as it serves to paint the Herculean traits
of the man whom we have just brought on the scenes
and who, though not one of the principals, is yet
destined to play an important part in this story.

A house was on fire in the city; the staircase, eaten

by the flames, had already fallen; yet a man, woman
and child were crying for help from a window on the
second floor. The man, who was a plasterer, asked
for a ladder or even a rope; with either he could save
his wife and child; but the onlookers lost their heads.
They brought ladders that were too short and ropes
that could not possibly support the weight of three
people. Meanwhile the fire was mounting and smoke
was pouring from the windows in great gusts, pre-
cursor of the flames, close behind and already visible.

"Hullo!" said John Bull, stopping before the
house. "Haven't you a ladder or a rope? Those
people will be burnt."

Indeed, the danger was imminent. John Bull
looked round and seeing that nothing of the sort was
to hand, he held out his arms.

"Throw down the child, Plaster Saint!"

The plasterer didn't wait to take offence at the nickname; he kissed the child, and threw it into the waiting
arms of John Bull. There was a cry of fright from
the onlookers. John Bull caught the child in his
arms and passed it to those standing behind,

"Now throw down the woman!" he cried.

The plasterer took his wife in his arms and despite
her cries forced her to take the same path as his child.
John Bull caught her, but he recoiled a pace. "There
you are!" he said, setting down the half fainting
woman whilst the watchers burst out into shouts of
applause.

"Now it's your turn, my brave!" he cried and
poised his weight as firmly on his legs as he could,
bracing himself for the shock.

Of the two thousand people who assisted at this scene not one seemed to breathe during the next five seconds. The plasterer got onto the window sill and made the sign of the Cross. Then, shutting his eyes, and murmuring a prayer, he leaped out. This time the shock was terrible. John Bull bent in two with the weight and reeled backwards step by step. But he did not fall. There was a shout from the whole crowd and everyone rushed to the man who had brought off this amazing *tour de force*. But before they could reach him, he had opened his arms and fallen insensible, vomiting blood.

Neither child, woman nor man had so much as a scratch, but John Bull had broken a blood vessel in his lung. They took him to the hospital but he was out again in two days' time.

The third fellow whose face was as black as that of Sac-à-Plàtre was white, and who evidently belonged to the Honourable Company of Charcoalburners, was called Toussaint. John Bull who had heard a thing or two from the architects he met over his work, nicknamed him after a certain famous negro who had been the presiding genius of a revolution in St. Domingo—Toussaint Louverture.

The fourth man was fifty or thereabouts, with darting eye and rapid gestures, from whose person was exhaled a strong odour of valerian. He wore a cotton velvet suit, and a cap of cats-skin, and answered among his friends to the name of *la Gibelotte*.[2] It was he who furnished the cabarets of the market with those roof-top rabbits that our friend Jean Davy feared to

² Which may be translated "Rabbit Pie."

have served up to him in place of the usual rabbit of the fields. The smell of valerian came from the bait with which he ensnared the poor beasts, whose carcases he sold for ten sous to the innkeepers while their skins brought him in some fifteen sous from the furriers. The industry was paying but dangerous, and we remember to have read, in the year 1834 or 35, an account of the trial of a confrère of la Gibelotte, who was condemned to a year's imprisonment and five hundred francs fine in spite of the eloquent pleading of his counsel who treated the gastronomic question in the manner of Carême or Brillat-Savarin, trying to convince the judges of the incontestable superiority of cat to rabbit.

The fifth acolyte—whom we have kept for the last —was John Bull himself, whom we need not describe particularly after the story we have already told of his physical prowess. Yet it would be as well to prepare by as exact a portrait as possible of his appearance for the moral development of one of the most singular characters I ever came across.

John Bull stood about five feet ten inches high, and was as sound and solid as an oak. By trade a carpenter, he was a Hercules of Farnese, hewn from one block of granite. To look at him, it would not be thought he would need help in the task of over-throwing our three friends. On the contrary, he seemed capable of crushing them, one by one, between his finger and thumb. He wore black whiskers, which grew round his throat like a collar, so thick were they, and was about forty years old. His hair was short and crisp, like that of the son of Jupiter

and Semele—that electric hair that the Ancients took
for a sign of power. His throat justified his name,
and completed the insignia of this unintelligent and
brutal type. He was dressed in a cotton-velvet vest
and trousers with a velvet cap, now going green with
age. From the pocket of his waistcoat protruded a
square rule and sticking out from the top of his
trousers was a long compass of iron, one leg of which
was tucked into the pocket while the other hung
outside.

Such were the five antagonists with whom our
three friends, Pétrus the painter, Ludovic the doctor
and Jean Davy the dramatist, were about to join
issue—that is, unless they decided to withdraw and
even that measure might well fail to bring the quarrel
to an end.

CHAPTER III

THE FIGHT

PÉTRUS still stood with his arms crossed, leaning
against the window-sill, regarding the five men with
defiance.

Ludovic examined John Bull with so much interest
as to make him lose sight of the gravity of the situation, and, man of science as he was, he was thinking
that he would willingly give a hundred francs to have
a subject like that for dissection. Perhaps, indeed,
he would the more gladly have given that hundred
francs if he could have had John Bull himself, for
he might well have preferred to have such an athlete
dead and stretched flat on a table than standing
before him full of life and spoiling for a fight.

Jean Davy, as we have said, had advanced to try and arrange matters; his negotiations having failed he kept his position that he might receive or give the first blow. He was young but he had read a good deal and was conversant with the theories of Marshal Saxe on moral influence; this led him to realize the great advantage if it came to blows of being able to lead the attack. Some knowledge of boxing and wrestling, acquired from a teacher then unknown but celebrated later, gave him confidence, especially as he was endowed with sufficient bodily strength to hold his own had his antagonist been anyone less redoubtable than John Bull. He meant, however, to do all in his power to smooth things over right up to the point beyond which it would be cowardice to go. Thus he was the first to break the silence which fell on both parties as the four men rose from the table to come to John Bull's aid.

" One moment ! " he said. " Before we start fighting, cannot we settle this affair amicably ? What is it you gentlemen want ? "

" He has insulted us ! " cried the scavenger. " We are not gentlemen ! Do you hear ? "

" I hear and agree," retorted Pétrus. " You are not gentlemen. You are scoundrels ! "

" He called us scoundrels ! " howled the cat-killer.

" We'll scoundrel them ! " shouted the plasterer.

" Let me get my hands on them . . ." the charcoal-burner began but John Bull interrupted.

" Stop it ! It's not your affair. This is my business ! "

" Why yours more than ours ? "

"We don't fight five against three—especially when one is enough! Back to your seats!" The two men obeyed, grumbling. "That is better. Now, my fine gentlemen, will you shut that window if you please!"

"No," replied all our three young men together, for the tone of this request discounted the politeness of the wording.

"Oho!" John Bull lifted his great arms as high above his head as the low ceiling permitted. "You want to be smashed to pieces, do you?"

"I don't advise you to try!" said Jean Davy, advancing a step nearer to the carpenter, but Pétrus leaped forward to place himself like a buckler between Davy and the Hercules. "Keep the other two back, you and Ludovic! I can manage this fellow." Putting Pétrus aside with a movement of one hand, Jean Davy touched the carpenter on the chest with the other.

"Were you talking about me, Your Highness?" sneered the Colossus.

"I was."

"And why have you picked me out for your special attention?"

"Because you are the most impudent and so deserve the sharper lesson. But that is not my only reason. There is another."

"And that is?"

"We both have the same Christian name. You are John Bull; I am John Davy."

"John Davy, are you? Liar! You are Johnnie . . ."

The young man did not let him finish. With a wrist of steel he struck the Colossus on the temple, and John Bull, who had not budged when a woman fell into his arms from a second storey, now staggered back several paces. He fell backwards onto a table, two legs of which broke beneath his weight.

At the same time a similar evolution was taking place between the other four combatants. Pétrus was a past master at both single stick and wrestling, and as he had no stick in hand he slipped his leg behind that of the plasterer and sent him rolling down by John Bull; whilst Ludovic, the anatomist, sent his fist between the charcoalburner's seventh rib and the neck of the femur, somewhere in the region of the liver, the effect of which was to whiten his victim's black face pretty considerably.

John Bull and the plasterer got up. Toussaint who hadn't fallen, sank into a chair, his two hands on his hips, and struggled to get back his wind.

But this, as you will understand, was only the beginning; a sort of flourish before the actual fight and the three young men realized this for each stood prepared for an attack.

Nevertheless, the surprise had been great, both for spectators and actors. At sight of their two comrades, John Bull and Plaster Saint, tumbling backwards, and of Toussaint Louverture doubling up on a chair, the other two rose and without bothering further about John Bull's prohibition, they advanced in fighting order, one with his stick and the other with a bottle in his hand.

The plasterer had simply been taken by surprise and he now rose little the worse for his fall.

As for the carpenter he felt as if the end of a rafter hurled by a giant had struck him on the head. The shock to his brain extended quickly to his whole body; he was as if stunned for a few moments, a mist of red before his eyes and a loud humming in his ears. He literally "saw red" for Jean Davy's fist had broken the skin on his forehead and the seal ring had left a bloody mark just above the brow.

"Damnation!" cried he, as he advanced unsteadily on his antagonist. "What it is to be taken by surprise! A child can get the better of one!"

"All right. Say when this time, John Bull. But look out! For I mean you to break the other two legs of that table!"

John Bull lifted his great fist, thus delivering himself into the hands of his enemy, as untrained brute force is always apt to do when confronted by skill. The whole theory of boxing rests on this assumption; that it takes less time for a fist to travel along a straight line than to describe a parabola.

Yet this time Jean Davy merely meant to defend himself. He used his right hand simply to turn aside the terrible blow John Bull aimed at him and just as that fist was about to descend on him he dodged, and, thanks to his great height, launched the savatte full on his adversary's body above the waist.

Jean Davy had spoken truly. John Bull again fell onto the table. Nor could he even cry out. The breath was driven from his body.

As for the three others, Pétrus with his usual agility had faced two adversaries. He had thrown his snuff-box full into the face of the scavenger who was advancing on him, stick in hand, and whilst Croc-en-Jambe was kept busy with the flying snuff, he sent the plasterer over onto his back, by the simple process of ramming his head into his abdomen. Ludovic, therefore, only had to tackle the cat-killer but being ignorant of the gentle arts that were standing his two comrades in such good stead, he simply threw his arms round the man's body and the two were now rolling over and over on the floor.   La Gibelotte, however, was underneath !

Unfortunately, Ludovic, instead of profiting by the advantage of the position, having got his knee on his enemy's chest, stopped to sniff and wonder where the smell of valerian was coming from.   He was still reflecting on this problem when the scavenger and the plasterer, seeing John Bull knocked out for the second time, Toussaint scarcely recovered from the blow in the ribs and the cat-killer reposing under Ludovic's knee, began to shout:

" Knife them ! "

At this moment the waiter entered with the oysters. He took in the situation with a glance, placed the oysters on the table and flew back down the ladder, no doubt to carry the alarm.

But his brief apparition on the scene was but a detail in the eyes of the other actors.   They had too much to do to give another thought to him, and he had come and gone so rapidly that if the oysters had not remained as evidence of his entrance, they might have thought it a mere dream.

What passed on the fourth and lower floors though, was no dream.   The noise of the carpenter's falls,

the smashing of the table, the cries of " Knife them ! "
had awakened the drunkards asleep below. The least
overcome had listened and one of them had crept to
the door, and seen the waiter hurrying down. They
were men of experience and knew what that meant !
Suddenly our three young men heard a sound of
hurrying footsteps and smothered growls like the
roaring of the waves on a stormy sea. The spawn of
the Market were rising and soon, through the open
door came crowding strange, twisted, debased-looking
creatures, furious at having been aroused from their
sleep.

" Who's cutting throats up here ? " cried some
twenty hoarse, thick voices.

At sight of this pack of wolves Jean Davy, the most
impressionable of the three, felt the blood turn to ice
in his veins—that cold terror that will seize the
strongest man at the touch of a reptile. Turning
towards the painter he could not forbear murmuring :

" Pétrus, what have you brought on us ? "

But Pétrus was improvising a new system of defence. To the cries " Knives ! Knives ! " which the
four madmen had uttered (for the carpenter and
Toussaint who had now found his voice again took
their part in the quartette), Pétrus replied with a cry
of :

" To the barricades ! "

This battlecry had not been shouted in the streets
of Paris once since the famous day to which this
system of defence has given its historic name. Later,
though, the Parisians claimed damages for a silence
that had endured 250 years.

4

Shouting his slogan, Pétrus drew Jean Davy after him and forcing Ludovic to get up, the three companions took refuge in a corner, piling up a barricade of tables and benches between themselves and the other occupants of the room. Pétrus, moreover, had profited by the moment's truce, short though it was, which his victory had given him, to snatch the curtain pole from the window, a weapon which it had been his ambition to possess from the very beginning of the fight. Jean Davy had taken up his cane, but Ludovic was content with the arms with which Nature had provided him.

The three friends quickly found themselves in the comparative safety of their improvised fortress.

" Look there ! " said Pétrus, pointing to the corner where were piled all sorts of débris—broken plates, oyster shells, empty bottles, iron forks, knives that had lost their handles and handles without blades. " You see we shan't want for ammunition."

" No," said Jean Davy. " But how do we stand as regards damage ? I haven't a scratch."

" Neither have I," said Pétrus.

" What about you, Ludovic ? "

" I think I got struck on the angle of the jaw. But I'm not bothering about that."

" Then what *are* you bothering about ? " asked Jean Davy.

" I'm wondering why that man I was fighting with smelt so strongly of valerian."

But at this moment the howling of the mob furnished a new preoccupation for all three of our young friends and that of a sufficiently grave character.

CHAPTER IV

M. SALVATOR

THE sight of the crowd produced on the working-
men an effect entirely opposite to that which it had
on our three friends. The carpenter and his companions felt that help was coming to them. Jean
Davy and his comrades realized that fresh enemies
had arrived on the scene, for, naturally, the sympathy of the mob would be with their own class.
With threatening glances at the three young men
who were by now withdrawn into their fort, the
crowd surrounded John Bull and his companions
asking what all the noise was about. The explanation was difficult for the carpenter was first in the
wrong when he demanded that the gentlemen
should shut the window. Then there was a second
offence even more grave than the first and that was
having allowed Jean Davy to give him a blow and a
kick which had marked his face and knocked all the
wind out of his body. He related the affair to the
mob as best he could, but however he put it, he could
not get away from these two facts : " I insisted on
the window being shut and it's still open. I wanted
to give him a good thrashing and he's thrashed
me ! "   Naturally the crowd, having at bottom
plenty of good sense in spite of its prejudice against
the aristocrats, realizing—if I may make use of a
vulgar expression which, however, fits the case—
realizing that John Bull had made a fool of himself,
started laughing at him. The carpenter did not
need this new provocation : already angry, the

laughter made him mad. He looked for our friends, saw them entrenched in their corner, and saw, too, that his own four companions, as furious as he was himself, were already attacking them.

"Stop!" he cried. "Stop! Leave those young bloods to me!"

His four companions were deaf to his cry; deaf, but by no means dumb. The scavenger had just received part of a broken bottle in his eye, thrown by Ludovic in such wise that it had cut open his cheek. Jean Davy, with the leg of a table had broken Toussaint's head, while Pétrus with the point of his stick, through the interstices of the barricade, had struck the cat-killer in the chest and the plasterer on the thigh.

The four wounded men were now crying at the top of their voices:

"Kill them! Kill them!"

It had indeed become a fight to the death.

Exasperated by the laughter of the crowd, and by the sight of blood on his clothes and those of his companions, John Bull had taken his iron compass from his pocket and armed with that terrible weapon, advanced alone upon the barricade.

Pétrus and Ludovic came to meet him simultaneously, each armed with a bottle, hoping to break the carpenter's head, but Jean Davy, seeing that he was the only serious adversary left, and that it would be advisable to finish with him for good and all, pulled his two friends back by their coat-tails, kicked an opening in the barricade and came out, cane in hand.

"So you aren't satisfied?" said he to John Bull.

The crowd shrieked with delight.

" No," replied the carpenter. " I shan't be satisfied till I've thrust six inches of this compass into your belly."

" You mean that as you aren't the strongest you'll be the first to use foul play? In other words, as you can't conquer me, you'll murder me? "

" Hell and blazes, I'll have my revenge! " cried the carpenter, intoxicating himself with his own words.

" Take care, John Bull, for, on my honour, you've never been in greater danger than you are at this moment." Then, addressing the crowd, Jean Davy added : " You are men. Make this man listen to reason. You can see that I'm calm but he's lost his head."

Four or five men moved out of the throng and came between the carpenter and Jean Davy. But the intervention, instead of cooling John Bull, seemed to redouble his exasperation.

He lifted his arm and it was enough to disperse the men.

" Oho," said he. " So I've never been in greater danger than now, haven't I ? Is it with nonsense like that that you think you can defend yourself against my compass, eh ? "

He brandished the instrument over his head. Now it was pulled out to its full length it was at least 18 inches long.

" That's just where you're wrong, John Bull," said the young man. " My nonsense is no nonsense. It's a viper and if you doubt that, look! " He drew from his cane the slender sword of which it was the sheath. " Here is its sting ! "

A triangular blade, fine, sharp, about twelve or fifteen inches long flashed in the young man's hand as he threw himself on guard, as if about to fight a duel.

The crowd howled with delight and shivered with horror.

Wine had been drunk and blood was going to be shed; things were following the ordinary procedure; incidents were following one another in accordance with all the laws of dramatic art, each more interesting than its predecessor.

" Ah ! " said the carpenter, visibly relieved. " So you are armed too. So much the better ! "

Head down, arm raised, leaving his chest uncovered with the inexperience of brute force, John Bull rushed on the young man, as he stood there in his black clothes, with his drawn sword in his hand.

But suddenly a strong hand seized John Bull's wrist, shaking it so violently as to make him drop the compass, which fell to the ground.

The carpenter turned with a terrible oath. But when he saw who had hold of him, his voice lost its menacing note and took on a tone of respect.

" M. Salvator ? " he said. " I'm sorry. That's quite another matter."

" M. Salvator ? " cried the crowd. " That's a good thing. Things were looking ugly."

" M. Salvator ? " repeated Jean Davy, Pétrus and Ludovic. " Who's he ? "

" Anyway his name's of good augury," declared Pétrus. " We'll see if he's worthy of it."

The person who, like a Greek God, had intervened, miraculously, to substitute, as it promised, a pacific dénouement for the bloody catastrophe that was imminent, and who seemed, indeed, to have stepped *ex machinâ*, so opportune and unforeseen was his appearance, looked about thirty years old.

As he sent a dominating glance over the crowd he presented the very picture of a man in his prime, at the age when manly beauty is most potent and power assuming its most beautiful form.

A moment later, however, it would have been difficult if not impossible to guess his age, even within ten years. His brow had indeed the candour and serenity of youth when he was glancing round him with good-natured curiosity. But when he took in the scene with disgust, his black brows came together and his furrowed forehead gave him a marked appearance of virility.

When he had seized the carpenter's wrist and made him drop the compass with which he was threatening his adversary, he glanced rapidly at our friends and recognized them for men of the bigger world who had strayed into this strange place inadvertently. He then took in all the details of the scene that as yet he had but half understood—saw the scavenger lying on a table, with his face cut open, the clothes of the plasterer stained with blood, the charcoalburner pale under his black mask, and the cat-killer holding his sides and declaring that he was dead. The sight of these things, though he must have expected them, caused a look of severity to settle on his face, a look so stern that even the most ruffianly there bowed their heads.

As this newcomer is our real hero, our readers must allow us to do for him what we have done for less important characters; that is, paint his portrait as exactly as we can.

His black hair was soft and curly; which made it appear shorter than it really was, for had the hair been straight it would have touched his shoulders. His eyes were blue, clear and limpid as the water of a lake. His face was a pure oval, Raphaelesque in its contour. His nose was straight and strong without being too large; his mouth small with good teeth and apparently delicate in shape, though under the black moustache which shadowed the upper lip it was difficult to see its exact form. His face was framed in a thick black beard and the fineness of the hair shewed that neither scissors nor razor had ever touched it. But the most striking thing of all was the tone of his skin. We can only give an idea of its immaculate whiteness by comparing it to the melancholy luminosity of the moon.

As for his costume, it consisted of a black velvet coat which only needed to be drawn in at the waist to look like a fifteenth century doublet. Waistcoat and trousers were also of black velvet. A cap of the same material was on his head and an artist was not needed to look instinctively for a feather, eagle, heron or ostrich to turn this cap into a noble's " bonnet." In all that crowd, what gave a touch of aristocracy to this costume, completed as it was by a purple silk scarf tied loosely round the throat, was that, instead of being in cotton velvet as were the coats of the working-men, it was made of silk velvet, like the dress of an actress or a duchess.

This picturesque costume not only struck Jean Davy and Ludovic but Pétrus too. Indeed, the effect it produced on the last-named was so great that he whispered :

" Why, here's the very model for my Raphael at the house of the Fornarina. I'd give him six francs a time instead of four if he'd only pose for me ! "

As for Jean Davy, who, as a dramatist, was always looking for types and effects for his plays, he was struck by the respectful reception this young man had met with from the angry crowd, which reminded him of the " quos ego " of Neptune quelling the angry waves of the Sicilian Archipelago with his godlike trident.

CHAPTER V
JOHN BULL RETREATS AND THE CROWD FOLLOW

A PROFOUND silence had reigned since the entrance of the stranger called M. Salvator; indeed the breathing of the thirty or forty people assembled there could scarcely be heard.

This silence was taken by the carpenter to imply a tacit condemnation of himself; he had been stupified by the appearance of the newcomer and the way in which he had been disarmed, but now getting back his self control little by little he spoke, softening the harsh tones of his voice as best he could.

" M. Salvator, let me explain . . ."

" You were in the wrong," interrupted the young man.

" But I tell you . . ."

" You were in the wrong," repeated the young man.

" But how can you know when you weren't there, M. Salvator ? "

" Do I need to be present to know how things passed ? "

" Well, I should think . . ."

Salvator stretched out a hand towards Jean Davy and his true friends, who were standing in a group for mutual support.

" Look," said he.

" I'm looking," replied John Bull.

" What do you see ? "

" I see three nobs to whom I promised a thrashing, and who'll receive it, one day or other."

" You see three well-bred young men, who should not have come to a place like this, but that wasn't sufficient reason for starting a quarrel with them."

" Me, start a quarrel with them ? "

" You are not going to tell me that they provoked you and your four companions ? "

" You could see for yourself that they were standing up to us."

" Because they had right on their side. You think force is everything, having changed your name from Barthélemy Lelong to John Bull. Well, now you've had proof to the contrary."

" But when I tell you that they called us swine, rogues, blackguards . . ."

" Why did they call you that ? "

" They said we were drunk."

" But why ? "

" Because we wanted them to shut the window."

" And why didn't you want the window opened ? "

" Because. . . . Because . . ."

" Because what ? Go on ! "

" Because I don't like a draught," said John Bull.

" Because you were drunk, as these gentlemen said. Because you wanted to have a row with someone and seized the occasion. Because something has put you out, and you wanted to make these innocent people pay for the caprice and infidelity of . . ."

" Stop, M. Salvator. Don't mention her name," interrupted the carpenter quickly. " Wretched girl, she'll kill me ! "

" You see I put my finger on the spot." Then, frowning, he added :'

" These gentlemen were right to open the window. The air here is poisonous and as two open windows aren't any too much for forty people you will, this instant, go and open the other."

" Me ? " said the carpenter, seeming to cling to the floor with his toes. " Me go and open a window when I've just asked them to shut one? Me, Barthélemy Lelong, my father's son ? "

" You, Barthélemy Lelong, drunkard and brawler, disgrace to your father's name, so that it's just as well you've taken another. I tell you you're going to open that window just as a punishment for having insulted these three gentlemen."

" May a thunderbolt fall on my head if I obey ! " cried Barthélemy Lelong, lifting a fist on high.

" Then I shall decline to know you under any name. You are nothing to me now but a worthless fellow and I'll have nothing more to do with you." He extended his hand. " Go ! "

" I won't go," shouted the carpenter, foaming with rage.

" In the name of your father which you invoked
just now, I command you to go."

"No, by Heaven. No! I won't go!" replied
Barthélemy Lelong, sitting astride a bench which he
clutched tightly with both hands, as if he were prepared to use it as a weapon if necessary.

"Then you force me to go to extremes?" said
Salvator so quietly that one would never have thought
he was using a severe threat. He took a step towards
the carpenter.

" Don't do that ! " cried the other, recoiling to the
end of the bench. " Stay where you are ! "

" Will you go? " demanded Salvator.

The carpenter raised the bench as if to strike the
young man . . . but he threw it away and cried :
" You know you can make me do anything you like
and that I'd cut off my right hand before I'd strike
you.—But, of my own free will, no, I won't
go."

" Obstinate fool ! " cried Salvator and he seized
John Bull by his cravat and waistband.

The carpenter emitted a howl of rage.

" You may throw me out," said he, " but I won't
go of my own accord."

"Then you shall have your own way," replied
Salvator.

With a violent heave he uprooted the Colossus
from the floor as he might have uprooted an oak
and carrying him to the staircase, over which he held
him suspended, he said :

" Will you go down stair by stair or all at once? "

" I'm in your hands. Do as you like. But I won't
go of my own accord."

" Then you'll go by force, you fool."

And he threw him like a bale of cotton from the fourth floor to the third. You could hear his body bumping from stair to stair. Not a sound did the crowd make; they were content to look on and admire.

The three young men, however, were deeply concerned. Pétrus, the joker, was now quite serious; Ludovic, the phlegmatic could hear his own heart beat; while Jean Davy, the sensitive poet, was the only one who apparently remained cool. But when he saw Salvator come back without the carpenter he slipped his sword back into its sheath, and passed his handkerchief across his brow which was bedewed with perspiration. Then he went straight to Salvator and offered his hand.

" Thanks, monsieur," said he, " for having come to our rescue. You've delivered my friends and me from that drunken fellow, but I hope that fall won't hurt him."

" Don't worry about him," Salvator replied, putting his white well-bred hand, the hand which had just shown evidence of amazing strength, into that which was held out to him. " He may have to stay in bed for a week or two, that's all, and he'll spend the time bitterly regretting his conduct to-night."

" That brute regret? "

" He has the softest heart in the world, I assure you. Don't worry about him. Look out for yourself."

" For myself? "

" Yes. . . . May I give you some friendly advice? "

" Please."

Salvator dropped his voice so that no one else should hear what he said.

" If you do as I advise you'll never set foot again in this place, M. Jean Davy."

" You know me ? " cried Jean Davy, astonished.

" But of course," replied Salvator with exquisite courtesy. " Are you not one of our most famous dramatists ? "

Jean Davy blushed to the roots of his hair.

" And now," said Salvator turning to the crowd, and changing voice and manner completely, " are you satisfied, all of you ? You've had enough for your money, I hope ? Then will you kindly get away as soon as possible ? There's not room for more than four here, which is another way of saying that I want these gentlemen to myself."

The crowd obeyed as a group of schoolchildren might have obeyed the voice of their master. They filed out in good order, saluting this young man who seemed to have command over them, with voice, head and hand. Yet his expression was unmoved.

John Bull's four comrades, including the scavenger whose wound had removed the clouds of intoxication from his mind, passed before Salvator with their heads down, each bowing respectfully, saluting like soldiers before a general.

When the last had gone the waiter appeared at the door.

" Am I to serve supper for these gentlemen ? "

" Rather ! " cried Jean Davy. Then, turning to Salvator, he added : " Won't you give us the pleasure of supping with us ? "

" Willingly, but don't order anything more for me. I was about to sup downstairs when I heard the noise and came up."

" You hear, waiter? " said Jean Davy. " Bring M. Salvator's supper with ours."

" Very good, sir," said the waiter.

He left the room and five minutes after our friends were sitting at table. They drank first to the victors, then to the vanquished, then to the man who had so happily arrived in time to prevent a greater effusion of blood.

" I must say," said Salvator, laughing to Jean Davy, " you seem to have an excellent knowledge of boxing, wrestling and fencing. And you were admirably encamped in that corner; if I were M. Pétrus I'd make a sketch of the affair."

" Oh, so you know me too, do you ? " cried Pétrus.

" Yes," replied Salvator with a sigh as if this admission awakened some unhappy memory. " Before you took your present studio rue de Ouest, you lived in rue du Régard. It was then that I had the pleasure of seeing you several times."

Then, turning towards the third friend, who had kept silent, as if pursuing the solution of a difficult problem :

" What's the matter with you, M. Ludovic ? You seem full of care. I could understand it if you still had your examination to pass and your thesis to deliver but you did that with honours some three months ago."

Jean Davy looked at him with astonishment and Pétrus burst out laughing.

" Well, of course, if you know everything, M. Salvator.—" said Ludovic.

" I wish I did," said Salvator laughing.

" Since you know that Jean Davy is a dramatist, that Pétrus is a painter and that I am a doctor, do you know Monsieur, can you tell me why that cat-killer smelt so strongly of valerian ? "

" Are you an angler, M. Ludovic ? "

" When I've time," replied Ludovic, " but I always seem so busy."

" Anyway, you know that anglers scent their bait for carp with musk or aniseed ? "

" One doesn't need to be an angler to know that. It's a little matter of natural history."

" Well, then, valerian is to cats what musk and aniseed is to carp. It attracts them. And as our friend la Gibelotte is a fisher of cats—"

" Oh . . ." Ludovic started talking to himself with that amusing absentmindedness that made one of the most original sides of his character. " Oh, the mysteries of science ! Is it always mere chance that lifts a corner of her veil ? . . . To think that if we hadn't put on these silly disguises to-night . . . if Pétrus hadn't insisted on supping at this thieves' den . . . . if we hadn't had this stupid brawl, I shouldn't have fought with a cat-killer, you wouldn't have had to interfere and science might have waited, perhaps, another ten years before discovering that valerian attracts cats as musk does carp."

The supper was a gay one. Pétrus told studio anecdotes, telling how once he had painted twenty portraits in a little inn to make enough to pay his bill which only amounted to ten francs twenty centimes —each portrait averaging the exorbitant price of 51 centimes.

Ludovic proved with mathematical accuracy that no pretty woman was ever seriously ill, and he maintained this paradox for a whole quarter of an hour with a verve and gaiety that one would never have expected from so phlegmatic an individual.

Jean Davy told them the plot of a new play that he was writing for Bocage and Mme. Dorval and received from the man in black velvet some valuable advice.

Bottle followed bottle, and as Pétrus and Ludovic were intent on making M. Salvator drunk in the hope that he would become garrulous, that happened which was sure to happen. It was M. Salvator who remained sober and the young men who succumbed.

As for Jean Davy, he drank water—as usual.

Step by step Pétrus and Ludovic, leading each other on, passed the border that they had marked for Salvator. They took to telling long stories, repeated jokes that all had laughed at already, and so fell into complete stupor, overcome by the sleep of intoxication.

CHAPTER VI
WHILE PÉTRUS AND LUDOVIC SLEPT

SCARCELY had the snores of the two sleepers indicated that they had abandoned the conversation to whomsoever cared to take it up than Salvator, leaning his elbows on the table, dropped his head in his hands and looked at Jean Davy fixedly.

" Tell me, sir poet, why did you come here to-night ? "

" To please "—and he (Davy) pointed to Pétrus and Ludovic.

" Was that the only reason ?   Was there no other ? "

" None that I know."

" You are sure ? "

" As sure as one can be of anything."

" You are not deceiving me, but you may be deceiving yourself.   Those good sleepers are not the cause; they are only the pretext.   Do you know why you came here?   I'll tell you.   You came in your capacity of philosopher and observer, painter of character, romancer, poet; you came to study the human heart as shown in the lower classes; now, didn't you ? "

" There is truth in what you say," replied Jean Davy, smiling.   " I've written nothing but plays so far, but I don't mean to limit myself to the drama ! I want to write a psychological novel, only I want to do it as Shakespeare did his plays; I want to embrace a whole historical epoch and bring in every class of society from the gravedigger to the Prince of Denmark himself.   And, mind you, the gravedigger is not the least interesting figure in ' Hamlet.' "

" Yes, you are right.   I agree with you in the main but you haven't chosen your scene well.   How does Shakespeare show us his gravediggers?   At their work, with their feet in their grave, pickaxe in hand and not at Yaughan's tavern, though the first grave-digger sends the second there to fetch him a stoup of

wine. You want to be a poet ? Then fall in love and
roam the woods. If you want to write a play go into
society till midnight, read Shakespeare or Molière till
two a.m., take six hours' sleep to let your reading
mingle profitably with your experiences, and then sit
down and write from nine till mid-day. If you want
to write a romance, read Lesage, Walter Scott and
Fenimore Cooper, masters of their different kinds of
romance. Study man at his work whatever it is and
wherever that may be, but not at the Inn when he's
tired and half drunk. And then, to choose a Carnival
night, when they're all wearing fancy costumes and
aping the rich.—A night when they're anything
and everything—except their true selves ! *Monsieur*
Observer," Salvator gave an expressive shrug, " you
have an odd method of observing."

" Well ? " said Jean Davy. " Go on. I'm listening."

" Chance brought us together and soon the
ordinary course of things will separate us again. Before this occurs may I offer you my advice. I, who
have fashioned my romance."

" You have ? "

" Yes, but I haven't written it. I've lived it.
That's why I claim to be something of an observer
myself. It's in society that we find our novels, poet.
Exert your imagination as you will, you'll not invent
in a whole year anything to equal what chance,
fatality . . . providence—call it what you like—
brings about in one night, in a city like Paris. Have
you a plot for your novel ? "

" No, not yet. I like writing plays, but a tale

. . . with its ramifications, its incidents, its flights from the highest classes to the lowest . . . the boudoir of a princess and the attic of a workgirl . . . I confess I shrink from the hard labour. It's like carrying a world on your shoulders."

" Well, I think you're wrong," said Salvator.

" Why ? "

" In what you want to DO."

" How do you mean ? "

" Don't think out a plot. Let it make itself."

" I don't understand."

" How did Asmodeus behave ? "

" He climbed on to the roof tops and said to Don Cleophas : ' Look there ! ' "

" Have you the power of Asmodeus ? No. So I advise you to try even more simple methods. Leave this den and follow the first man or woman you see. It's unlikely that he, or she, will be the hero or heroine of your story but they will be one of the threads of the great human story. You may be sure that you must be on the trail of some adventure, terrible or grotesque."

" But it's night time."

" Well, all the better ! Night was made for poets, lovers, patrols, thieves and novelists."

" Then you want me to begin my novel now at once ? "

" It has begun."

" You mean that ? "

" I do."

" But when ? "

" Directly your friends said : ' Come and have supper in the Market.' "

" You're joking."

" No, on my honour. It's up to you. John Bull might be a character in your story, his four friends, your two, myself if you think me worthy.—But don't drop it immediately after the prologues."

" You're right. I ask nothing better than to go on with it ! "

" Then just remember that you are not the author creating the situations, but an actor in this great human drama of which the world is the stage— where each acts according to his interests, his own will apparently, but really moved by the invisible and omnipotent hand of Destiny. The tears shed in that story will be real tears, the blood real blood, and you yourself will mingle your tears and your blood with others."

" What does that matter if art is to gain by it ? "

" I was right in my estimate of you. Why, its freezing—a lovely moonlight night. Let's go and seek the continuation of the story of which we have just lived the first few chapters."

" But I can't leave my two friends."

" Why not ? "

" Suppose they came to some harm ? "

" There's no danger. I'll speak to the waiter. When it's known that they're under my protection the most hardened rascal here wouldn't dare to touch a hair of their heads."

" All right," said Jean Davy. " But do you mind speaking in my presence ? "

" Certainly."

Salvator went to the staircase and gave a soft whistle of a peculiar note.

It was evidently not the custom to keep M. Salvator waiting, for the singular modulation had scarcely died away before the waiter appeared.

" Sir ? "

" Those two gentlemen "—pointing to the two sleepers—" are my friends. You understand, Babylas ? "

" Yes, M. Salvator," replied the waiter, simply.

" Come along," said the young man to the poet and left the room.

Jean Davy stayed to ask for the bill. Then, giving the waiter a tip of five francs, he said :

" Do you mind telling me who that gentleman is ? "

" He isn't a gentleman. He's M. Salvator."

" But who is M. Salvator ? "

" You don't know him ? "

" I shouldn't ask if I did."

" He's the commissionaire of the rue aux Fers."

" What ? "

" I said he was the commissionaire of the rue aux Fers."

" I think M. Salvator was right," murmured Jean Davy to himself. " We have to-night begun a story unlike any that has ever been written."

CHAPTER VII
MOONLIGHT AND MYSTERY

IT was two o'clock by the Market clock and, as the commissionaire of the rue aux Fers had said, a beautiful moonlight night, for the fog had disappeared almost magically.

The fountain of the Innocents—*chef-d'œuvre* of

Jean Goujon, the only architect-sculptor whom we have ever had—was to the right of the young men as they came out of the cabaret.

Lit by the splendid lamp that the hand of the Creator had suspended in the firmament, its elegant grooved pillars, marvels of Corinthian architecture, were outlined in all their grace and purity. The naiads, those drops of water turned into women that the chevalier Bernin so admired, bending forward in supple curves, seemed to throw off their draperies and descend into the basin of the fountain to bathe their small white feet.

The companions, in spite of the social barrier that the difference in their ranks seemed to raise between them, linked arms and started up the rue St-Denis, towards the *palais de justice*. When they reached the place du Châtelet they stopped. The river ran at their feet and Notre Dame reared up before them with the majesty of stillness. Sainte-Chappelle lifted its toothed comb above the houses as Leviathan his hump above the waves. The illusion of the Paris of the fifteenth century was almost perfect.

To complete it a band of young people dressed in the costume of the time of Charles VI appeared, shouting at the top of their voices:

" Fourteen minutes past two ! Sleep in peace, citizens. All's well ! "

Indeed they looked like one of those bands of malcontents whom the good citizens of Paris, of the worshipful company of Butchers, used to dispatch from time to time to King Charles VI to drag some fresh concession from him. They might have been the Gois, Tibers, Lhuillers, Meulotts, with the terrible knacker Caboche at their head.

They seemed to be waiting for the setting of the moon or the rising of the king to begin their riot.

Our two friends let them go by, before they rapidly crossed the Exchange bridge, and reached the little square between the St. Michel bridge and the rue de la Harpe.

Some thirty students were dancing here with grisettes in fantastic costumes, round a bonfire of straw.

Jean Davy, who was studying the history of France, looked for the boundary post on which was carved a head with a purse hanging from the neck and which stood here, so the old chroniclers say, till the seventeenth century.

It seemed as if these young people all dressed in mediaeval costume, for that period was coming into favour, were here to protest, some four hundred years after the event, against the horrible treason of which this spot was the scene.

It was indeed on just such a moonlight night at two in the morning, that on the twelfth of June, 1418, Perinet Leclerc, having stolen the keys of the Porte St. Germain from under his father's pillow, opened the gates of the town to 800 of the Duke of Burgundy's men who were waiting outside the walls under the command of Villiers, Lord of l'Isle-Adam. Everyone who fell into their hands was slain without mercy, women, children, old men; the Bishops of Coutances, Bayeux, Senlis, d'Évreux, all killed in their beds; the constable and chancellor dragged forth and massacred, their limbs cut off and their heads carried through the streets. The massacre lasted eight days, at the end of which time the Parisians chased the Burgundians from the town, remaining the victors. Then they started to find out what traitor had been the cause of this disgrace and misery. They searched Paris from end to end to find Perinet Leclerc. He had disappeared and no one ever heard of him again. A sculptor then quickly carved a huge image of the traitor and after it had been carried through the streets by the mob, after they had struck it, and spat at it, the same sculptor carved on the boundary post the Judas of his century, with his purse round his neck.

This memory was occupying Jean Davy's thoughts, who had turned from the gay dancers glowing in the light of the flames to peer into the darkness of the corners while he whispered :

" I wish I knew where that boundary post used to stand."

"At the corner of the square and the rue St. André-des-Arcs," replied Salvator as if he had followed all Jean Davy's thoughts of which his whisper was but the culmination.

" How do you know? I didn't know," said Jean Davy.

Salvator smiled.

" Doesn't that implication savour slightly of vanity? Do you really think, Mr. Poet, that it is the people who ought to know who always do know? I think the ignorance of your friend Ludovic on the subject of valerian rather proved the contrary."

" I am sorry ! " said Davy. " It slipped out. It shall not occur again. I will take it for granted that you know everything."

" By no manner of means everything ! " replied Salvator, laughing. " But I live among the people who are everybody ! You know the fable of Argus with his hundred eyes and Briareus with his hundred arms who were stronger than kings and had more wit than M. Voltaire? One of the qualities of the People is their habit of remembering grievances, especially treasons. Certain traitors whom kings have re-
• habilitated and loaded with honours—to whom the nobles have opened their doors—whom the middle classes salute as they pass—remain for ever traitors in the eyes of the People. It may not be long —" Salvator's eyes grew sombre, taking an expression of which one would not have believed them capable —" before you have an example of what I say ! Well, the name of Perinet Leclerc, barely remembered by the higher classes, is a hated memory to the People even though they are vague about the details of his treason—and hated the more because that treason was never expiated . . . because Providence for once seemed impotent when the guilty man escaped. Come along ! "

Salvator turned into the street of St. André-des Arcs and Jean Davy followed him, finding the place empty and dark. Between the rue Maçon and the square of St. André-des Arcs his companion halted before a small house, clean and white, but with only three windows showing in its front.

A little door grained to resemble oak admitted

them when unlocked by a key that Salvator drew from his pocket.

" Now it's agreed that we pass the rest of the night together, isn't it?" he said to Jean Davy.

" You made the offer and I accepted it. You don't want to withdraw it?"

" On the contrary! But, humble as I am, there are two who would be anxious if my absence were too long prolonged. A woman and a dog."

" Go and reassure them. I'll wait here."

" Is it discretion on your part to refuse to enter? If so you're wrong. I'm one of those mysterious creatures who have nothing to conceal. My way of preserving my incognito is to keep in the light of day. Wasn't it Talleyrand who said that if a diplomat would only speak the truth he'd deceive everyone? I am that diplomat; only I don't try to deceive any-one since no one takes any notice of me."

" In that case," said Jean Davy who was all curi-osity to see the home of this commissionaire, " as the Italians say, ' *Permesso!* ' "[1]

" Si," replied Salvator in excellent Tuscan. " *Sottante vederete il cane, ma non la signora.*"[2]

The door opened and the two young men entered the passage.

" Wait while I get a light," said Salvator. Draw-ing a phosphoric tablet from his pocket he was about to strike a match when suddenly a light appeared at the top of the stairs sending long rays down the wall.

Then a gentle voice said :

[1] By your leave.
[2] Yes, now you will see the dog but not the lady.

" Is that you, Salvator ? "

" Yes," replied the young man. Then, turning to Davy : " It wasn't you who were wrong, but
I," he said. " You will see both the lady and the
dog."

The dog appeared first. At the sound of his
master's voice he bounded down the stairs like a
waterspout. When he reached his master, the enormous animal put his two front paws on his shoulder,
rubbed his nose affectionately against his cheek and
emitted little cries of affection as a tiny King Charles
might have done.

" All right, Roland. Let me pass," said Salvator.
" Your mistress Fragola wants to speak to me."

But the dog, seeing Jean Davy, pushed his great
head over his master's shoulder with a growl that
was more a question than a threat.

" That's a friend, Roland. So be good," said
Salvator. And having kissed the dog's black
muzzle, he pushed him down, saying :

" Let me pass, Roland ! "

Roland let his master pass and sniffed at Jean
Davy; then, licking the poet's hand, took his place
behind him at the end of the procession.

Jean Davy had glanced at the dog with the eye of
a connoisseur.

He was a magnificent beast of the St. Bernard
species. When he stood up on his hind legs he must
have been near six feet high. His coat was as tawny
as a lion's.

Making these observations as he went up to the
first floor, Jean Davy there promptly forgot the dog
in the lady.

Fragola was about twenty and her thick golden hair framed a sweet pale face, with the tint of a blush-rose under the creamy skin. The candle that she held in a crystal stand lit up her great blue eyes and her half-open, smiling mouth which showed within two rows of pearls behind two lips as red as fresh plucked cherries.

A tiny mark under the right eye, such as is called by the vulgar a "beauty spot," took on at certain periods of the year the colour of a strawberry and probably was the origin of her name, Fragola, whose poetic quality had already struck Jean Davy.

The sight of our friend had caused her some hesitation even as it had Roland, but, like Roland, she had been reassured by Salvator's statement that he was a friend. She offered Salvator her smiling brow on which he printed a tender and one might say a respectful kiss. Then, addressing Jean Davy, she said, with a charming smile:

"Friend of my friend, you are welcome."

And, candlestick in one hand, the other on Salvator's shoulder, she went back into the room. Jean Davy followed, but had the discretion to wait for a moment in the first of the two rooms which seemed to serve as a dining-room.

"You haven't waited up because you were anxious about me, I hope," said Salvator. "I should not forgive myself if that were so, child."

The young man spoke in a tone that might well be described as paternal.

"No," replied the young girl gently. "I received a letter from that friend I spoke to you about."

" Which one? You have three friends of whom you constantly speak."

" You might say I have four."

" Yes. Well, of which are you speaking ? "

" Of Carmélite."

" Has anything happened to her ? "

" I'm afraid so. We were to meet to-morrow, she, Lydia, Régina and I, at Mass at Notre Dame as we always do every year and now, instead, she asks us to meet her at seven."

" Where ? "

Fragola smiled.

" She asks us not to say, my friend."

" A secret, eh ? " said Salvator. " You know my opinion. Secrets are sacred."

Then, turning towards Jean Davy, he added : " I'll be with you in a moment. Do you know Naples ? "

" No, but I hope to go there in a year or two."

" Well, do you mind amusing yourself by looking round this little room ? It's an exact replica of the poet's house at Pompeii. When you've finished you can talk to Roland."

So saying, Salvator went into the inner room with Fragola and shut the door behind him.

CHAPTER VIII

CONVERSATION BETWEEN A POET AND A DOG

LEFT alone, Jean Davy took up the candle and went to examine the walls of the room, while Roland with a sigh of satisfaction, lay down on a rug placed before the door through which the young man and girl had gone out, which rug seemed to be his accustomed bed.

Jean Davy held the candle to the walls for some
moments without seeing anything, for his eyes were
turned inwards, as one may say, and thoughts took
his mind from his surroundings. He was thinking
of that beautiful young girl, candle in hand, bending
over that dark and narrow staircase in this low
quarter of the town. Her long gold hair, her eyes
as blue as Heaven, her exquisite fine skin, like the
petal of a rose, that neck a trifle too long which
gives such grace to man or animal as in the swan or
the woman Raphael loved to paint—that form of
hers, as supple as silk, yet which he knew intuitively
had been touched by illness and misfortune; in short,
the whole apparition of Fragola as astonishing as
Salvator himself and in some way completing him,
seemed in the poet's eyes a vivid dream. It was all
so strange. Strange, even that little scarlet spot
below her eye, which made them call her Fragola
with its charming diminutive, Fragoletta. Then the
name of Régina that the young girl had mentioned,
recalled to the poet an aristocratic lady who could
have nothing to do with the humble folk of this
house but the thought of whom set something
vibrating in his young heart.

But his abstraction gradually passed, and he
turned to view the paintings that covered the walls.
The artistic side of his nature instantly got the upper
hand and reality drove away dreams. He saw before
him a marvellously exact copy of the decorative work
of antiquity. The four walls each held a picture
in a panel, and each picture showed a landscape seen
through the columns of a peristyle or the windows

of a room. The frames of the panels were graced by every imaginable fancy, such as the hours of day and night, dancers, a grasshopper drawn in a chariot by two snails, doves drinking from a cup and so on. The whole was copied with perfect taste and a fidelity of tone that denoted the colourist.

Jean Davy would again have been astonished if by now anything could astonish him where his singular friend was concerned. Thoughtful, he placed his candle on the table, which seemed small for the room, and sat down. His eyes roved vaguely about the room and then fell on the dog.

He remembered that Salvator had said : " When you have finished, talk to Roland." He smiled at the recollection. The words might have seemed a mere joke to another, but to him were natural enough. They were proof of yet another sympathy between himself and his new friend, for Jean Davy, simple and good-natured, was not vain enough to believe that God had given souls to men and men alone. Like the poets of the East, the Brahmins of India, he believed that animals had souls which were slumbering or enchanted, either by the fascination of nature, as on the banks of the Ganges, or the spell of Circe in more Western regions. He had often thought of Man when the world was born, preceded there by the animals, his brothers, and he fancied that the animals and the plants, which are their sisters, were the guides and teachers of humanity. To him it seemed as if the beings we rule now were then our leaders, guiding our wavering reason with their sure instinct, and that they counselled us, those simple creatures whom, to-day, we despise. Even so, the Baobab which began as a tree and became a forest and has seen the centuries pass like a chain of old men hand in hand; the migrating bird who travels a league with each stroke of his wing and so sees the whole world; the eagle looking at the sun before whose rays we have to turn away our eyes; the bird of night with eyes like embers, flying through darkness that to us is a thick wall; the cattle ruminating under the green oaks or sombre pines, treading under foot in the fallow fields races and civilizations destroyed by the vast campaigns of Rome;—have not all of these something unknown to tell to Man if Man could but understand their language and would take the trouble to question them?

Jean Davy believed that in his own childhood he had had his hand on universal brotherhood; that he had for a moment understood the baying of dogs, the songs of birds, even the perfume of roses to whom he used to offer the bits of sugar his mother gave him, when he saw their petals beginning to unfold.

Then, as he grew older, it seemed as if this almost human intercourse of the child with animals and plants had vanished.

What was the cause of this breach in the link that bound the human child with the simple and the humble, with animals and plants? Pride. It was as the difference between East and West.

India, common mother of the human race—India whose symbol is the milch cow—to India we turn when Europe needs to replenish its soul by immersion once again in primitive sources. Greece and Rome deified art and destroyed nature. They made slaves of men; to them animals were but brutes, and they exhausted the land, without troubling to help it to renewed fecundity. Then one day Athens found herself a ruin; Rome a desert. Magnificent roads down which no one journeyed, triumphal arches beneath which tramped a ghostly army, and aqueducts which still conducted water to dead cities where were none to thirst !

All these ideas surged through our poet's brain at sight of the dog to whom he now began to talk.

He called his name in the short commanding tone of the hunter, and Roland, who was sleeping with his nose upon his paws, lifted his head and looked at him.

Jean Davy called him again, slapping his leg. The dog rose on his two front paws, sitting on his haunches like a sphinx. A third call induced him to come and lay his nose on the poet's knee, looking at him in friendly fashion.

" Good old dog ! " said Jean Davy caressingly.

Roland gave a whine, half affectionate, half plaintive.

" Your master Salvator was right, old man. We are going to understand one another, aren't we ? "

At the word Salvator the dog gave a friendly bark and glanced at the door of the inner room.

" Yes, he's in there with your mistress Fragola, isn't he, Roland ? "

Roland went to the door, put his nose down to

the slit at the bottom, gave a loud snort and came back to lay his head again on our poet's knee, half-shutting his intelligent, almost human eyes.

"Now let us see who were our father and mother. Please give me your paw."

The dog lifted his huge paw and placed it in Jean Davy's hand. He examined the interstices of the toes.

"Ah, I thought so. Now tell me your age."

He opened the animal's powerful jaws, uncovering a double row of teeth as white as ivory but a little worn at the back of the mouth.

"We're not quite in our first youth; if we had been a woman we should have begun hiding our age some years ago, but being a man, we are only just about to start, eh?"

The dog made no sign. He seemed quite indifferent on the matter of his age. This being so, Jean Davy went on with his examination, hoping to find some point on which the dog would be more sensitive. This he soon did.

Except that his hair was longer and more curly, especially underneath, Roland's coat was like the tawny fur of a lion. Yet Jean Davy noticed on his right flank, between the fourth and fifth ribs, a white spot.

"Oho!" said he. "What have we here, Roland?"

He put his finger on the spot and Roland whined.

"Why, it's a scar," said Jean Davy, who knew that wounds or burns destroy the colouring matter in hair; he had seen a white star formed on a horse's forehead by the application of a red-hot knob. He guessed that this white spot indicated a wound or burn. A wound, probably, since his finger felt a cicatrice. He looked on the left flank and there, a little lower down, was a similar place. Davy touched this with his finger and the dog whined again even more dolefully than before, which Davy understood when he felt the rib, for on that side it had been broken.

" Poor old Roland. So, like your namesake, you've been in the wars? "

Roland lifted his head, opened his jaws and emitted a howl that made Jean Davy shudder. It had so mournful a note that it brought Salvator from the inner room.

" What's the matter with Roland? " he asked.

" Nothing. You told me to talk to him and so I asked him his history. He was just telling it to me," replied Davy, smiling.

" What has he told you? I'm curious to know. The truth, I hope."

" Why should he lie? He isn't a man."

" All the more reason for telling me what he told you," repeated Salvator with some insistence which seemed to spring from a secret uneasiness.

" Here's our conversation, word for word. I asked about his parents and he told me he's a cross between a Newfoundland and a Mont St. Bernard. That he's between nine and ten years old; and when I asked what this white patch meant, he told me it was left by a bullet which entered his right side and came out on the other, breaking a rib in its passage."

" That's all perfectly true."

" Good. Then you'll admit that as an observer I'm deserving of your pains."

" You are a sportsman; the membrane between Roland's toes and the colour of his coat told you he was a cross between the water dog and the mountain hound; you guessed his age from his teeth, and of course you felt his scar and found out about the bullet wound. That's right, isn't it? "

" You make me feel small ! "

" And that's all he told you? "

" When you came in he was telling me that he hadn't forgotten his wound and that he would prob- ably recognize the man who shot him. Now I count on you to tell me the rest."

" Unfortunately, I know no more than you."

" How's that? "

" I was out shooting one day round Paris . . ."

" Shooting? "

" Poaching, I should say.—A commissionaire doesn't shoot.—I found this poor animal in a ditch, he was covered with blood and dying. His state moved me and I carried him to a fountain and washed his wound with cold water and a drop or two of brandy. It restored him wonderfully. His master didn't seem to set much store on him, or he would never have left him in that state, so I thought I might keep him. I nursed him, giving him much the same treatment that wounded soldiers receive and he recovered. That's all I know. Oh, I forgot to say that he shows a gratitude which would put men to shame and that he'd die for me or anyone I cared for. Wouldn't you, Roland? "

Roland gave a joyful bark and again put his fore-paws on his master's shoulder.

"All right, old fellow. You're a good dog. Down!"

Roland went back to his rug again.

"And now," said Salvator, "are you ready to come out with me?"

"I'd like it if I'm not interfering . . ."

"Interfering?"

"Doesn't your companion want you to go out with her early in the morning?"

"No. You heard her say she couldn't tell me where she was going."

"And you let her go out like that without know-ing where?"

"My dear poet, there can be no affection without trust. I love Fragola with all my heart, but I'd as soon suspect my mother as suspect her."

"Yes, but isn't it imprudent to let a young girl go out like that at six in the morning?"

"She will have Roland with her, and with him she'd be safe all over the world."

"Oh, of course that's another matter." Jean Davy threw his cloak gracefully round him and added: "By the by, when your companion was speaking of her friends, she mentioned the name of Régina."

"Yes."

"It's an uncommon one. I know someone so called. She's the daughter of a Marshal of France."

"You mean the daughter of Marshal Lamothe-Houdan?"

" Yes."

" That is Fragola's friend. Come along."

Jean Davy followed without a word. He felt that he was proceeding from one surprise to another.

CHAPTER IX
THE SOUL AND THE BODY

SALVATOR now wore a long white coat, a waistcoat buttoned to the throat and dark trousers. Thus dressed, it was impossible to say to what class of society he belonged. With his hat cocked over one ear, he seemed a working-man in his Sunday clothes, but with it straight on his head he looked a man of the world in morning dress. Jean Davy noticed this particularly.

" Where do you want to go ? " asked Salvator, shutting the door behind him.

" Where you like. You're in command to-night."

" Then let us do as the Ancients did. Throw a feather into the air and follow it."

Walking to the centre of the square, Salvator tore a scrap of paper from his pocket-book and tossed it up. The wind wafted it towards the rue Poupée. They followed it to the rue de la Harpe. There a second scrap of paper took them towards the rue St. Jacques.

They wandered on without knowing where they were bound, entranced in one another's company. Two or three times Jean Davy tried to surprise his companion's secret, but each time Salvator turned off his questions, till at last he said plainly to his interrogator :

" We're looking for a tale in the making, aren't

we ? Mine's a story that is told. If I give you your wish and stop to tell it, we shall be going back into the past. Let us go forward ! "

Jean Davy saw that his companion wished to remain incognito and did not insist. At that moment, they came upon a group of men and women collected round someone lying on the ground.

" He's drunk," said some.

" He's dying," said others.

A rattle was heard from the man's throat.

Salvator broke into the crowd, knelt to lift the man's head and said to Jean Davy :

" It's Barthélemy Lelong. He'll die of congestion if I don't bleed him at once. There must be a chemist's near. Knock one up. They have to attend when they're wanted."

Jean Davy saw that they had reached almost unconsciously the faubourg St. Jacques, near the Hospital. Facing the hospital he read over a shop window :

LOUIS RENARD. Chemist.

He knocked with a full sense of the need for promptitude, and in a few minutes the door oponed and M. Louis Renard appeared in cotton nightcap and fustian trousers, asking what he wanted.

" Bandages and a basin," replied Jean Davy. " There's a man with congestion of the brain who must be bled at once."

They brought the poor carpenter to the shop. He was unconscious.

" Is there a doctor here who can bleed him ? " asked the chemist. " I can't. I'm a herbalist really."

" All right," said Salvator. " I've studied surgery. I'll do it."

" I've no lancet," said the chemist.

" I've my case," said Salvator.

The crowd filled up the shop.

" Do you want to be of service to this man ? " Salvator asked them.

" Of course, M. Salvator," said one of the men and offered his hand. Salvator took it and Jean Davy thought he saw him exchange a masonic sign with the newcomer.

" While I bleed this poor wretch, knock up the hospital and tell them we're bringing him along."

Several of the crowd, led by the man who had spoken to Salvator, went off to the hospital. Mean-while, the chemist had taken off poor John Bull's cravat and drawn his arm from his shirt. The veins in his neck were swollen to bursting point.

" Do you bandage the arm ? " asked Jean Davy.

" Have you bandages ready ? " Salvator asked the chemist.

" I'll get them," replied he.

" Press tightly just above the vein please, M. Davy. I think I can manage."

Davy obeyed, while one man held the arm, one the basin and another the lamp.

" Mind the artery," said Davy, anxiously.

" Don't be afraid. I often bleed people at night with no other light than that of the moon or the street lamp. This sort of thing is common with these poor fellows, especially when they leave the wineshop."

Even as he spoke he used his lancet and the blood came spouting out, black and slimy.

"It was high time," he said, shaking his head. The operation had been accomplished with the quickness and dexterity of a practised surgeon.

Barthélemy took a deep breath.

"Tell me when you've taken away enough blood," said the chemist, who now came up with a bandage.

"He's got plenty. He won't miss it," replied Salvator. "Let it run for a bit."

When they had taken about two basinsful, the invalid opened his eyes. His first glance was dull and unintelligent, but, little by little, his eye lit up. He recognized Salvator.

"That you, M. Salvator? Glad to see you."

"So am I to see you," replied Salvator. "It looked as if we might not see you again!"

"Oh . . ." said Barthélemy, with a little more consciousness of his surroundings. "So you've been bleeding me, have you?"

"Yes." Salvator wiped his lancet carefully and put it back in his case.

"Then you didn't want me to die?"

"Me? Why should I want you to die?"

"Well, you threw me downstairs, so I supposed you wanted to kill me."

"Don't be a fool."

"Oh, why shouldn't you? I'd made you angry refusing to have that d——d window open! But you see I couldn't give way. I'd have felt so ashamed of myself. And that d——d dandy gave himself such airs!"

" That d——d dandy has just helped to save your life."

Barthélemy turned and looked at Davy, who smiled at him.

" I say, is that true ? " he asked.

" Don't let us bear malice, my friend," said Davy, offering his hand.

" Oh, I'm not given to sulks," replied Barthélemy. " And since you want to shake hands . . ."

" I wanted to begin that way but you will do me the justice to admit that it was you who refused."

" That's true," said Barthélemy, frowning. " A man is a fool to let a woman work him up like that. Would you believe it, M. Salvator ! She's gone back to that little worm from Bobino's. I can't fight a threadpaper that size and he reckons on that. Oh, she knows what she's doing in taking up with a thing you can't call a man ! "

" Now, now, steady ! "

" It is easy to talk like that. You live with one of God's angels, M. Salvator. Well, you deserve it ! But whatever I am, I've been a good father and it's a shame that anyone should run off with my girl. I've been looking for her everywhere; she's hidden herself somewhere with her hag of a mother. I can't get at her there, for whenever the old thing sees me she screams out : ' Murder ! ' I've done two nights in chokey, but I'd do cells for weeks and months if I could only get my girl back. . . . My little Fifine ! "

The Colossus began to cry like a woman.

" What did I tell you ? " said Salvator to Davy,

who was watching this curious scene with interest. "Now, now. You shall have your girl back," he added to John Bull.

"You'll get her for me, M. Salvator?"

"I promise."

"Oh, if you do, you won't have to throw me downstairs. You'll only have to say, 'John Bull, throw yourself down,' and I'll do it!"

"The hospital gate's open, M. Salvator," said the man who had gone to give the alarm.

"Not for me?" said Barthélemy.

"For you."

"Oh, I won't go!"

"You won't?"

"I don't like hospitals. They're for the poor. I'm able to pay to be nursed at home."

"Yes, but you won't be nursed at home. You'll just eat and drink until you go to the hospital to come out no more. Now, now, Barthélemy. Come along."

"I won't, I tell you!"

"All right. Then go back home and look for your girl yourself. I'm tired of you!"

"M. Salvator, I'll go wherever you please! Where is that d——d hospital? I love hospitals, damn them!"

"Ah! That's better."

"But you will find my girl?"

"I promise you news in three days."

"And what am I to do for those three days?"

"Just keep quiet."

"Can't you let me know before that?"

" I'll try."

" All right, I'll go. Why, where have my legs gone to? I can't walk ! "

Salvator made a sign and two men helped Barthé-lemy to get up and took him away. As he left the shop he cried :

" You promise to give me news of my girl in three days at latest, M. Salvator. Don't forget ! "

They got him across the road to the hospital, but he stopped at the gate to shout again :

" You won't forget my poor little Fifine, will you, M. Salvator ? "

" You were right," said Jean Davy. " One shouldn't go to a cabaret to see what men are really like."

CHAPTER X
WHAT WAS HEARD AT A CHEMIST'S SHOP

THE operation finished, the patient in hospital, there was nothing for our friends to do but go on their way with the consoling thought that if caprice had not taken them through the streets of Paris at three o'clock in the morning, a man, who might now be reasonably expected to live some thirty or forty years, would have died.

Before leaving, however, Salvator asked his host for some water in a basin to wash the blood from his hands.

There was plenty of water but a basin was not forthcoming. The only one our worthy chemist possessed was full of the carpenter's blood and Sal-vator had ordered that to be kept and shown to the doctor at the hospital. The demand for a basin, therefore, seemed a trifle inconvenient.

The chemist looked round and at last said :

" Suppose you come and wash your hands at the pump."

Salvator agreed, and as Jean Davy also had received a stain or two, he followed his friend. When they reached the little yard, they stopped and looked at one another, in astonishment, for through the open door of the kitchen came the sound of melody.

Where the music came from and what instrument caused it, they did not know. Near was the high wall of a convent. Did the delightful harmony come from the organ there, borne on the wind to the few passers by ? Or had Ste. Cecilia herself descended from Heaven to celebrate Ash Wednesday ?

The air they heard was no opera air, nor even the gay singing of someone returning from the masked ball. It seemed more like a psalm or canticle from some old Biblical story—the voice, perhaps, of Rachel mourning for her children, for as they listened they seemed to hear all the sacred hymns of childhood, all the inspirations of Bach and Palestrina. Had they named the air, they would have called it Resignation ; no other name could express so well its effect.

It made them feel that the player must be gentle and unhappy like the music. Our two friends hastened to wash their hands, resolved to set forth in search of the musician.

The chemist brought them a napkin by way of towel, and Jean Davy offered him in return five francs, for which sum he seemed as if he would have been content to be roused three times a night !

His thanks were so profuse that Jean Davy asked to be allowed to stay a few minutes longer, to listen to the music.

" Stay as long as you like," replied the chemist. " It won't matter to me if I may shut the door and go back to bed."

" But how shall we get out ? "

" The street door is only latched. You've only to undo the bolt to get into the street."

" But who will shut it again ? "

" Oh, that doesn't matter. I wish I had an extra pound a year for every time it remained open all night ! "

" Then all's well," said Jean Davy.

" It is, indeed," replied the delighted chemist, and shutting the door, he left the two young men masters of the kitchen and yard.

Salvator meanwhile had gone up to a lighted window on the ground floor, through which the music seemed to come. Pulling at the shutters, he found they were not fastened. He then moved the curtains gently aside and looked in. He saw in the room a man of about thirty seated on a high stool, playing the 'cello. This man might well have sat for the portrait of Liszt.

Though a music score lay open on the desk before him, he kept his eyes on the ceiling and seemed wrapped in thought, almost unconscious of what he was playing; though his hand guided the bow mechanically, his thoughts were elsewhere. He seemed to be waging an inward struggle between self-control and despair; he closed his eyes as if to shut out the sight of his surroundings, hoping so to shut away his grief. Then with a cry of agony, his bow slipped from his hand.

Was his soul vanquished? Tears coursed down his cheeks.

He took out his handkerchief and wiped his eyes; then picked up his bow and started playing again.

Our two friends had watched with intense interest.

"Well?" whispered Salvator.

"It's astonishing," replied Jean Davy, brushing away a tear from his own eye.

"There's the story you were looking for, my friend."

"Do you know the man?"

"No. I've never seen him before, but I don't need to know him to see that here is a great tragedy. He's a strong man. One can tell that by the way he goes on playing, and for him to shed tears betokens an immense sorrow. Let us ask him to tell us his story."

"You don't mean that?" said Davy, trying to stop him.

"Of course I do," said Salvator, going to the door and looking for knocker or bell.

"You think he will talk about his affairs to anyone who likes to ask?" cried Davy, again trying to stay him.

"We aren't exactly anyone," remonstrated Salvator. "We are . . ."

He stopped, and Jean Davy hoped that he would

let slip something that would clear up the mystery surrounding him, but he merely added :

" We are philosophers."

" Oh ! "   Jean Davy was disappointed.

" We aren't drunk nor are we actuated by vulgar curiosity. I don't know what you thought of me when you first saw me, but I'm sure that anyone seeing you would trust you with a secret as one would trust you with his hand."

He offered his hand as he spoke as if offering a certificate of honesty and added, smiling : " All men are brothers. We may be able to help."

" Oh, if you insist," said Davy and shrugged his shoulders.

Salvator, finding neither knocker nor bell, rapped three times with his knuckles, whilst Davy watched through the window to see what effect this interruption would have on the man within. He saw him rise, lay down his bow, lean the 'cello against the wall and open the door without giving any sign of surprise. Either he expected someone or he was so abstracted from the things of this world that nothing could astonish him. In either case, his demeanour seemed to bear out Salvator's opinion.

" Who are you ? " he asked.

" Two unknown friends," answered Salvator.

This seemed to satisfy the 'cellist.

" Come in," said he, showing no surprise at the strange time of night at which their call was made. They followed him into the room and Jean Davy shut the door.

It was a very small room but with a simple charm.

7

White walls gave it the semblance of a nun's cell, especially as it contained so little furniture; yet the delicate and modest taste that had dictated the choice of decoration would have made it a perfect setting for a young girl. It seemed odd to find a man there; it gave the impression that a woman must share it with him; his sister probably. Yet the musician seemed to live alone. Nor could one believe that some woman of another type had a right to visit him there, for the room was chaste and the man honest and straight. There must be some other explanation. He lived there and his sister took care of the room for him. Was that it? But if so, why was he so sad?

Their host offered them chairs, but they felt they must first explain.

"Before we sit down, may we ask you a question?" said Salvator. "Is it in the power of man to help you in the trouble from which you are obviously suffering?"

"No, sir," replied the 'cellist simply, showing no more surprise than when he had admitted them.

"Then we will go," said Salvator. "We heard you playing from the courtyard out there, and, looking through the window, saw your grief. It moved us so profoundly that we ventured to come in that we might offer you money if you are poor or sympathy if you are in trouble."

The 'cellist's eyes again became wet, but they were tears of gratitude. There was something in the tone in which Salvator spoke—something in the whole personality of the man—such sincere sympathy for his fellow men—that one felt irresistibly drawn to him.

The 'cellist offered them his hand.

" It is terrible to have to hide one's sorrows," said he, " especially when one's heart is full of them. Besides, to speak of them may serve as a warning to others. Sit down and let me tell you. . . ."

Jean Davy sank into an armchair, but Salvator, characteristically, leant against the wall. The 'cellist told his tale.

It is we who will narrate it here, for we know many things which his modesty prevented him from mentioning.

Let us begin by bringing him and one of our heroines together. There are some of us who do not begin to live until the path towards love is opened.

CHAPTER XI
JUSTIN AND MINA

IT was a wonderful moment for Pierre Justin Corby —child as he then was—when he first heard his teacher, Professor Müller, playing his violoncello, and drawing from it strains as gravely melancholy as the soft plaint of the wind stirring in the woods. He had always been a favourite pupil; and henceforward the bond between them became a strong one, riveted by their common love of music. Justin gave the old man no peace till he shared with him those treasures of harmony which set vibrating every fibre of his being. Every day he presented himself for his music lesson, or, in other words, he gave up his whole recreation time to the pursuit of study in the disguise of pleasure. They deciphered together the works of the Great Masters, comparing old with new, Porpora with Weber, Bach with Mozart and Haydn with Cimarosa. Their was a " solitude à deux " : a fairy-tale : a dream : and the dream lasted seven years. Then it was broken by tragedy.

" Poor Justin ! How good he is ! " his mother would sigh.

" Do not pity him," cried the Professor stoutly. " He is magnificent ! He reminds me of my dear friend Weber when he was young."

This was the highest praise M. Müller could give, for Weber and he had been boys together, and it was Justin's fancied likeness to Carl Maria that had first awakened in the old musician's breast a feeling of interest in the studious lad.

Yet, in spite of the harmonious vibrations of his beloved 'cello, life became burdensome to Justin. He fell into a melancholy which alarmed good M. Müller.

" You are growing old before your time ! We must take some little excursions together as soon as the holidays begin."

So when the holidays came, they walked in the country outside Paris. And thus it was that Justin met Mina.

It was at the close of a perfect June day, when all Nature seemed holding festival, that the two friends, in the best of spirits, were returning from an excursion to the plain of Montrouge. They were crossing a field of barley, Justin a few steps ahead of his companion on the narrow path, when he stopped short. A child lay at his feet, asleep among the poppies and cornflowers.

She seemed to be about ten years old, in a white frock with a blue ribbon round her waist. Her little feet, in their blue shoes, hung down into the ditch with an air of abandonment that suggested extreme fatigue. Her sweet face was so fair and gentle that she looked like a dove in its nest.

The men looked round in vain for her friends. There was no one in sight. That they could leave the child to sleep alone in the field all night never even occurred to them, so they gently awakened her. She opened her eyes, as blue as the cornflowers, but she showed neither surprise nor fear.

" Why are you here, child? " asked the old man.

" I was asleep, sir. I was so tired that I couldn't walk any further."

" Then you've come a long way? "

" Oh, ever so far ! "

" Where are your parents? "

" I have no parents. I lived with nurse."

" Where is she? "

" Dead, sir," replied the poor child and burst out crying. The two friends turned away to hide their own emotion.

" But how is it you are here all by yourself? " asked the old man, gently.

" I came from La Bouille, near Rouen," she replied, drying her eyes with the backs of her little hands. "I was driven to Paris and walked from there. I want to find the faubourg St. Jacques. M. the Curé has given me a letter to deliver to my nurse's brother. But the diligence was so late reaching Paris that everyone is in bed, so I thought I would sleep out here in the fields."

" Weren't you afraid ? "

" Why should I be ? Don't the birds and flowers sleep out of doors ? "

" Won't you come back with us ? " suggested the young man. " You shall go and find your nurse's brother in the morning."

" It's very late, sir," replied the child. " Soon it will be daylight. It's not worth while to trouble you."

" If you stay here you might be taken up."

" What for ? " asked the child with that directness that is sometimes embarrassing in children. " I haven't done anything wrong ! "

" As a vagabond."

" Oh ! . . . Oh, then please take me with you ! " She held out her little hand to the young man, as willing to go with him now as before she was reluctant.

" I will carry you, with M. Müller's help," he said. " You must be too tired to walk." In spite of her denials, he and the old man crossed hands, and she slipped a little arm round each of their necks. But just as they were about to start, she cried :

" I am forgetting the letter the good Curé gave me ! "

Slipping from her perch, she ran back to the field for her baggage, which consisted of a little package, a basket with some cherries and bread and a coronet of cornflowers which the child had twined for herself while resting among the barley. The old man tied the package to his buttonhole and she managed to carry the basket herself, but the coronet of corn-flowers kept getting in the young man's eye, as she sat with her arm round his neck, and at last he managed to pick it up with his teeth and place it on her head ! Crowned with the blue flowers, her white dress shining against the men's black coats, the little girl looked like a young child-druidess being carried in triumph to the sacred forest.

The more the two friends induced her to talk, the more delighted they were with her, and soon they learned the whole of her history, as her nurse had told it to her, and it had, indeed, a touch of mystery about it. It seemed that one day when the good woman returned to her cottage, she heard to her great surprise, a child crying. She hastened to light the lamp and then she saw lying on her bed a little baby, about a year old, while on the table were a purse and a letter. She opened the letter, and with some trouble, for she was no scholar, she read these lines :

" *Mme Boivin,*
    " *You are known to be a good woman and that is why a father, obliged to leave France, is trusting his child to your care. You will find twelve hundred francs in the purse on the table; that is the allowance for the first year, which is being paid in advance. Regularly, dating from this day next year, you will receive a hundred francs a month, which will be paid you through the Curé of la Bouille, but even the Curé will not be told from whom they come. Give the child the best education you can and make her a good housewife, for God knows what trials may be in store for her! Her name is Mina; that must be her only name till I can give her the surname that should be hers.*"

This letter was dated the 28th of October, 1812, and for seven years the sum mentioned was regularly paid, but then the payments suddenly ceased. The nurse, Mme Boivin, was a good-hearted woman and still continued to keep the child who wanted for nothing while she lived. But now she had been dead a week and the good Curé had care of the child with instructions to send her to Mme Boivin's brother, a wheelwright in Paris, whom she had not seen for some time but whom she declared trustworthy. His name was Durier. When they heard this, the two friends exchanged glances. Durier! The name brought to the young man's heart a fear . . . which was really a hope in disguise.

This little girl was to him a dream, a revelation. He felt that Providence had looked kindly on his struggles, for is it not a mark of favour when a life is entrusted to us?

And so they bore the little weary Mina home to the shabby little house in the faubourg St. Jacques.

It was seven years before the day on which Salvator and Jean Davy saw and wondered at the 'cellist's charming room. Its appearance then was very different.

Instead of the white muslin curtains, which gave the alcove the air of a tiny chapel, in place of the statue of the Virgin and the two rose-coloured candles from which an impression of peace and meditation seemed to flow, we find it cold and damp, with low ceiling and flagged floor. No flowers perfume the air, no birds sing at the window, which is uncurtained even as the walls are unpapered. Its sole

furniture is a bench to seat some eight children, a
desk with a large volume on it—at a guess the works
of Handel—a blackboard, an old table and one cane
chair. At the end of the room hangs a serge curtain
which conceals a miserable bed. A more wretched
room can hardly be imagined. Its tenant is our
Justin, a poor schoolmaster, and the quarter of the
city that of St. Jacques, a squalid one, overflowing
with children but singularly void of the means of
paying school fees. The suburb of St. Jacques is
one of the most primitive in Paris. Is this because,
surrounded by four hospitals as a citadel by four
bastions, these hospitals keep tourists away? Or is
it that, as it is not on the way to any place of
importance, vehicular traffic is comparatively rare;
so rare, indeed, that directly a carriage does appear
there, the urchin who has the distinction of being the
first to see it makes a trumpet of his hands and
announces the news to all the other inhabitants.
Then everyone drops his work, rushes out of doors,
stares and chatters. Gossip was the principal amusement of the faubourg, and a subject to gossip about
was hailed as a godsend by all the neighbours.

How did Justin come to be an inhabitant of this
quarter? We must go back to the tragedy which
interrupted his happy absorption in music by the
side of his friend and teacher, M. Müller.

Justin was barely sixteen when the death of his
father, a farmer, left him the sole support of a blind
mother and a little sister too young to work. By the
advice of his old friend he brought them to Paris,
and, with his help, procured rooms for them in the

small house in the faubourg St. Jacques. The struggle was a severe one. He succeeded in getting two or three private pupils, and also obtained the post of music-master at a school. This gave them a meagre living; but he was determined to repay the assistance he had had from M. Müller, an enormous sum, more than he could earn in a year! His days were full; but he had his evenings free. By dint of enquiry he heard that a timber-merchant was in need of a book-keeper twice a week. The last man to hold the post had been paid fifty francs a month; the timber-merchant offered Justin twenty-five, and he accepted. With the strictest economy, he might now hope to pay his debt to the Professor in some four years. This was not enough. His teaching took up eight hours a day, his book-keeping four hours twice a week. He still had four hours of four days a week to dispose of, to say nothing of twelve hours every night! He set about finding still more work; and thought himself fortunate when he secured the post of proof corrector at the printing office of a Royalist newspaper. It only took up some two-thirds of his nights. And in the course of one year, day for day, he had managed to repay his whole debt to the good Professor. Surely it was with reference to courage like this that a holy man once said, " To work is to pray ! "

But his happiness was short-lived : he fell ill. Typhoid had him in its grasp and carried him to death's door. He had to keep his bed for two whole months; and when he rose from it he found himself out of work. His pupils had gone to other masters; the book-keeping had been given back to his predecessor in the job; and the Royalist newspaper had failed. Once more he started the weary task of looking for work; and ended by opening a school at his own house. It was, as we know, a wretched dwelling, dependent for light and air on a courtyard surrounded by much higher buildings, dark, damp and insalubrious. Mother, son and daughter slowly withered there; the mother, poor blind woman, kept her room, not venturing over its threshold three times a year, but her son and daughter met in that room every evening; and she never complained. She had the sublime resignation of a Spartan matron and practised the same austere virtues. Sparta would have given her divine honours, but French society martyred her, as it martyrs so many. When face to face with the Supreme Judge, their answer to the question " What have you done ? " will be : " We have not conquered but at least we have died fighting.",

Her daughter, Céleste, a wild flower transplanted to a cellar, was delicate and anæmic; she suffered from aneurism which made even breathing difficult, and all excitement and exertion were dangerous for her. Even the neighbours, in spite of their gossipping tongues, looked on her as a saint, for, like her mother, she never complained; yet the sadness of her life was gradually wearing her away. The one relaxation of the little family was to welcome the good old Professor, who came to spend many an evening with them. On these occasions hospitality always led them to propose to light the fire, but the offer was always declined, and to make up for the cold hearth M. Müller would tell them amusing tales. His gay spirits warmed his hearers like a genial ray from Heaven.

Justin's pupils were too young to require any skilled training. Their parents only wished them to be taught the rudiments, and so his mother and sister were able to help him with his school. Céleste would take the arithmetic class, while Justin sat with his mother who received the youngest of the little scholars each day in her room. There they knelt round her chair while she heard their prayers and told them some simple Bible story. It was a charming sight to watch the fair childish faces while the rosy lips murmured a prayer. It might have been supposed that they were praying for the restoration of the blind woman's sight. Thus laboriously passed the days for all; but at night, when the women were in bed, Justin went to his own room and took out his 'cello. His family consisting of two delicate women, and his only friend the old Professor, he found family and friends and youth itself in his instrument. Was it not another self? A speaking mirror, to which he could confide his every care, and which with sonorous melody faithfully echoed his thoughts?

Thus passed his life in a monotony of work that ground him down. Too poor to afford himself any relaxation, or even to seek relief from his drab life among friends of his own age, he was chained like a galley-slave to his duty to his family; yet, heart of gold that he was, nothing would have caused him greater distress than to lose either of the frail and suffering women for whose sake he was renouncing all the pleasures of youth.

And now we come to the moment when Justin and the Professor returned from their ramble, bringing with them a little fair-haired girl, half asleep. What an astonished, yet overjoyed welcome they received! Céleste is amazed at the child's beauty, and though poor blind Mme Corby cannot see Mina's sweet face, she has eyes in her finger-tips which convinced her of the child's beauty. Both women are eager to hear Mina tell her story, but the little girl is dropping with sleep, and Céleste sets to work to make up a bed for her. Taking from its wooden easel the great board on which Justin chalked sums for his scholars, she lays it on four stools and spreads a small mattress on it. Mme Corby lays her hand on the child's head in gentle blessing, and little Mina climbs into bed, where she instantly drops off to sleep.

*   *   *   *   *   *

The next morning Justin went forth in search of information about the wheelwright Durier, who was, as he knew, a friend of a worthy plasterer of his acquaintance and ours, named Toussaint, but the news he heard from Toussaint only confirmed his own expectation. Durier had been concerned in a conspiracy with a Corsican named Sarranti, and both men had found it advisable to leave the city. There was no one to whom Mina's letter could be delivered. Thus Justin returned home to break the bad news to his mother and sister, who hailed it, as he had done, as good news.

" God has sent us an angel ! " cried the good

women, and indeed the little girl was a godsend, for she prevented our hardworking family from becoming weary of their own narrow life. They had been too long constricted in the sacred Ark of duty; here was a dove arrived, carrying in its mouth the olive branch. They adopted the child, one and all, with delight; poor as they were, they were eager to live even more poorly if they might have the joy of keeping Mina. Whatever sacrifice it might entail, to add her to their household seemed to them adding to their treasures.

" I will see to her education ! " cried Justin.

" I to her religious instruction," said his mother.

" And I," said Céleste, " will make her clothes ! "

But the next morning, when they were happily awaiting the child, with breakfast on the table, they heard her crying. The sight of poor Justin's dull, bare room made her unhappy, for she was used to fresh air and bright flowers, to blue skies and country milk and fruit. She found herself in a dark street, ever so close and depressing, and, worst of all, she found she was expected to drink on waking that terrible beverage which Parisians call *café au lait!* Why, who knows, since it is more than half chicory ? Mina had been in the habit of taking milk drawn from Mme Boivin's cow, and she found it hard to believe that the " coffee " was made with milk at all. When she put a teaspoonful of the horrible beverage in her mouth she had to reject it instantly !

The melancholy of that close, airless house, with its drab walls, spread over her like a thick veil.

Everything surprised her—the sad-coloured paper in Céleste's room, the dull brown curtains in the mother's chamber, and above all the sombre face of the young schoolmaster—and when, that same evening, Justin took out his 'cello and started playing, the poor child burst into tears! She fought against her own inclinations and made up her mind to resign herself to the semi-monastic life of the austere little house, but, poor child of the fields and hills, she was promising more than she could fulfil. She tried in vain to repress the treasure of gaiety that she carried in her bosom. One day, when cutting the meagre grass growing in the damp little yard, she began unconsciously to sing a folk-song she had heard in her country village, but Céleste appeared at the window and little Mina trembled with fright, to think she had so far forgotten herself as to sing. She felt as if she had been caught chattering in church! Another time, when arranging Justin's books, she saw the 'cello standing in a corner, out of its case. She hated the instrument, the deep tones of which made her feel most unhappy, but on the other hand, she was full of curiosity as to how those tones were produced! Taking the bow gingerly between her fingers, she stole up to the 'cello and twanged one of the strings. At this moment Justin appeared at the door and the poor child went white with terror. He only smiled at her and, taking her on his knee, showed her how to pass the bow over the strings. All his care and gentleness failed to soften her dislike of the poor instrument.

But in a short space of time the light-hearted child

learnt that, instead of assimilating the sadness of her benefactors, she could please them better by sharing with them her gaiety of heart. Instead of blaming her, they encouraged her to follow the impulses of her charming nature, making of all her little duties a pleasure, and every day for her became a fête-day. In the end, it was she who ruled the household, all the other members seeming to recover their own youth in hers. The old blind mother, the invalid sister, the overworked schoolmaster—indeed, the whole house—underwent a complete transformation; her care-free innocence reviving and rejuvenating all around.

She brought flowers from her country walks for the old mother, and found a little kitten to be a pet for Céleste, while as for Justin's own bare room, she redecorated it entirely. She saved her sous to buy for the walls a pretty paper and made the simple muslin curtains for the windows with her own hands. Every day she had a fresh inspiration—a new thought for the happiness of those about her. All the inventive genius of childhood was concentrated in her little blonde head; it seemed as if, like Zephyr, she only lived to breathe the spirit of spring and strew roses and jasmine round her path. They called her the Angel of Joy. But she never liked Bach or Palestrina. Justin had to lay aside his beloved scores and teach his instrument the gayer strains of comic opera!

But this was not all. One day a well-known notary who wanted a tutor for his sons, called to see Justin, and was so charmed by the little room as redecorated by Mina that he not only gave Justin the post, but used his influence in his favour elsewhere, with the result that better days dawned for them all.

*   *   *   *   *   *   *

One day, some few years later, a young man stood watching with others in the streets as a procession passed. A carpet of flowers was spread under the feet of the priest bearing the Host; the houses were decorated, the scent of incense perfumed the air, vibrating with the ringing of the church bells. The young girls in their white veils who followed the procession, made a charming spectacle, and groups of youths stood on the roofs and at the windows to watch them pass. Mina was among them and our friend Justin stood in the street to see her go by. He was there merely for that purpose, and it was quite by chance that he raised his eyes to a window; there he saw a young man devouring with ardent gaze the girls as they went by. Was he merely an ordinary spectator or was he watching with special attention any one of the white figures? Justin could not help thinking that he had come there for Mina and for her alone.—A flush—it would be more correct to say a flame—swept over Justin's face, and in a flash he saw the truth of his own heart.

That evening Mina came to him for the usual good night kiss, but as he gave it to her he trembled.

"What is the matter, Justin?" asked she, anxiously. "Are you ill?"

He *was* ill—with love. When anyone but himself so much as glanced at Mina, jealousy devoured him. He took to shutting himself into his room, where he alternately sat in a sort of trance or paced up and down, muttering and gesticulating. He would sing and laugh and then suddenly drop into a brooding silence. Then his appetite failed! Alarmed at these symptoms, his mother and sister sought advice from the old Professor, who had his suspicions as to their cause. Taxing Justin with it, our friend admitted the truth of the old Professor's surmise.

"Yes, it is true. I love Mina," he said. "But I am so afraid she does not love me!"

"Are you mad?" laughed the old Professor. "Of course she loves you!"

"But I am nearly thirty and she is only sixteen!"

"You don't look more than twenty-five, my boy. That fair hair of yours takes years from your age. But it is true that Mina is still very young!"

They were walking slowly along the street as they talked, and at this moment Justin was accosted by a boy of some twelve years old.

"*Monsieur*," said he. "Here is your handkerchief. You dropped it when you went out this morning."

"Why didn't you give it to me before?" asked Justin, taking the handkerchief.

"I wasn't sure it was yours, but the neighbours told me it belonged to the gentleman where the pretty young lady is living."

Justin took the handkerchief and gave the boy a ten sous piece.

"Oh, I must get that changed!" cried the boy. "Otherwise my old Grannie will take it all from me. I shall tell her you only gave me five sous."

He was about to run off with the coin when he

suddenly stopped. "*Monsieur*, do you want to know if the young lady loves you ? . . ."

"What's that?" said Justin sharply, his heart beating at these words. "What young lady? And what do you mean?"

"Why, the young lady who lives with you. Everyone knows you are in love with her. If you want to find out whether she returns your love, come and see my old Grannie. Brocante's the name. I'm Babolin Brocante, rue Triperet, number eleven. But everyone knows where old Mother Brocante lives. She'll tell the cards for you for ten sous."

But Justin was no longer listening, for the boy's words had seriously disturbed him. So everyone knew he was in love with Mina, did they? They were all talking about it, all talking and gossiping about him and Mina! He winced at the thought. In India there is a horrible insect called a moschite whose bite is dangerous. Not content with merely sucking one's blood like a gadfly, or pricking one with a sting like a wasp, it deposits in the hole which it makes in the skin of its victim a tiny egg, from which in three days is hatched a worm which in its turn engenders a host of other worms to eat their victim up alive! Now round us here in Europe, in France and even in Paris, there are insects different in form but even more dangerous than the moschites of India. We call them neighbours. "More dangerous" we said, and it is true. You can apply a remedy for the bite of a moschite, but the wounds inflicted by one's neighbours are mortal. They steal one's secrets as a thief one's property ; indeed, thieves have this point to the good over neighbours—that they risk their own lives, but neighbours attack the lives of others.

Justin, knowing his neighbours in the faubourg St. Jacques, was horrified at what he had heard from Babolin.

"We must stop this gossip for Mina's sake!" he cried. "Can I not marry her at once? She has no parents to be consulted."

M. Müller shook his head.

"She is too young," he objected. "It would be better to send her away to school for six months, during which time you can get the consent of the good Curé of la Bouille who stands to her practically in the position of guardian. He won't refuse it, and in six months' time you can fetch her away from school and she can then become your wife."

This arrangement seemed advisable to all except Mina herself. The news that she was to go to school at Versailles, under a governess known to M. Müller, came as a thunderclap to her. She could not understand why she must not remain with her friends—could not believe that anything should separate her from those who had grown so dear to her! One day Justin's mother said to her:

"What would you do, dear child, if I were to die?"

"I should follow you," replied Mina, smiling. "You would want someone to look after you in Heaven!"

"But in Heaven I should have all the angels with me, Mina dear," remonstrated Mme Corby.

"Oh, yes," replied the girl. "But they haven't lived with you for five whole years as I have!"

Why was she to go away to school? She could not understand it. In vain they told her that a grown-up girl of sixteen must not go on living in the same house as a grown-up young man. Why not? Neither the old mother nor the wise Professor himself could make her accept the fact that it was wrong for her to stay when Justin's sister Céleste was allowed to remain. Her heart was breaking and her eyes full of tears when at last she left her happy home for school.

* * * * * *

The six months soon passed away and our good people were plunged in preparations for the marriage. Directly the month of January began, all their thoughts were bent on arranging a home for the young couple. On the same landing as the rooms occupied by Justin's mother and sister, were two other rooms to be let;—the very thing they wanted;—and soon the whole household was turned upside down to furnish them. Nothing they had already was good enough and they started to haunt the shops. They had set their hearts on mahogany but, alas, in that poor quarter, they could find nothing better than walnut, with which they had to be content. Céleste undertook to get the carpets and curtains, and it was quite an adventure for her, for the invalid girl had not left the house for six months. There was not a shadow of jealousy in Céleste's heart, and though she might well have wondered why one young girl should marry the man she loved and the other be condemned by illness and affliction to remain an old maid, she was as happy as if she had been buying her own trousseau.

Mme Corby, whose blindness prevented her taking an active part in the preparations, drew from its hiding place the fine old lace which had adorned her own bridal gown and gave it to Justin to have cleaned for Mina. The good Professor also wanted to give his present, and one morning the neighbours, already intrigued by the quantity of new pieces of furniture which kept arriving at the house, saw to their astonishment a huge waggon draw up at the door. It was instantly surrounded by all the good wives, urchins, dogs and fowls of the neighbour-hood. They crowded round the vehicle, passing their hands over its varnished sides, combing the horses' tails with their fingers, and even mounting on the box while the coachman refreshed himself. In the midst of loud hurrahs from the sightseers standing in all the shop doors and windows, and even on the roofs, the cover of the waggon was raised and within was seen. . . . Oh, thrice in-credible luxury!—a large piece of furniture made of mahogany! The whole neighbourhood trembled with excitement, the pavement swarming with an attentive crowd, while cries of delighted astonishment passed from house to house. No one could make out what this huge object was, but as the mahogany glittered with polish they admired it excessively.

This enigma in wood was lifted with care from the vehicle and carried into the house, the door being shut in the faces of the curious onlookers; but they continued to discuss the nature of the object. Was it a sideboard? or a large writing desk? But neither suggestion seemed very probable, for the object had no visible drawers, and a sideboard without drawers, even of mahogany, scarcely seemed satisfactory. Someone suggested that it might be a wardrobe, but it had no doors! After much debate they waited round the house to waylay and interrogate the men who had brought the thing when they came out again. Breathlessly, the crowd watched for their re-appearance, and a portly dame, hands on hips, took on herself to be the spokeswoman. But, alas, for their curiosity! One of the porters was deaf and the other from Auvergne. The deaf man couldn't hear and the man from Auvergne couldn't make himself understood! The two men mounted the empty waggon without more ado, and with a crack of the whip it disappeared, forcing the crowd to disperse right and left to avoid being run over.

Not one of the neighbours ever heard the solution of that mystery! Even now they still talk it over during the long winter evenings. If any of our readers have guessed that the mysterious mahogany object was a piano, we beg them not to mention the fact to anyone! Let the neighbours continue in ignorance; it serves them right for having gossiped about Justin and little Mina!

We can imagine the astonished delight of our poor friends on receiving such a magnificent present, and when it was placed in the future home of the young couple everything was ready. It was a doves' nest in pink and white, simple and charming, and at the head of the bed, in an oval frame of gilded oak, was the small coronet of cornflowers that the little girl had woven while resting in the field: It hung like a votive offering in the simple room, for was it not from the very day that that coronet had been twined that all the clouds had lifted as by a miracle from the Corby family?

On the fifth of February all the Corbys set out with the Professor to fetch Mina back from school. The old blind mother had surprised them all the night before by insisting on going with them to Versailles. It was in vain to tell her that the fatigue would make her ill; she held to her resolution.

"I was the first to bid the child good-bye," she said, "and I want to be the first to bid her welcome home again."

The next morning, to the astonishment of the neighbours, a huge yellow barouche drew up at the Corbys' door. There are no carriages like that nowadays. They were the mammoths and the mastodons of the species—a sort of ark in which, on a rainy Sunday, a whole family could take refuge. Eight people could crowd in, but nowadays they would require four carriages; four times as comfortable, no doubt, but also four times as expensive. Is this progress? Who shall say?

The eyes of the neighbours were haggard with curiosity when the huge barouche drew up and the Corbys came out to take their seats in it—Justin, his sister, his mother whom the neighbours had never seen before! and, to crown all, the Professor. But before he got in he gave a small object and a message

to M. Renaud, our friend the chemist. The yellow
barouche was scarcely round the corner before all the
neighbours rushed to the chemist's shop to ask what
the message was about. M. Renaud was too profes-
sional to part lightly with a secret, but unfortunately
his old housekeeper was not troubled with scruples
of etiquette.

"They have left the key of their house with us,"
she explained. "And when the country Curé
arrives, Miss Mina's guardian, we are to give it to
him and ask him to wait."

"A Curé! They are going to be married!" cried
the neighbours, and as it happened to be a Sunday
and no one was at work, groups stood about the
street all day long discussing the news and waiting
either for the Curé to arrive or for the family to
return. Even when mealtime came round and took
some of them indoors, they left a sentinel with instructions to call them the moment anything happened!

Meanwhile the barouche arrived at the school and
just as it turned into the street another barouche was
driven away from the door. This, too, was yellow,
but it only contained one passenger, a young man.
Our friends, however, were too impatient to get to
their destination to notice him. Justin's heart,
indeed, beat so fast that he felt faint.

The schoolmistress, Mme Desmarets, received
them and sent at once for Mina, but the maid came
back to say she was not in her room.

"Look in Mlle de Valgeneuse's room," advised
Mme Desmarets, and turning to her guests, she

added : " I expect she is with her friend, Mlle
Suzanne de Valgeneuse, a charming girl, and very
highly connected. Her father has a fine place near
Rouen. She and Mina became great friends at once
and I congratulate you on the fact. Oh, here she
is ! "

Mina appeared at the door, flushed with pleasure
and breathless with excitement. She ran straight to
Mme Corby with a happy cry of :

" Mother ! "

Glad as she was to see them, however, there was
a shade of sadness in her joy when she was told
that she was to leave the school. During her stay
there she had grown fond of three things; her
governess, her friend Suzanne de Valgeneuse, and
her little bedroom overlooking the recreation ground,
and she soon begged leave to go and say good-bye to
her room and to her friend. Running back to her
room, she religiously greeted everything it contained,
passing her little hand lovingly over the furniture
and kneeling at the prie-dieu chair to say a final
prayer. Meanwhile Suzanne had reached the par-
lour. She was a handsome girl of about nineteen
with great black eyes that seemed a little hard, black
hair and brows in keeping with her eyes, and a tall,
slender figure. Her voice was imperious—even
haughty—and it was evident that she regarded herself as a member of the privileged classes. Justin
was not prepossessed in her favour, but when she
heard that Mina was leaving school for good, she
seemed so upset that he thought he had done her
an injustice.

" Mother ! " whispered he. " I do not want Mina to want her friend on her wedding day. Cannot we invite Mlle Suzanne to spend the day with us ? "

" She would refuse," replied his mother, for with the sensitiveness of the blind, her ear had detected certain hard notes in the young lady's voice that led her to doubt the reality of her friendship for Mina.

" We can but ask her . . ." began Justin, not satisfied.

" Our home is too humble for the daughter of rich people," interrupted his mother.

But she had to yield, and when it was proposed that Suzanne should accompany Mme Desmarets on a visit to Mina's home, that young lady accepted at once.

"Now I am ready to go home ! " Mina cried joyfully, and with a final *au revoir* our five travellers got into the yellow barouche again and returned to Paris. As for Suzanne, she ran to her own room and scribbled the following note to her brother, M. Lorédan de Valgeneuse :—

" *You had no sooner left than the Corby family arrived to take Mina away. I fancy something extraordinary is to take place and am going to see them to-morrow with Mme Desmarets. If you want to keep yourself informed, arrange to drive there too, in your barouche.*
" *Your loving sister,*
" *S. de V.*"

* * * * * *

Justin spent the night before his wedding playing airs from *il Matrimonio Segreto*, enriching them with fantastic ornament and gay variations; at three o'clock in the morning he decided to go to bed, but he was too happy to sleep, and at six he got up again, wondering why the dawn was so long coming! Surely all the clocks were slow! He went down to the street door, opened it and stood looking out. He seemed to be expecting something, though what, he himself did not clearly know. . . . He was expecting happiness! But happiness rarely comes to those who would open the door in advance. He went back to his room and began to dress, taking a good hour over his toilet. There were silk stockings and patent leather shoes to put on, to say nothing of the black coat and trousers or the white waistcoat and cravat. At eight, he heard the two girls getting up in the room above.

When Mina saw the petticoat of white taffetas, the muslin frock with its beautiful lace, and the white silk shoes and stockings, she was astonished and delighted.

" Who is going to be married? " asked she.

" It is a secret."

" Who will tell it to me? "

" Justin."

" Oh, I then will soon be dressed! Come and help me, Céleste."

Mina was as good as her word, for it is the hair dressing that, as a rule, delays a woman's toilet, and hers curled naturally. Just a touch of the comb and beautiful long curls fell gracefully each side of her neck, losing themselves in her modest bosom and all was ready!

" I am dressed, Céleste. Where is Justin? "

" Come along and find him,'' said Céleste . . .

but before they could get to the stairs they had to pass through Mme Corby's room and the blind woman heard their steps. Mina flew to her arms and Mme Corby laid her hand on her head; she seemed to be feeling for something. . . .

" This way ! " cried Céleste, and led the girl into the room so carefully prepared for the young couple. There stood Justin, waiting, with Mina's bridal wreath in his hand, the wreath of orange blossoms.

Mina understood all ! She stretched out her arms as if to find a support. And she did so, for Justin caught her to his breast and asked her to marry him. Four minutes later Mina was at Mme Corby's feet.

" Bless you, my child, and may you enjoy as much happiness as you have given me," said the blind woman as she felt the wreath.

At that moment the three guests arrived; the old Professor, the governess and Mlle Suzanne de Valgeneuse. While the others were congratulating the bride and bridegroom, Suzanne stepped to the door and looked out into the street. There she saw a small boy dressed as a groom, in white breeches and a cocked hat. He was elbowing his way through the gaping neighbours, and when he saw Suzanne he touched his hat and offered her a note.

" From M. Lorédan, miss," he said in English. " He told me to wait for a reply."

Suzanne unrolled the bit of paper and saw :

?

She wrote as follows:

> **?** *"She is marrying her goose of a school-master! No chance for you now . . . but who knows? Later, perhaps. . . ."*
>
> *"S. de V."*

"Here, Dick. Take this to your master," said she.

Justin, who had seen all that passed from within the house, wondered for whom the note was meant. He did not understand what it was about, but, some-how, he felt himself shiver as if seized by a presenti-ment of misfortune. He saw a barouche standing a little way down the street and by it a young man, fashionably dressed; this, of course, was M. Lorédan de Valgeneuse. When he turned to take the note from the groom, Justin caught a glimpse of his face. —He was the same man who had watched Mina so persistently on the fête day.—Once again the school-master felt jealousy stirring in his heart. . . . Yet, no sooner had the little groom climbed to his seat than the barouche drove rapidly away.

Someone else was now approaching the house, someone whose soutane and three-cornered hat pro-claimed his identity. It was the good Abbé Ducornet from la Bouille. He seemed surprised when the excited neighbours surrounded him.

"Of course M. the Curé has come for the mar-riage?"

"Why, yes, I have," replied the Curé, stopping.

"For M. Justin's marriage?" suggested one good woman.

" With little Mina, whose guardian you are ? "
cried a second.

" Well, yes."

" Don't bother him with your gossip," urged a
brewer's man who was rolling along a barrel.
" Can't you see he's in a hurry ? "

" I really am rather."

" There you are, M. l' Abbé. Only a few steps
further ! "

" That's the house with the yellow carriage outside ! "

" We'll go with you, M. le Curé."

" Babolin, run along ahead and tell them M. le
Curé's coming ! "

" You should just see the fine things they've been
buying, M. le Curé."

" There's nothing finer in the Tuileries, M. l'
Abbé."

" Then is M. Justin a rich man ? " asked the Curé,
bewildered.

" Oh, there are some folk who spend what they
have and others who spend more than they have ! "

" Come along, M. le Curé. They're waiting for
you ! " cried Babolin, who had been to the house
and back again while the good neighbours were pouring out their scandal.

" I'm coming ! " panted the little Curé, trying to
hurry. " Oh, Paris is a big place ! Much bigger
than la Bouille ! "

With a final effort he reached the house to find
Justin and Mina waiting for him at the door.

" Oh ! " cried the good man when he saw them,
" God surely made them for one another ! "

Mina ran to him and threw her arms round his neck, as she used to do when she was only eight years old. He felt he would never have recognized in this beautiful young girl the child he had sent to Paris only six years before. But he easily recognized her pretty, caressing ways!

" Come upstairs, M. le Curé. We need not start for the church just yet."

They took him gaily to the new rooms, where he found all the others assembled.

" It's our dear Curé from la Bouille, mother! " cried Mina. " The Abbé Ducornet."

" Yes, I've got here and I've brought the bride's dowry with me! " explained M. Ducornet.

" Her dowry! "

" Yes! Just think! I received a letter a few days ago—a registered letter from Germany, and in it was a draft on MM. Leclerc and Louis, the Rouen bankers, for ten thousand eight hundred francs! "

" What? " cried Justin, and his voice showed that he had received a shock.

" There is the draft," said the Curé, showing it, "and this is the letter that came with it."

" A letter? " murmured Justin. " What does it say? "

The Abbé opened the letter and read it aloud :

" *My dear Abbé,*

" *I have been travelling in India for the last nine years and that is why you have received no news from me. But I know you and our good Mme Boivin and I am sure my little Mina will not have suffered through my negligence. I have now returned to Europe and am detained at Vienna by business which may take some time, but I hasten to send you the sum of ten thousand*

*eight hundred francs which I owe you, and you shall
now receive regularly the twelve hundred francs a month
that I promised you for the maintenance of my child till
I can come myself.*

" Mina's Father."

" Oh, Justin, how lovely ! My father is living ! "

Justin glanced at his mother, who had turned very
pale.

" Mother ! " he cried; the blind woman rose and
came to him, her arms outstretched, groping her way
but guided by his voice.

" You understand, don't you, my son ? You could
have married Mina a poor orphan, but you cannot
marry her now she is rich and has her father ! "

Justin could not reply in words, but he fell on his
knees at her side.

" God bless you, my son ! God help you ! "

" Oh, mother," cried poor Justin. " With your
spirit to give me courage, I can find strength to do
this thing, but I could never have resisted the
temptation alone ! "

" What is the matter ? " cried Mina. " Oh, what
does it mean ? What does it mean ? "

" It means, Mina dear, that till your father gives
his consent—and he may never give it—we must
remain just brother and sister."

" Oh," cried the poor girl. " Let father keep his
money ! And leave me my happiness . . . leave
me you, Justin ! Oh, Justin, you are not going to
cast me off ? " She fell back into his arms unconscious.

In about an hour's time Mina was on her way back

to school again, one hand in that of her friend
Suzanne and her head on the shoulder of her school
mistress. But before they got into the carriage
Suzanne had found time to write and send another
little pencilled note :

> *" The marriage is broken off. It appears that*
> *Mina is rich after all, and has a father. We are*
> *taking the broken-hearted beauty back to school*
> *at Versailles.*
>
> *" S. de V."*

But if Mina was broken-hearted, so was Justin
—and above all, so was his mother. So courageous at
first, she had collapsed in the end and was taken to
her room, for her face was livid and her lips violet.
The terrible thing was that no one was to blame;
everyone had acted with the best intentions, but Fate
had intervened. Justin sat by his mother's bed till
nightfall and then she insisted that he should go to
his own room. She knew that he must be alone with
his grief. He went downstairs again to the little
room that Mina had arranged for him, carrying with
him her crown of orange blossom.—He went to the
door of the cupboard where his 'cello was shut up,
but he did not open it, for he had not the power to do
so. He paced up and down the little room for hours
till at last, overcome with fatigue, he threw himself
on his bed exhausted.

Luckily, the next day was a holiday, and all day
long he fought with his grief, striving for self-control. For hours he walked, fighting with himself,
till at last he felt that he could return and show a
smiling face to his mother and sister. But when they

had gone to bed he returned to his little room to count the hours till midnight. Then once again he went to his cupboard and this time he opened the door and took out his 'cello.

" I have been ungrateful, old friend! I shut you away when I was happy, but to-night, in my grief, I come to you for comfort."

Placing his music on the desk, he passed his bow across the strings, but as he played the tears ran down his cheeks. Slipping the bow under his left arm he took out his handkerchief to dry his eyes, and then began once more to play that strange sad air that, as we have described, Salvator and Jean Davy had heard through the window.

CHAPTER XII
A CHRISTMAS ROSE

THE impressionable Jean Davy had been deeply moved by Justin's story. Salvator, on the other hand, had listened with apparent insensibility, but at the names of Mlle Suzanne de Valgeneuse and her brother Lorédan he had trembled.

" Monsieur," said Jean Davy to Justin, " we should be unworthy of your confidence if we offered you trite expressions of sympathy. Here are our addresses. If you ever have need of friends, please remember us."

Tearing a leaf from his note-book, Jean Davy wrote down the addresses and handed it to Justin who placed it in his music score where he would see it every day. As he was so doing they heard a knock at the door. Who could be knocking so late? Justin was so lost to everything but his own sorrow that he took no notice and let his guests depart. It was they who opened the door to the nocturnal visitor, or rather to the early caller, for the first rays of daylight were beginning to appear. To their surprise, they saw a boy of about thirteen, a ragged urchin with fair curly hair and rosy cheeks; a true Parisian *gamin* arrayed in blue blouse, a cap minus the peak and broken shoes.

"Is that you, M. Salvator?" he cried when he saw who it was who had opened the door.

"What are you doing here at this time of night, M. Babolin?" asked the commissionaire, laying a friendly hand on the urchin's collar.

"I've brought a letter for M. Justin, Old Mother Brocante found it on her rounds to-night."

"Talking about the schoolmaster, you know you promised me you'd have learned to read by the fifteenth of March!"

"Well, it's only the seventh of February! There's plenty of time!"

"You know if you can't read fluently by the fifteenth I shall take back the books I gave you?"

"Not the ones with pictures in? Oh, M. Salvator!"

"Every one, without exception!"

"All right. Then I'll have to show you I can read," said the boy, resignedly and glancing at the letter, he read aloud:

> "*For M. Justin, faubourg St. Jacques, number twenty. A reward of a louis will be given to anyone who takes him this letter.*
>
> "*Mina.*"

" It's all written in pencil too, M. Salvator ! "

" Take it to him quickly, boy," cried Salvator, pushing the boy towards Justin's room.   Babolin rushed across the hall and burst into the room, crying :

" M. Justin !   Here's a letter from Mlle Mina ! "

" What shall we do ? " whispered Jean Davy.

" Let us wait," replied Salvator.   " That letter may tell of some new event in which our assistance might be useful."

Salvator had scarcely spoken when Justin appeared at his open door, looking as white as a ghost.

" You are still there ? " he cried.   " Thank God ! Read this ! "   Salvator took the letter he held out and read :

" They have got me and are taking me . . . I don't know where. Save me, Justin . . . or avenge me ! "

                                        " Mina."

" My friends, it was Providence that brought you here," cried Justin, holding out his hands to them in a gesture of appeal.

" Well," whispered Salvator to Davy.   " You asked for a plot and here, I think, you have it." For a moment the three young men stood looking mutely at one another.   For that space of time all seemed stupefied, but the next instant Salvator, at any rate, had regained his usual presence of mind. " We must keep cool.   This is a serious matter and we must not act like silly children."

" But they're carrying her off !   They're abducting her ! " cried Justin.   " She has appealed to me for help.   She asks me to avenge her ! "

"Yes, that is just why we must first find out who has abducted her and where she is being taken."

"Oh, God, how can we find out?"

"With time and patience, my dear Justin, we shall learn. You are sure of Mina?"

"As of myself."

"Then you may be sure she will defend herself. Now we must act quickly."

"Oh yes, act for pity's sake! Oh, I shall go mad!" All Justin's resignation vanished at the thought that Mina was in the hands of some blackguard who might do her grave injury.

"Is Babolin there?" asked Salvator. "Let us question him."

"Obviously that is the first move," agreed Jean Davy.

"First of all," said Salvator, going into Justin's room, "give the boy a louis for his mother and a tip for himself." Justin took two louis and two five franc pieces from his pocket and gave them to the boy, but Salvator seized his fist and forced him to disgorge one louis and one five franc piece which he handed back to Justin, greatly to Babolin's disappointment. "Put that money back in your pocket!" said he. "You'll find a use for it before another hour is over." Then turning to the boy, he added: "Where did your Grannie find that letter?"

"What say?" grumbled the boy sulkily.

"I asked where your Grannie found the letter. What streets has she been working to-night?"

"How do I know? Ask her yourself!"

"He's right. We must ask her. She is probably

expecting us to go round to her place. Now we must lay our plans well. . . ."

" You direct and I'll obey. I've lost my head ! " cried poor Justin.

" You know you can dispose of me, my dear Salvator," said Davy.

" Yes, I'm counting on your taking a part in this drama."

" As active a one as you please."

" Oh, hurry, gentlemen; hurry ! " cried poor Justin, feeling the precious moments pass.

" This is my idea. You, M. Justin, must go with this boy to his grandmother."

" Yes, yes. At once. . . ."

" Wait ! You, M. Davy, get a saddle-horse and meet him at rue Triperet number eleven."

" Nothing easier."

" And I'll go and inform the police."

" Do you know anyone in the police ? "

" Yes. The very man. Then I'll join you at number eleven and we'll take counsel."

" Come along, my boy," said Justin.

" Hadn't you better leave a word for your mother to ease her mind ? " suggested Salvator. " You may be very late back, or may not return at all."

" You are right. My poor mother ! I had for-gotten her." So saying Justin scribbled a few lines on a piece of paper lying on the table simply saying that a letter he had just received would take him away for a day. " Now, come along ! "

It must have been about half past six when the three young men left the house.

"That is your road," said Salvator to Justin, pointing to the rue des Ursulines; "and that is yours" to Davy, indicating the rue de la Bourbe. "I go this way," he added, taking the rue St. Jacques; "our rendezvous is rue Triperet, number 11."

Let us follow Justin as he sped towards the rue Triperet with Babolin at his heels. It is a small street, parallel to the rue Copeau and perpendicular to the rue Gracieuse. All that quarter still recalled in 1827 the Paris of Philippe-Auguste. The muddy lanes circling round the walls of Ste. Pélagie gave the prison the air of an ancient fortress built on an island; the lanes were barely eight or ten feet across and were obstructed by dunghills and rubbish heaps, while the unsavoury abodes of the inhabitants were hovels rather than houses. It was before such a hovel that Babolin stopped.

"This is the house," said he.

It was a wretched place, smelling vilely and literally sweating dirt and filth, but Justin scarcely noticed it.

"Go on," he said. "I'll follow."

Babolin went in as one accustomed but after a step or two Justin had to stop him. "Where are you?" he cried. "I can't see you."

"Here, M. Justin," said the boy, retracing his steps. "You'd better take hold of my blouse." This Justin did and step by step they climbed up the ladder, pretentiously called "staircase," that led to Mother Brocante's dog-kennel; the name seemed justified, since even from the stairs they had heard the barking and yapping of some dozen dogs.

"It's me, Grannie!" shouted Babolin, making a speaking trumpet of his hands. "Open the door. I've got someone with me."

"Will you be quiet, you mad creatures?" cried Mother Brocante, obviously addressing the livestock. "I can't hear myself speak! Still, Cæsar! Shut up, Pluto. Silence, all of you!"

At this command, uttered in a threatening tone, there was such an instant silence that one might have heard a mouse stir—and certainly there must have been plenty of mice in that house!

"Come in! Open the door; it isn't bolted."

Babolin, lifting the latch, let in the impatient Justin, who found himself facing a picture which, without being poetic, merits description. He was in a garret, the roof supported by cross beams, the daylight filtering through the broken tiles; in places the ceiling bulged so that it was evident it would fall on the heads of the inmates at the first storm. The walls were running with damp and infested by spiders, who sat in their webs watching disdainfully insects of all varieties. A dozen dogs, hounds, lurchers, half-bred Danes and little Toys growled in one of the corners, all packed into one basket that might have held comfortably some four or five at most. On the angle of the crossbeams was perched a large black raven flapping its wings and croaking joyously at the dogs' growling.

Seated on a stool with her back against one of the beams, surrounded by a heap of rags of every sort and colour, reaching some four feet up the wall, was a woman of about sixty, tall, and bony; emaciated, indeed to a degree; and between her knees knelt a girl whose long black hair she was combing with a care that either indicated a real love of its beauty or for the girl herself. This scene, which did not lack picturesqueness, owing to the diversity of objects composing it, was lit by a sandstone lamp similar in shape to those found in Herculaneum or Pompeii.

The old woman, obviously Babolin's "Mother Brocante," was dressed in rags and pieces picked up here and there and sewn together, looking like a row of samples of brown. The young girl's whole costume consisted of a long shift of écru linen, like that in which Scheffer dresses Mignon; round her waist was a rope of cotton, grey and cerise, having at each end a great tassel like that at the end of a curtain band; round her neck, hiding her bosom, was a wool scarf of cerise, torn and old but harmonizing with the touch of cerise in her waistbelt. Her feet were bare and they were charming, like the little feet of a Princess of Spain or of the gypsies. As for her face which she turned to Babolin when he came in with the schoolmaster, it was pale as a drooping flower, but her features were regular and fine though her face was so thin that admiration must be tinged with pity. Her shadowed eyes, restless and deeply set, the poor hollow cheeks and lips parted as in remembered famine or with a gasp of horror; her lack of words, so unusual in a girl of thirteen, all combined to give a touch of strangeness to her aspect which would have suggested to our friend Pétrus the idea of a child Medea or youthful Circe. She only wanted a magic ring to be a witch—a circlet of flowers to be a fairy;

yet she was really the Parisienne incarnate. Lack of air, sunlight and nourishment were written in ineffaceable lines on her poor thin body.

At the risk of interrupting our story, let us tell all we know of this unhappy child.

About nine o'clock of the twentieth of August, 1820, Mother Brocante was driving her little donkey cart home after a journey to the paper factory of Essonne with a load of rags, when a child rushed panting towards her, crying:

"Help! Help! Oh, save me!"

Now Mother Brocante belonged to the gypsy race whose strange instinct it is to carry off children even as birds of prey carry off larks and doves; she jumped from the cart, seized the girl, mounted her cart again and whipped up her donkey, looking all the time more like a wolf stealing a lamb than a woman saving a child. This happened some five leagues from Paris, between Juvisy and Fromenteau. The little girl was bareheaded and her hair, having come undone during the run or the struggle was hanging down her back; her forehead was bathed in perspiration and her white frock was stained with a long trail of blood from a wound in her breast, apparently made by some sharp instrument. The child was about five or six and no sooner was she in the cart than she crouched in a corner, whispering pitifully:

"Oh, don't let her catch me! Don't let her catch me!"

Old Mother Brocante who appeared to dread pursuit as much as the child, kept peering from behind the cover of the cart and lashing her donkey on; it was midnight when they entered the gates of Paris where Mother Brocante was too well known to be stopped and at last they gained the rue Triperet. Directly they halted the poor child rushed into the shelter of the house, crying:

" She isn't after me, is she ? "

" Come in here, child. There's nothing to be afraid of."

Letting the child into her room the old woman went back to stable her donkey. When she returned to the garret she found the little girl kneeling in a corner, feverishly repeating all she could remember of her prayers.

Mother Brocante called her and tried to question her as to her name and identity but the child could not be induced to tell anything, merely repeating, terrified, to all questions:

" I daren't tell ! She'd kill me ! "

Mother Brocante could never find out her name, or address. She never mentioned her relations, nor did she say who it was who had given her that cruel wound in the breast. Yet at night, in her dreams, she would sometimes cry out:

" Oh, have pity, Mme Gérard ! I have never injured you ! Oh, don't kill me ! "

It seemed, therefore, that the woman who wanted to kill her was a Mme Gérard.

As for the child herself, as she had to have a name, old Mother Brocante called her Rose de Noël.

When the old woman had signed to her to sleep on the mattress beside a child some few years older than herself she had obstinately refused. The filthi-

ness of the mattress sickened her. Instead, she took
a chair on which she passed the night. Early next
day old Mother Brocante bought her a blue cotton
frock and some cheap shoes and stockings, the whole
costing about seven francs. These purchases she
spread out on a box.

"Those things aren't for me, are they?" asked
the girl disdainfully and not till the old woman told
her that they would serve as a disguise could she be
induced to put them on. Her own charming white
frock, silk stockings and dainty shoes with delicate
lacy underwear the old woman sold for some thirty
francs, and congratulated herself on her luck. However, when mealtime came a difficulty arose. The
child refused flatly to touch the coarse food that
furnished a hearty meal for Babolin and his Grannie
and declared pitifully that she was not hungry. The
same thing happened at the next meal.

"What does the girl want?" grumbled the old
woman. "Pheasants stuffed with orange or
partridges and truffles?"

"No, no. But I would like a bit of white bread
like we used to give to the poor every Sunday."

Mother Brocante, hardened as she was, was touched.

"Here! Go and get her her white bread," said
she to Babolin, handing him a coin.

The boy ran off and quickly returned with a roll
which Christmas Rose gratefully devoured to the
last crumb.

"Feel better now?" asked Mother Brocante
gruffly.

"Yes, madame, thank you."

No one had ever called Mother Brocante "madame" before!

"A fine madame I am! And now Mlle Precious, what would you like for dessert?"

"I should like a glass of water," replied the child.

Babolin offered her a jug without a handle and cracked in several places.

"Is that what you drink out of?" asked she, gently.

"Grannie does. This is my way."

He tilted the jug above his head and, opening a very wide mouth, absorbed into it the water as it came pouring down.

"Oh! I think I won't drink, thank you."

"Why not?"

"I don't know how to drink like that."

"She wants a glass, poor fool!" shrugged Mother Brocante.

Babolin found a dirty glass lying in a corner, filled it with water and offered it to Christmas Rose who again shook her head.

"No, thanks," said she. "It's so dirty. But, oh dear, I am so thirsty!"

And the poor child burst into tears. Babolin rushed downstairs, washed the glass at the neighbouring fountain, filled it with pure clear water and brought it back to Christmas Rose.

"Oh, thank you, *Monsieur* Babolin!" cried she and drank it down in one draught.

"She called me *Monsieur* Babolin!" shouted the boy with glee.

That night the same scene was enacted again

about the bed and again the child preferred to sit up in the chair. The next day old Mother Brocante made a great effort. She put in her pocket the thirty francs she had got by the sale of the girl's clothes and, going out, she bought a little bed, a mattress, a blanket and two pairs of sheets all as white as snow.

"That's for you, Miss Precious," she said. "Since you're a princess we must treat you as a princess, eh? Now where are you going to sleep? Shall we have to rent an apartment for you?"

"Give me that corner over there," cried the child, and little by little, that corner had become a tiny room with its own furniture for old Mother Brocante was not so poor as she seemed; she was simply miserly, to pay out money being an extremely painful process to her mind. She had a profession of her own; she "did the cards," and from her clients she demanded, by way of fee, all she needed for Rose. The child was almost happy, dressing in her own picturesque way and reconciling herself to her airless, sunless lot. Yet a hard little cough gave sign that the life was telling on her and that, as time went on, its influence on her health might well be fatal.

CHAPTER XIII
MOTHER BROCANTE

THE scene that met Justin's eyes might have attracted the attention of any man less absorbed than he was in the thought of Mina's danger, and her call for help, but he entered the garret with that thought and that only in his mind.

"Grannie," said Babolin, going in before him as an interpreter might precede him for whom he is the spokesman; " here is M. Justin the schoolmaster. He has come himself to ask you about what I couldn't tell him."

" And the louis? " whispered the old woman, smiling as if she had expected this visit.

" Here it is," replied Babolin, slipping the gold coin into her hand; " but mind you buy Rose a nice warm dress! "

" Thanks, Babolin," said the girl, offering her cheek to the urchin who gave it a brotherly kiss; " but I'm not cold."

As she spoke, she coughed in a way that gave the lie to her words, but all these details were wasted on Justin who, as we have already said, was lost in a mist, seeing but the one thing which engrossed his thoughts.

" Madame . . ." he began and at the word old Mother Brocante lifted her head to see if he could really be addressing her. Justin was the second person to call her madame, the first having been Rose.

" Madame, it was you who found this letter? "

" Looks like it," growled the old crone, " since I sent it to you."

" Yes and I am very grateful," replied Justin, " but I want to know where you found it."

" In the quartier St. Jacques, to be sure."

" I mean in what street."

" Don't remember looking but it must have been somewhere between the rue Dauphine and the rue Mouffetard."

" Oh, try to remember, please! " cried Justin.

"Why, it might have been in the rue St. André des Arcs."

An observer more familiar than Justin with the gypsy type would have seen that old Mother Brocante was feeling her way towards a purpose of her own.

Justin thought he understood.

"Here," he said, "perhaps this will help you to remember."

He handed her another louis.

"Come, Grannie," said Babolin, "tell M. Justin what he wants to know. He isn't just anyone. He's thought a lot of in the quartier St. Jacques, I can tell you!"

"What are you interfering for, *gamin?*"

"Oh, all right. M. Justin told me to bring him here and I've done it. He's old enough to look after his own affairs."

So saying, Babolin went off to play with the dogs.

"Mother Brocante," said Rose in her musical voice. "You can see how anxious and unhappy this poor young man is. Do tell him what he wants to know!"

"Oh, my dear child, implore her to tell me!" Justin clasped his hands in anxious entreaty.

"She will," said Rose.

"Yes, yes, of course I will," mumbled the old crone as if obeying a stronger will than her own. "You know my weakness, dearie; you know I can't refuse you anything."

"Well, madame!" cried Justin, mastering his impatience as best he could. "Make an effort to remember, I beg of you!"

10

" I think it was. . . . Yes, of course it must
have been.—And yet.—But the cards will tell us."

" Then . . ." Justin went on speaking as if to
himself, taking no notice of Mother Brocante's last
words. " Then they went along by the Seine to the
Pont Neuf, and probably passed the barrier Fontainebleau or perhaps the St. Jacques barrier."

" That's it," said Mother Brocante.

" How do you know ? " asked the young man.

" I only said ' That's it.' . . . I didn't mean
. . ."

" If you know anything, for God's sake tell me
what it is ! "

" I don't. Only that I found a letter addressed to
you in the Place Maubert and sent it on to you."

" That's naughty, Brocante. You know more
than that," said Rose, " and you must tell it."

" No, I don't know anything more ! "

" You are doing wrong to send this gentleman
away like that. He is a friend of M. Salvator."

" I am not sending him away. I'm only telling
him that is all I know. But even if you don't know
you can always ask them as does."

" Whom can I ask ? Tell me, quickly ! "

" Ask them who know. The cards."

" Oh . . . I see. Thank you. Well, you've
told me something, and now I'll rejoin M. Salvator
and the police."

The young man went towards the door but Mother
Brocante, changing her mind, called out his name and
he turned. The old woman pointed a skinny finger
at the raven beating his wings above her head.

" You see that bird ? " said she.

" Yes."

" He's flapping his wings, isn't he? "

" Yes."

" Well, there you are! When that bird flaps his wings there's very little hope. That's all! "

" But you don't mean that his flapping has any significance? "

" My God, you ask that? You, a man of learning you a schoolmaster, and not know that the raven is the prophetic bird? "

" Well, but what does the flapping of his wings mean? "

" It means of course that you won't find the person you're looking for easily . . . for you are looking for someone, aren't you? "

" Yes, and I'd give all I possess to find her! "

" Well, you see, that bird knows it as well as I do."

" But what does the flapping of his wings mean exactly? "

" It means. . . . Why, look you, his flapping . . . that figures your trouble; as he flaps his wings ·in the air, so you will beat about in the void. He's done it three times and each time signifies a year; that means your search will take three years. So I advise you not to begin searching wildly, without a plan. See what the cards have to say."

" Then let us see at once! " cried Justin and, like a drowning man clutching at every straw, he retraced his steps, quite ready to believe the cards no matter how improbable might seem what they had to say.

" Will you have a short reading or a long reading? " asked the old woman.

" Just as you like. Here is a louis."

" Oh! Then you shall have a long reading and the divination of Cagliostro. . . . Get me the full pack, Rose."

The young girl rose; she was slim, lithe and graceful as a palm tree; she took a pack of cards from the drawer of an old trunk, hidden in a corner and with her pretty little hands, white and well kept, though painfully thin, she handed them to the old woman. Though no doubt he was well used to these cabalistic experiences, Babolin sank down on his haunches by his Grannie, prepared to follow with naïve admiration the scene of magic that was about to begin.

Mother Brocante drew from behind her a piece of wood shaped like a horseshoe and placed it over her knees.

" Call Phares," she said to the young girl, indicating with a jerk of her head the bird perched on the beam which answered to that name, taken from one of the three cabalistic words from the Feast of Belshazzar. The raven had stopped flapping its wings and seemed to be waiting for the moment when he would play his part in the coming scene.

" Phares! " The young girl called the name so musically that she seemed to chant it. The raven hopped from the beam to her shoulder as she stooped above the old woman, inclining towards her the side on which the bird was now perched.

The old crone then uttered a strange sound, coming from throat and lips and seeming half whistle, half cry. At this piercing note the twelve dogs, with one

bound sprang out of their basket, jostling one another
as they did so and, knowing creatures that they were,
disposed themselves right and left of the sorceress;
sitting on their haunches with the gravity of doctors
about to hold a learned séance or theological discussion, and forming round the table a perfect circle the
centre of which was Mother Brocante. When these
preparations, apparently indispensable, had been
noisily achieved by the dogs who kept uttering
mournful whines, silence reigned. Mother Brocante
looked from the bird to the dogs and then pronounced
in a solemn tone syllables borrowed from a strange
tongue, which Arabs might have taken for French
though Frenchmen would certainly not have taken
it for Arabic. We do not know if Babolin, Rose de
Noël or even Justin knew what the words meant;
but we can state that they were certainly understood
by the dogs and the raven judging by the rhythmic
yapping of the dogs and the piercing cry of the bird;
a cry that seemed imitated from the raucous note that
the old woman had uttered to call upon her *troupe*.
Then when the yapping died down and the bird
ceased to croak, the dogs who had sat stiffly, gazing
at one another with the wistful eyes of their kind,
lay down as if to sleep. The bird, however, hopped
from Rose's shoulder to the old woman's head and
there it stayed, its claws buried in her grey locks.

What a picture for a painter of interiors! The
sombre garret, lit only by the straggling rays of
daylight that came through the gaps in the roof; the
old woman, sitting with the dogs around her, Babolin
at her feet and Rose standing by the beam; the whole

group bathed in the red light from the earthen lamp. Justin, standing pale and impatient in the shadow. The raven flapping his wings from time to time, uttering sinister cries, recalling the fable of the crow who would be an eagle, except that the crow had his claws fixed in the white wool of a sheep, and our raven had crooked his in the grey hair of the old woman.—It was a strange, fantastic picture, well calculated to haunt an imagination less preoccupied than that of Justin.

Lit, as we have said, by the red light of the smoking lamp, the sorceress lifted her skinny arms in the air, describing mystic circles.

" Silence, all ! " cried she. " The cards are about to tell their tale ! "

Both dogs and raven fell silent and the cards took up the spell. First of all, the old Sybil shuffled them and made Justin cut with his left hand.

" It is understood that you have come here to ask for news of a person you love ? "

" I adore her ! " said poor Justin.

" Very good. You are the Knave of Clubs; that is, an enterprising and adroit young man."

Justin smiled sadly ; initiative and address were the two qualities he most lacked.

" SHE is the Queen of Hearts, gentle and amiable."

That was true of Mina. The pack shuffled and cut, Mother Brocante turned up three cards to start with. She recommenced the same proceedings six times. Each time there were two cards of the same suit ;—that is, two clubs or two diamonds or two

spades;—she took the card of the highest denomina-
tion and laid it down before her, arranging the cards
from left to right. Having done this six times, she
had in front of her six cards. This first operation
finished, she shuffled again, made Justin cut again
with his left hand and recommenced the process
following the same system. One of the sets of three
this time showed three aces; the sorceress took them
all and laid them down with the other cards on the
table. This chance shortened the proceedings,
giving her three cards instead of one; then she continued as before till she had seventeen cards; the two
cards representing Mina and Justin had both come
out. The sorceress then counted seven cards from left
to right, starting from the Knave of Clubs and including him in her count.

"There!" said she. "The young girl you love
is fair and between sixteen and seventeen years old."

"That is true," said Justin.

She counted another seven and touched a seven of
hearts, turned upside down.

"A project overthrown. You had made some
plan with her which you could not accomplish."

"Unfortunately, yes!" sighed Justin.

She counted seven again and touched the nine of
clubs.

"The project was overthrown by unexpected
money; a pension or legacy."

Again she counted seven and this time stopped at
the ten of spades.

"And the strange thing is that the money which
would have delighted most people, caused you

tears." Counting once more, she came to the ace of spades, upside down. "The letter I sent you," said she, "was from the young person, who is threatened with imprisonment."

"Imprisonment?" cried Justin. "Impossible!"

"The cards say so. Imprisonment or reclusion or sequestration. . . ."

"Why, yes," murmured Justin. "If they abduct her they will hide her. Go on! You are right so far."

"The letter reached you when friends were with you."

"Yes, that is so. Good friends, too."

Mother Brocante counted seven again and touched the queen of spades upside down.

"This trouble has been helped by a dark woman whom the girl you love believes her friend."

"Could it be Mlle Suzanne de Valgeneuse?"

"The cards say: a dark woman. They do not mention her name."

She went on counting and touched the eight of spades. That, too, was upside down. "The project hindered was a marriage."

Justin listened breathlessly. So far, whether by magic or chance, the cards had been right.

"Oh, go on!" he cried. "For the love of God, tell me more!"

Still counting, she now touched one of the three aces which had come out together.

"Oh!" said she. "A plot!"

The next seven brought her to the king of clubs, upside down.

" You are being helped now by a man of loyal character, who loves to render services."

" Salvator ! " murmured Justin. " That's what he called himself."

" But he is thwarted," she continued. " Something he is trying now to do for you is delayed."

" The fair young girl ? " cried Justin. " Tell me of her ! "

The old woman again counted seven and came to the knave of spades.

" Oh ! " sighed she. " She has been carried off by a dark young man—a scoundrel."

" Tell me where she is, woman ! " cried Justin, " and I will give you all I possess ! "

He drew a handful of money from his pocket and was about to throw it on the table where the cards lay when he felt a touch on his arm. He turned. It was Salvator, who had come in without being seen and who wished to stop his reckless generosity.

" Put that money back in your pocket," said he to Justin. " Come along down and jump on M. Jean Davy's horse. Gallop to Versailles and see that no one goes into Mina's room or sets foot in the court-yard. It is half-past seven ; you can be at Mme Desmarets' by half-past eight."

" But . . ." said Justin, hesitating.

" Start without losing a moment ! " said Salvator. " It is most important."

" But . . ."

" Start at once or I won't answer for the con-sequences."

" I'll go," said Justin, and turning to Mother Brocante he added : " I'll see you again."

He then ran rapidly downstairs, took the bridle from Jean Davy, leaped into the saddle, like the farmer's son he was, accustomed from childhood to mount any sort of horse, and disappeared at a gallop down the rue Copeau, the shortest way to Versailles.

CHAPTER XIV
WHY THE CARDS ARE ALWAYS RIGHT

JEAN DAVY, relieved of his horse, felt about for the staircase, the position of which had been pointed out to him by Salvator, who had found him the first at the *rendezvous* when he returned from the police. We might show off our wit on the subject of garrets, dark stairways and poets, but as Jean Davy owned a horse who could do some five leagues an hour, he was not at all the type of poet to be associated with a garret.

When Salvator appeared, the old woman had let the cards fall with a deep sigh; the dogs had gone back to their basket and the raven to his beam. When Jean Davy entered in his turn, he merely saw the picturesque group which appealed at once to him as a poet; that of the old woman sitting on her stool, with Babolin at her feet and Rose leaning against the beam by her side. Evidently Mother Brocante was awaiting with some anxiety Salvator's next words, but the two youngsters smiled at him as at a friend, though with very different expressions. Babolin's smile was gay, but Rose's melancholy. To the great astonishment of old Mother Brocante, Salvator made no allusion to what had just been happening.

" So there you are, Mother Brocante," said he.
" How is Rose to-day ? "

" Very well, thank you, M. Salvator," replied the
young girl.

" I wasn't asking you, child."

" She has been coughing a little, M. Salvator,"
confessed the crone.

" Has the doctor been ? "

" Yes, M. Salvator."

" What did he say ? "

" That she must leave this place."

" Naturally ; I've been telling you that for ever so
long." He frowned and added, sternly : " Why are
the child's legs and arms bare ? "

" She won't put on shoes or stockings."

" Is that true, Rose ? " said the young man gently,
yet with a tinge of reproach in his tone.

" I can't wear those coarse woollen stockings and
the only shoes I have are so common and heavy."

" Why doesn't Mother Brocante buy you cotton
stockings and kid shoes ? "

" Because they are too dear, M. Salvator. I'm a
poor old woman. . . ."

" They are not dear and you are not poor," said
Salvator.

" Oh, M. Salvator ! "

" Silence ! and listen to me."

" I'm listening, M. Salvator."

" And you'll do as I say ? "

" I'll try."

" You will do as I tell you ? " repeated the young
man sternly.

" I will do as you tell me."

" If in a week's time . . . you hear me? . . . a week's time you have not found a room for your-self and Babolin, another room both airy and sunny for this child and a kennel somewhere else for the dogs, I'll take Rose away from you."

The old woman put her arm round the girl's waist and pressed her to her breast as if she feared that Salvator would execute his threat that instant.

" You would take away my child?" she cried, " after she's been with me seven years?"

" She isn't your child," said Salvator. " She is a child you stole."

" Saved, M. Salvator. Saved!"

" Stole or saved; you shall argue the point with M. Jackal." Mother Brocante did not reply to this, but she pressed the girl even more closely to her. " However," continued Salvator, " I didn't come here about that. I came about the poor young man you were fleecing when I entered the room."

" I wasn't fleecing him. I was only taking what he gave me of his own free will."

" You were deceiving him, anyway."

" I wasn't. I was telling him the truth."

" How did you know it was the truth?"

" By the cards."

" That's a lie."

" But the cards . . ."

" It's all a cheat."

" M. Salvator, I swear on the head of Rose that all I told him was true!"

" What did you tell him?"

" That he loved a fair girl between sixteen and seventeen years old."

" Who told you that ? "

" It was in the cards."

" Who told you ? " repeated Salvator, sternly.

" Babolin. He heard it from the neighbours."

" Oh, so that's the part you play in the game, is it ? " said Salvator to Babolin.

" Sorry, M. Salvator. I didn't know there was any harm in telling Grannie. Everyone knows M. Justin is in love with Mlle Mina."

" Go on, Brocante. What else did you tell him ? "

" I told him the girl loved him and that there was a project of marriage which had been overthrown by an unexpected sum of money."

" Who told you that ? "

" Why, M. Salvator, the ten of clubs means money and the eight of spades a project thwarted."

" Who told you, Mother Brocante ? " demanded Salvator, getting more and more impatient.

" A good Curé, M. Salvator,—a good old Curé with white hair who would certainly not lie. He said to a group of neighbours : ' When one thinks that a sum of twelve thousand francs '— twelve or ten, I forget which . . .'"

" Never mind."

" . . . ' When one thinks that a sum of twelve thousand francs which I brought news of has caused all this misery.' "

" I see. And what else did you tell him ? "

" I told him that Mlle Mina had been carried off by a dark young man."

"How did you know that?"

"Why, M. Salvator, the knave of spades came out and you know the knave of spades . . ."

"How did you know the girl had been carried off?" demanded Salvator, stamping.

"I saw it, monsieur."

"You saw?"

"As clearly as I see you."

"Where was this?"

"Place Maubert."

"You saw Mina in the place Maubert?"

"This very night, M. Salvator.—I had just done the rue Galande and was doing the place Maubert when all of a sudden a carriage came by so quickly you can't believe! The window was let down and I heard someone cry: 'Help! help! I'm being abducted!' and a pretty little head as fair as a cherubim's appeared at the window. But a second head followed—that of a dark young man with a moustache.—He dragged her back and shut the window, but she'd had time to throw out a letter . . ."

"And that letter?"

"It's the one addressed to M. Justin."

"What time was this, Mother Brocante?"

"It might be five o'clock in the morning, M. Salvator."

"Good. Is that all?"

"That is all."

"You swear on Rose's head?"

"On Rose's head."

"Why didn't you simply tell M. Justin what passed?"

" I was tempted, M. Salvator. He'll tell others and it will bring me clients."

" Well, here's a louis for having told the truth," said Salvator, " but out of that louis you will buy this child three pairs of cotton stockings and a pair of kid shoes."

" I should like red shoes, M. Salvator," said the girl.

" You shall choose whatever colour you prefer, child." Then, turning to Mother Brocante, he added : " You understand? If in a week's time to the hour I find you still here, I shall take Rose away."

" Oh ! deary me ! " sighed the old woman.

" And you, Rose—if I find you going barefoot again, I'll have you dressed in the clothes you had on when I first saw you five years ago."

" Oh, M. Salvator ! " cried the young girl.

" Now, don't forget, Mother Brocante," said he, going to the old woman and speaking in a whisper, "that you answer to me for that child with your head ! If you let her die of cold in this garret I'll see that you die of cold, misery and hunger in a prison cell."

Having uttered this threat he bent towards the girl, who offered him her cheek to kiss. Then he made Jean Davy a sign to follow him from the filthy room. Davy, however, gave one last glance at the old woman and two children before he, too, went out.

" Who is that strange young girl ? " he asked as soon as they had reached the street again.

" God alone knows," replied Salvator, and as they walked down the rue Copeau and the rue Mouffetard he told Jean Davy how the girl, whose savage beauty had had so powerful an effect on the poet, had come into Mother Brocante's hands that twentieth of August seven years ago. The tale was not a long one as we know, and it was finished as the two young men reached the pont Neuf.

" Here we are," said Salvator and leant against the railings of the statue of Henri IV.

" Are we to wait here ? "

" Yes."

" What for ? "

" For a carriage."

" Where's it going to take us ? "

" Oh, my dear fellow, don't be so inquisitive ! "

" But "

" As a dramatist, you must know that it is an important thing to sustain the interest."

" Oh, just as you like ! "

They did not have to wait long. In about ten minutes a carriage, drawn by two strong horses, turned the corner from the quai des Orfèvres and stopped before the statue of Henri IV. A man of about forty opened the door, crying :

" Jump in ! " And directly they had done so, he added to the coachman : " You know where to go ! "

The carriage started off in haste, turning at the extreme end of the pont Neuf and hurrying along the quai de l'École.

CHAPTER XV

M. JACKAL

WE will now tell our readers what Salvator had not thought it advisable to tell Jean Davy.

When he left Justin and Davy, Salvator, as we know, went straight to the police. He reached that horrible blind alley called the rue de Jérusalem, so narrow that the sun never succeeds in penetrating its muddy depths, and there he entered the Préfecture. It was seven in the morning and hardly daylight. The concierge stopped him.

"Where are you going, sir?" he cried.

"Eh?" said Salvator, turning.

"Oh . . . pardon, M. Salvator. I didn't recognize you. It's your own fault," he added, laughing. "You are dressed like a gentleman."

"Is M. Jackal in his office yet?" asked Salvator.

"He slept here."

Salvator crossed the courtyard, entered the sombre door and went up a little staircase to the left, mounting to the second floor, where he turned off along a corridor and asked to see M. Jackal.

"He is busy at the moment," replied the clerk.

"Tell him it is Salvator, the commissionaire of the rue aux Fers."

The clerk disappeared through a door to reappear immediately.

"He'll see you in ten minutes."

A few moments later the door opened and though no one was visible a voice could be heard crying:

"Find the woman, I tell you. Find the woman!"

Then the speaker appeared. Let us try to paint his portrait. M. Jackal was about forty with a very long body so tapering as to be almost vermiform, and very short legs. His head seemed to belong to the order of carnivorous digitigrades, and was covered with a

11

reddish grey hair or fur or what you please; his ears were both pointed and hairy and set close to his head like those of an ounce; his orbits yellow at night and green by day, resembled the eyes of a lynx or wolf; the pupils, long and vertical like a cat's, contracted and dilated according to the light; his nose and chin or as we may say his muzzle tapered like a grey-hound's. In short he had a fox's head and a pole-cat's body. His legs, moreover, restless and bony, promised that he could glide like a marten into any crevice however small, provided it admitted his head. His whole expression, like that of a fox, revealed astute finesse; like the nocturnal hunter of rabbits and fowls one felt that M. Jackal would only quit his lair in the rue de Jérusalem to go a-hunting in the dead of night.

He blinked when he saw who was awaiting him in the semi-darkness of the corridor.

"Why, it is you, my dear M. Salvator," he said, advancing with marked cordiality. "What brings me the pleasure of this early visit from you?"

"They told me you were very busy, sir," said Salvator, who seemed to have some difficulty in hiding the repugnance the man inspired in him.

"That's true, but you know I'd leave all my affairs to have the pleasure of a talk with you."

"Then let us go into your room," said Salvator, not returning the compliment.

"Impossible. There are twenty people waiting to see me there."

"Will it take you long to dispose of them?"

"About twenty minutes; a minute each. I must be at Bas-Meudon at nine."

" What are you going there for ? "

" I've got to investigate a suicide."

" Suicide ? "

" Two young people have killed themselves. The oldest of them is only twenty-four."

" Poor things ! " sighed Salvator. Then reverting to Justin's affair : " It's very inconvenient not to be able to talk to you; I had a serious matter to discuss."

" I know ! "

" What ? "

" I'm driving and shall be alone in the carriage. Come with me and you can tell me about it as we go. What is the matter ? "

" An abduction."

" Find the woman ! "

" We're trying to ! "

" I don't mean that one. I mean the other."

" Which other ? "

" The one who has arranged the abduction."

" You think there's a woman in it ? "

" There's a woman in everything, M. Salvator. That is what makes our work so difficult. Yesterday they told me a slater had fallen from a roof."

" And you said : ' Find the woman.' "

" I did and they laughed at me; they said it was an obsession. But I looked for her and found her ! "

" But how ? "

" The man had turned round to have another look at a woman in the garret opposite and he was so absorbed in watching her that he didn't attend to his footing. He slipped and fell. And there you are ! "

" Was he killed ? "

" Dead as a doornail, the fool.   Well, is it understood ?   You come with me to Bas-Meudon ? "

" Yes, but I have a friend with me."

" There's room for four in the carriage. Fargeau,"
he added to the clerk, " have the horses put in."

" I must go to rue Triperet . . ."

" I'll give you half an hour."

" Where shall we meet ? "

" At the statue of Henri IV.   I'll stop the carriage
and take you up and then off we go ! "

With this M. Jackal went back to his room and
Salvator set out for the rue Triperet; things had
passed according to programme and the two young
men got into M. Jackal's carriage and were now
driving rapidly towards Bas-Meudon.

M. Jackal's marvellous attributes had raised him
from simple commissioner to Chief of Police. He
knew every thief, every criminal and every vagabond
in Paris; ticket-of-leave men, escaped convicts, experienced, amateur and retired thieves, they all
swarmed within his ken in the muddy pandemonium
of the old Lutetia Parisiorum and no matter how
dark the night, how tenebrous their course nor how
infinite their hiding places, they could not escape his
eye. He was master of lodging-houses, gambling
hells, and resorts of vice as Philidor of the squares
of his chessboard. He no sooner saw a rifled shop, a
broken pane or a knife-thrust than he would cry:
" Aha !   That's So-and-so's work ! "   And he was
seldom wrong. He seemed superior to the needs of
Nature; if he had no time to dine he went without

dinner and if he had no time for sleep he did without sleep! He could wear any disguise with equal success; gentleman of means, general of the Empire, member of the Caveau, concièrge of a great house or porter of a small one, grocer, shopman, quack, peer of France, Dutch tumbler, he could be anything he wished and put to shame the finest and most versatile actors. Proteus himself would have been but a mountebank compared to him.

He had neither father, mother, sister nor brother. He was alone in the world and it seemed as if Providence had left him without relatives that his mysterious ways might have no witnesses and he could be free to choose his own path. His bookcases contained four different editions of Voltaire, one for each case! At a period when every one, and especially the police was jesuitical he claimed the right to Free Thought, quoting the Dictionnaire Philosophique on every occasion and knowing 'La Pucelle' by heart. The four editions of the author of 'Candide' were bound in shagreen; funereal emblem of his buried beliefs. M. Jackal did not believe in good; evil dominated his world. To repress this evil seemed to him the sole object of life; he could understand no other. He was a sort of Archangel Michael of the nether regions; the Last Judgment had already sounded for him and he used the powers Society had conferred on him as the exterminating angel uses his sword. Men seemed to him a collection of marionettes or puppets of every profession; the woman pulled the strings and he had a monomania on this subject of which we have already had an example, yet that monomania led him to the detection of crime after crime. Whenever a conspiracy, assassination, theft, abduction, escape, sacrilege, or suicide was announced, he merely replied : " Find the woman ! " They looked for her and if they found her there was no more to do. The rest went without saying. He had seen a woman at the back of the slater's accident where anyone else would but have seen an accidental slip and he was right. He was, therefore, faithful to his principles when he said to Salvator àpropos of Mina's abduction : " Find the woman ! "

Such was M. Jackal, and we have not said the half of what we wished to record of him. We have forgotten one characteristic touch; he always wore green-tinted glasses, not that he might see better but that others might see less of him. When he wished to use his eyes freely he would hurriedly push the glasses up on to his forehead; then his eyes would shoot one quick glance from beneath his half-shut lids and he would lower the glasses again without touching them, merely by a slight movement of his frontal muscles. They would then fall of themselves into the rut their steel bridge had cut across his nose. He rarely needed a second look, his observation was so rapid and so exact. His glance indeed was like summer lightning flashing from dark clouds, on a hot August night.

CHAPTER XVI
FIND THE WOMAN

WHEN M. Jackal had the two young men in his carriage his first action had been to thrust up his glasses and flash on Jean Davy one of those lightning glances that seemed to lay bare a man's whole character. Then the glasses instantly fell back to their place, either because he recognized Jean Davy, already a dramatist of some reputation, or because the young man's honest face had satisfied him.

"Ah!" said he, when he was comfortably established in the corner of his carriage, which corner he had wished to yield to Salvator who had firmly refused it; "so it's an abduction, is it?" He took out his snuffbox—a delicate bonbonnière that may well have held pastilles for the Pompadour or the Dubarry —and inhaled with rapture a large pinch. "Now tell me all about it."

Every man has his weak side, his heel of Achilles, his vulnerable point. M. Jackal had his and we should be unfaithful chroniclers if we omitted to mention it. He could do without food and even without sleep, but he could not do without snuff. His snuffbox was indispensable. One might almost say that it was there he found those wonderful countless ideas with which he astonished his contemporaries. He had heard Salvator's story once but vaguely, and when preoccupied with other things so he needed to hear it all over again. This second recital, however, though augmented with all the details that Salvator had heard from Mother Brocante, left his opinion unchanged.

"You haven't looked for the woman?" he said.

"We haven't had time. We only heard of the affair at seven o'clock."

"Oh, the devil! They will have rearranged the room and stamped all over the garden."

" Who will ? "

" Those fools ! " By this unflattering term M.
Jackal referred to the schoolmistress, her under-
mistresses, and the pupils.

" No," said Salvator. " There's no danger of
that."

" Why not ? "

" Justin went off at a gallop on this gentleman's
horse " (he pointed to Jean Davy) " and he will stand
sentinel at the door."

" If he gets there ! "

" What ? "

" Does a schoolmaster know how to ride ? If you
had told me I would have put the Hussar on to the
job." The Hussar was one of M. Jackal's subordin-
ates, so called because of his fine horsemanship.

" That's just what I said to Justin but he replied
that he had ridden from childhood, being the son of
a farmer."

" Good. Then once we find the woman all will be
well."

" But," objected Salvator, " I can't think of any
woman to suspect."

" Suspect all women."

" Isn't that a trifle arbitrary, M. Jackal ? "

" You say it is a young man who has abducted
your Mina ? "

" My Mina ? " smiled Salvator.

" The schoolmaster's Mina; the Mina in question."

" Yes, Mother Brocante, who saw them pass, says
it was a young man and he was dark."

" At night all cats are grey." As he quoted the proverb M. Jackal shook his head.

" You doubt that he's dark ? " asked Salvator.

" It doesn't seem natural for a young man to abduct a young girl; we don't do that sort of thing, unless the young man is of good family, has influence at Court and is not afraid to assume in the nineteenth century the mantle of Lauzun or Richelieu. If he were the son of a noble or nephew of a Cardinal or Archbishop. . . . It's the old men who go in for abductions. Listen to this, M. Salvator and you too, M. dramatist."—He jerked his head slightly towards Jean Davy.—" Old Age is blasé and has lost its charms, but a young man, good looking and attractive—for him to abduct is monstrous."

" Yet so *it is*."

" Then find the woman. Evidently a woman has inspired this crime. I do not know to what degree, but a woman must play some part in this strange drama. You say you can't think of any woman about your Mina, but I think of her as surrounded by women; mistresses, undermistresses, school friends, servants. . . . Oh, you are too naif to know what girls' schools are like." He took another pinch of snuff. "They are just so many incendiaries where young girls of fifteen live in the flames like the salamanders mentioned by our naturalists of old. I know one thing; if I had a daughter of marriageable age, I'd rather lock her up in my cellar than send her to boarding school. Oh, you've no idea of the complaints we receive of the morals of those places; not that the mistresses are to blame, but simply that the

girls are always ready and anxious to fall in love.
It's the old story of Eve; mistresses, undermistresses,
and all the rest are constantly on watch like watch-
dogs round a farm; but how can one prevent the wolf
from entering the sheepfold when the sheep herself
opens the gate?"

"That isn't the case this time. Mina adored
Justin."

"Then a friend has done it; that's why I keep
saying: Find the woman."

"I am beginning to agree with you, M. Jackal,"
said Salvator, wrinkling his brow as if to force his
thoughts to halt at some suspicious detail which
evaded him.

"I am not doubting your Mina," explained the
Chief of Police. "I mean your schoolmaster's Mina.
Brought up as she was she couldn't bring with her
the germs of corruption; but for one candid perfumed flower, how many evil weeds may not be in-
fecting the air with the poison they have imbibed
from their own families? We think children careless and lighthearted but they forget nothing. Remember that! They may have seen some innocent
fairy play when ten years old; and so at fifteen, a
boy will dream of a knight's lance to transfix the
giant persecutors of the princess of his choice; a girl
may fancy herself that persecuted princess, victim of
her own parents and to rejoin the lover they have
torn her from will employ the cunning of the en-
chanter Maugis or the wicked fairy Colibri. Our
theatres, museums, walls, shops, walks, all con-
tribute to awaken in the child's mind a thousand

impulses of curiosity that the first passer-by may serve to satisfy, if the parents are not there. Everything concurs to excite that thirst to know about everything that is the danger of childhood; and the mother who cannot satisfy this curiosity and reveal to her daughter the things that puzzle her, sends her away to a school where she can talk about it to girls a little older than herself. That is why I say that girls carry poison with them even when they come from honest families."

" But surely . . ." said Salvator who, with Jean Davy was listening to all this with surprise, " but surely there is a remedy ! "

" Oh, there is a remedy for everything. But, in this case, there is first a wall higher and stronger than the Great Wall of China to be overthrown —the wall of custom, that plague of Society. That is why a fatal tendency is spreading among our young people."

" What ? "

" Suicide. A young man loves a girl who as yet does not love him; he will not wait for her to fall in love; he kills himself ! A young girl loves a man . . . and perhaps counts on him to cover with his name a certain fault. . . . She kills herself ! Or two young people love each other and their parents refuse their consent. They kill themselves ! And do you know why they do this as a rule ? "

" Surely because they are tired of life," said Jean Davy.

" One is never tired of life," replied the Chief of Police, " and the proof of that is that the older one gets the more one clings to life. There are a hundred suicidal young people to twenty-five septuagenarians. It's horrible—but the young man kills himself to be remembered by his girl, or the girl by the man she loves; the loving couple that they may remain a ghastly memory to their parents. And it is all the more terrible because if they had only waited six months or a year it would have been unnecessary. It used not to be so. In the Middle Ages; that is only some three or four centuries ago; we only hear of ten proved suicides."

" But in the Middle Ages they went into convents," Jean Davy ventured to suggest.

" You have put your finger on the spot, young man. If they were unhappy and felt life unbearable, they took the veil or entered a monastery; that was their way of blowing out their brains or drowning themselves. And here I am to-day on my way to Bas-Meudon to investigate the suicide of Mlle Carmélite and M. Colomban. Heigho ! "

" Of whom ? " cried both the young men, shuddering.

" What is the matter ? "

" Was not Mlle Carmélite a pupil at St-Denis ? " asked Salvator.

" She was."

" And was not M. Colomban from Brittany ? " asked Jean Davy.

" That's right."

" Then now I understand the letter Fragola received this morning," murmured Salvator.

" Poor young fellow ! " sighed Jean Davy. " I

have heard Ludovic speak of him. But I thought he was a saint.''

'' And the girl was an angel,'' said Salvator.

'' I daresay,'' replied the old Voltairian. '' That is why they have gone to Heaven; they were not in their right place here on earth, poor children.'' He spoke with a singular mixture of sarcasm and feeling.

'' Fragola will be heartbroken,'' sighed Salvator.

'' And poor old Ludovic will be upset,'' commented Davy. '' But is the cause of their death a secret or could you tell us . . .? ''

'' All the details? Yes, if you like. You need only change the names to make a story or play out of it; I tell you there is plenty of material! ''

So, as they rolled along from the quai de la Conférence to the pont de Sévres M. Jackal poured into their attentive ears the following history, which, though at first sight it may seem a digression, will in the end fall into its place in the events we are already relating.

We shall take the liberty of retelling it in our own words.

CHAPTER XVII
COLOMBAN AND CARMÉLITE

THE Twelfth District was in 1827 and is still the poorest in the capital. It is divided into four Quarters, the Observatory, the jardin des Plantes, St. Jacques and St. Michel, and since most of the events take place in this Twelfth District, as our story progresses we shall show our readers the physiognomy of these four quarters one after the other. We may say at once that the most picturesque is St.

Jacques, lying between the rue du Val de Grace and the rue de la Bourbe, to-day known as the rue du Port Royal. Indeed, all the houses to the right as one goes up the rue St. Jacques from the rue du Val de Grace, though old, ugly and ill built, are situated in charming gardens such as are seldom seen round more aristocratic residences.

It is to a house between numbers 330 and 350 in the rue St. Jacques that we must now conduct our readers. We fancy we shall introduce them to a country quite unknown and those who, when thinking of the Quarter of St. Jacques, scent in imagination the stale odour of poverty will be surprised and, we hope, charmed to inhale with us the perfume of roses and jasmine which enters the windows of those privileged apartments, looking on to a terrestrial paradise.

The entrance to the house was through a narrow door leading to a dark passage, so drear indeed that one might well expect it to lead to some cut-throat's den. No sooner had its last step been passed, how-ever, than was found a tiny Eden, for the passage ended in a courtyard leading to a large garden culti-vated by a florist who grew roses of every kind in profusion. Many of them are there to this day, though the garden has shrunk in size. Green lattices were covered with climbing roses, honeysuckle and clematis, all springing from a verdant lawn. The house itself consisted of a ground floor and two other storeys whose windows all looked on to the garden. Each floor was divided into two sets of apartments, each consisting of three rooms and a kitchen. Those on the ground and first floors were tenanted by work-people, but on the second floor lodged, one to the right and the other to the left of the staircase, the two principal people in this particular history.

A young man of twenty-three had the rooms to the left; a good-looking fellow, with fair hair and blue eyes; though not tall the breadth of his shoulders indicated exceptional strength. He had been born at Quimper and he bore the stamp of loyalty and energy characteristic of that fine Gaelic race. His father was poor but of noble family and lived in the old tower which was all that remained of the thirteenth century feudal chateau, sadly battered by the wars of the Vendée. His son, however, stayed in Paris to study law. Young Colomban de Penhoël had come to these rooms when he left college and had now been there for three years, that is to say since 1823, when this true story begins. His father made him a small allowance of 1,200 francs a year and as his rooms only cost him 200 francs a year he had a thousand left for his other expenses—quite a fortune for such a steady, sober and reliable young man. His only luxury was the hire of a piano, to make good the old Breton axiom which according to Augustin Thierry places the musician beside the agriculturist and artisan as one of the three pillars of the State.

At ten o'clock one January night in 1823, Colomban was seated in his chimney corner studying the Justinian Code when he heard a cry for help. He opened his door and saw at the door opposite a young girl, very pale and with disordered hair. He knew that those rooms were occupied by a girl and her

mother, the widow of a captain killed at Champ-
Aubert in 1814. Mme Gervais had her pension of
1,200 francs which she augmented by taking needle-
work; her daughter Carmélite, her father having
been an Officer of the Legion of Honour, had been
educated at St-Denis. Only a few days before, the
young girl had timidly begged Colomban to refrain
from playing the piano, telling him that her mother
was seriously ill and he had greatly wished to ask if
he could be of any assistance, but his nervousness
overcame his good nature and kept him tongue-tied.
So it was only when he heard the young girl call out
for help that he ventured to offer his services.

Unfortunately, it was too late; Mme Gervais was
suffering from aneurism in its final stage. Oppressed
with a feeling of suffocation, she had asked her
daughter for a glass of water and the girl had gone
to the next room for it when an appealing moan
caused her to hurry back. She found her mother
speechless lying with her head fallen back; raising
the poor head the young girl saw her mother's eyes
through which her whole soul seemed to speak.
Carmélite held the glass to her lips but Mme. Gervais
gave a long, shuddering sigh; then her head fell
heavily on her daughter's arm. The girl with an
effort raised it once more and again held the glass to
her mother's lips, saying:

"Drink, mother dear."

But the invalid made no reply. Her teeth were
clenched and the water ran out of the corners of her
mouth; her staring eyes seemed as if immovably
fixed on her daughter. Carmélite felt the beads of

perspiration forming on her forehead—yet those wide-open eyes gave her courage.

" Drink, mother, drink ! " she cried again, but still the sick woman was silent. Then it seemed to Carmélite that the neck she was supporting on her arm was growing cold! Frightened, she let her mother's head drop back on the pillow and threw her arms about her, covering her with kisses. The poor child, who but a moment ago had heard her mother's voice, could not believe that she could pass from life to death without a sound; she pressed her lips to her mother's forehead, but they touched a brow of marble. . . . Carmélite fell back a few steps, terrified but not convinced, but the immobility of the dead held her spellbound. She cried her mother's name but dared not touch her—then not daring to stay within the range of those terrible eyes, she opened the door of the room and called for help.

" Monsieur ! " she cried when she saw Colomban. " My mother looks at me but she does not reply ! "

" Perhaps she has fainted," said the young man and entered. When he saw the dead body he shuddered. He remembered having seen his mother, the noble Countess de Penhoël, lying on her bed of state and he recognized on the forehead of this poor woman the violet hues of death.

" Why does she not answer me, monsieur ? "

" Come closer, mademoiselle," said Colomban.

" I daren't ! Why does she look at me so ? What does she want me to do ? "

" She is asking you to close her eyes, mademoiselle, and to pray for the repose of her soul."

12

" She isn't dead ? " cried the young girl, as if
struck with lightning. " Oh, I see . . . I see.
. . . My mother is dead ! "

She fell back as if she, too, were struck with death
and the young man caught her and laid her, fainting,
on her bed in the alcove of the adjoining room.

The girl's cries had brought on the scene two of
the workmen's wives who lived on the floor below.
One of them poured water on the orphan's face till
she came to herself, trembling. The women wanted
to undress her and put her to bed, but with an effort
she got on her feet and turned to Colomban.

" Monsieur, you said that my mother wished me
to close her eyes. Take me to her. . . ." She
whispered these words in terror and the young man
feared they indicated the beginning of delirium.
Leaning on his arm she crossed the room and bending over the dead woman, gently closed her eyes;
then she fell across her mother's body and fainted for
the second time.

Leaving the women to undress her, Colomban retired to his room, but ten minutes after one of them
followed him.

" She has come to herself, M. Colomban, but she
is talking nonsense."

" Has she any relatives ? " asked the young man.

" Not that we know of; nor friends either. They
were very quiet people and seemed to know no one."

" What can we do? She can't remain in that
chamber of death."

" I would offer her mine," said the neighbour,
" but we have only one bed. But I could send my

man to sleep in the attic and I could pass the night in a chair."

Devotion like this towards a stranger is only to be found in certain women of the people who will offer their food, room, bed, with more disinterested kindness than a banker will offer a glass of water. When sorrow, either physical or moral, comes across her path the woman of the people offers consolation and help of all kinds with a generosity and self-abnegation that form one of her principal claims to the admiration of the philosophic observer.

" The best thing," said Colomban, " would be to take the young lady's bed into my room and put mine up in the alcove here. Then kindly bring a priest to watch by the bed of death, and I will go and fetch a doctor."

The woman hesitated.

" I would rather go for the doctor and let you find the priest."

" Why ? " asked Colomban.

" The good lady died suddenly and consequently she died . . . you understand . . .? "

" No, I do not."

" She died without confession."

" But you said yourself that she was a good woman."

" Yes, but a priest, you see. Well, he might not look at it like that."

" You don't mean that a priest would refuse to watch by the dead ? "

" If she died unconfessed and unabsolved."

" Very well. You go for the doctor and I'll get

the priest, if you can find someone to take a letter for me to the rue du Pot-de-Fer.''

Colomban then sat down and wrote as follows :

'' Come, my friend. The living and the dead both have need of you.''

This letter he addressed to : '' Brother Dominique Sarranti, Dominican monk, rue du Pot-de-Fer, No. 11.''

While waiting for the answer to his letter, Colomban went out to buy a candle, which he lit, and falling on his knees, began to recite the prayers for the dead. Many people would have laughed to see this handsome young man on his knees by the bedside of a strange woman, reading the prayers for the dead from his prayer book, stamped with his family arms, but Colomban was Breton and religious, as they were in the old days when his ancestors sold land and castles to follow Gaultier-sans-Argent to Jerusalem, saying : *Diex le volt!* He was praying with real fervour when the door behind him opened and the priest he had sent for appeared. Brother Dominique, in his white and black gown, stood on the threshold.

This young monk was almost the only friend Colomban had in Paris. He had heard him preach one day on Resignation. Young in years but aged by austerity and sorrow, the monk stood in the pulpit in his white robe; dividing his subject into two parts he said that to all such ills as death, accident or incurable illness . . . one must resign oneself, for resignation in such cases is a virtue; but with regard to misfortunes such as ruined fortune or thwarted projects, he said :

" Fight, my brothers! Rise up, strong in your confidence in God in your right and in yourselves. Resignation in such cases is cowardice! "

At the end of the sermon Colomban asked to shake the hand of this man in whom he respected the three qualities his own character fitted him to appreciate; simplicity, honesty and strength. From that day the two young men—for the monk was but four or five years older than Colomban—found themselves in unusual sympathy and it was rarely that they did not meet once or twice a week.

Let us glance back a moment at the sad past of our young monk, for he is to be one of our chief characters.

His name was Dominique Sarranti and he had more than one resemblance to the sombre saint whom Chance had made his patron. He was born at Vic-Dessos, a little town of Ariège, on the edge of a forest, six leagues from Foix, a stone's throw from the Spanish border. His father was Corsican, his mother a Catalan, and he resembled both, for he had the brooding memory of the Corsican, the terrible tenacity of the Catalan. Anyone seeing him in the pulpit, with his powerful gesture and his grave and austere eloquence would have taken him at once for a young Spanish monk on a mission to France.

His father, born at Ajaccio the same year as Bonaparte and attached to his compatriot's fortunes, suffered the same vicissitudes; he had accompanied the defeated Emperor to Elba; and followed him to St. Helena. In 1816 he had returned to France. Why did he leave the illustrious prisoner? Gaetano

Sarranti gave as pretext the insalubrious climate and the devouring heat of the sun, but those who knew him did not believe in this motive and they looked on Sarranti as one of the mysterious agents sent by the Emperor to France to engineer an escape from St. Helena as he had escaped from Elba or at least, if this proved impossible, to watch over the interests of his son. Sarranti took a place as tutor to two children. His employer, M. Gérard, was a rich man, but the children were his nephew and niece. Suddenly, in 1820, at the time of the conspiracy of Nantes and Bérard, Gaetano Sarranti had disappeared and it was said he had gone to rejoin in India one of Napoleon's former generals, who had taken service in 1815 with the Rajah of Lahore. We mentioned Sarranti's flight àpropos of the flight of the wheelwright of the rue St-Jacques, the brother of Mother Boivin. Durier's disappearance had closed his door to little Mina and left her free to be adopted by the schoolmaster and his family.

Sarranti's son was our Brother Dominique, or as they called him because of his Spanish appearance, *Fra Dominico*. The young man had always been destined for the church and on his mother's death his father had sent him to a seminary, but on his return in 1816 his father had looked with displeasure on this vocation for a young man who might have been anything he pleased. He had a sufficient fortune to assure independence for his son but the youth had obstinately refused to give up his chosen vocation. In 1820, when his father disappeared, he had been called several times to police headquarters. He was then a boarder at St-Sulpice and his comrades noticed that he was even paler and more sombre than usual when he returned for he had been told that an accusation far graver than that of political conspiracy hung over his father. Gaetano Sarranti was not only accused of having wished to overthrow by violent means the established Government, but there was also a warrant out against him for the theft of 300,000 francs belonging to M. Gérard. Even this was not all. He was also accused of having brought about the disappearance of his two pupils. It is true that the pursuit after him was soon abandoned; but nevertheless the exile remained under a terrible suspicion.

All this combined to render Dominique more and more melancholy as a man and more and more austere as a priest, and when he took the vows he announced his wish to enter one of the more severe Orders, choosing the Order of St. Dominic, called in France the Order of the Jacobins because the first monastery of that Order was built in the rue St-Jacques. He pronounced the vows and was ordained priest the day after he came of age, on the seventh of March, 1821. He had therefore been a Dominican some two years when this history opens. He was now 27 or 28 years old, with large black eyes, quick, clear and penetrating. His glance was thoughtful, his brow careworn, his face pale and austere, his carriage proud, energetic and resolute; his stature was tall, his gesture restrained, his speech concise, his walk noble, slow and rhythmic. When seen passing along the street, looking for shade in which to veil his dreamy brow which bore always the trace of sombre care, he might have been taken for one of those beautiful monks from Zurbaran, stepped from the canvas;—fleeing the sepulchre to make a re- appearance in this world with the firm and sonorous tread of the Statue who came at the invitation of Don Juan. In short, the inflexible will and profound energy crowning this fateful figure revealed rather the rigidity of unshrinking principles than the war of ambitious passion. His was, moreover, the straight- est judgment, the sanest mind and the warmest heart in the world. The only crime that seemed to him unforgivable was that of inhumanity, for love of man- kind was to him the principal element in the life of a people; he contemplated the future with wonderful enthusiasm, for he foresaw, though distant still, a uni- versal harmony founded on the fraternity of nations liked unto the universal harmony of the planets. When he spoke of the future independence of nations it was with a magnetic eloquence; his auditors felt transported towards him and with him with irre- sistible sympathy; his words seemed but a reflection from his heart and carried to them all his strength! His hearers felt illuminated by the rays of his flam- bouyant energy; ready to take hold of a corner of his gown and say:

" March onward, Prophet; we will follow you! " Yet a terrible canker gnawed at his heart—the accu- sation of theft and murder hanging over his absent father.

Such was the young monk who appeared at the threshold and halted there, struck by the spectacle before his eyes.

"Friend," said he in that gentle voice to which he could give at will the accent of consolation. "The woman lying there is, I hope, neither your mother nor your sister?"

"No," replied Colomban, and as the monk was about to kneel before the dead body, he added: "Wait, Dominique. I sent for you because that woman, struck down by the breaking of a blood-vessel in the heart, though a good Christian and a saintly woman, died without confessing."

"It is for God, not man, to judge how she died," said the monk. "Let us pray." And he knelt at the bedside.

*   *   *   *   *   *

From that day the intimacy thus formed between Colomban and Carmélite, the two young tenants of the house in the rose garden, was uninterrupted. Colomban soon found that the girl loved flowers; he taught her the rudiments of botany, and from botany passed to astronomy. Then Colomban reopened his piano at Carmélite's request and drew from it a thousand melodious notes while the scented air from the garden came softly through the window to caress the sorrowing young girl. Thus she had both perfume and melody, but within was sadness. . . . Poor Carmélite! She was in the worst—or the best— mood to fall in love, according to whether love is considered as a grief or a joy, a misfortune or a blessing. Let us try to describe her as she then was, that is to say when seventeen years old. She was tall and graceful with wonderful chestnut coloured hair, sapphire-hued eyes, and well-modelled features

set off by a perfect complexion—in fact, a queen
of beauty and charm was this Carmélite Gervais.
One night, punctuated by the perfume of roses from
the garden, which enveloped them as the clouds en-
velope Virgil's goddesses, they looked out of the
window together.

" What is that tomb ? " asked Carmélite.

" It is the tomb of Mlle de la Vallière," replied
Colomban, leaning his elbows on the sill.

" But how does it come to be here ? "

" All this ground now, as you know, a florist's
garden," replied Colomban, " was once that of a
convent belonging to the religious Order whose
name you bear. As a Sister of that Order the gentle
victim of love passed the last thirty-six years of her
life and there she lies still . . . among the roses."

" I wish I could have a rose from the spot," sighed
Carmélite.

" Come and get one," replied Colomban.

" To-night ? But surely the gardener is in bed."

" I think that will-o'-the-wisp glancing in between
the roses is his lantern. He is probably chasing some
cat ! Come along ! "

They felt their way down the stairs and soon found
themselves before the great wooden gate which serves
as entrance to the old garden of the Carmélites. The
gardener heard their knock and let them in, introducing this new Adam and Eve to Paradise. Nothing
can express the feeling of charm and intoxicating
freshness which seized the two young people as they
gained this Harem of roses, for every variety of the
queen of flowers blossomed there. Arm in arm they

strolled till they, the young man of twenty-three and
the girl of seventeen, came to the tomb of Sister
Louise de la Miséricorde. Carmélite hesitated, but
on Colomban's invitation she entered the tomb, only
to retreat, for instead of the religious emblems she
expected to find there, she saw hanging to the wall
or leaning against it shovels, spades, rakes, watering
cans, wheelbarrows and all the gardening tools used
by a nurseryman. She then walked round the little
tomb, consumed by curiosity and found that it was
surrounded by rose trees some six or eight feet high.

"What are those magnificent rose trees?" she
asked.

"The Alexandria, a white rose," replied the
gardener. "They come from the South of Europe
and the coasts of Barbary. Otto of roses is made
from their flowers."

"Could you sell me a tree?" asked the young
girl.

"Which would you like?"

"This." Carmélite pointed to the one that
adhered most closely to the tomb. The gardener went
into the tomb to get his spade.

A nightingale was singing his lovesong twenty
paces from them and the moon was not alone the
moon but the Phœbe of the Greeks, looking long-
ingly on earth in the hope of seeing once more the
shadow of Endymion. The night breeze passed so
gently over the hair of the young people that it
seemed a kiss. It was indeed a scene full of colour
and poetry in which figured the lovely young girl in
her mourning black, the fair youth, also dressed in

black and the old gardener, working in the fresh
night breeze, in the light of the moon, to the music
of the nightingale's song. The young couple seemed
to say with every breath :

" Oh, how good it is to be alive ! We give thanks
that our paths through life have touched ! "

Alas ! The first blow of the spade sounded omin-
ously in their hearts; to disturb the earth where reposed the body of the Egoist-Monarch's unhappy
mistress almost resembled sacrilege. They left the
garden bearing away their rose-tree, but as fearful as
children who have gathered a flower in a cemetery.
Once beyond the garden, however, they forgot these
sad fancies and casting a last glance at the nursery
which seemed now but a perfumed shadow, they
looked up at the stars and absorbing the sense of life
which hovered round them, thanked Providence for
the happiness of that ineffable spring night.

The next morning they met on the stairs.

" How happy you look this morning, M. Colomban ! " cried Carmélite.

" Yes, mademoiselle, I am happy ! " replied
Colomban, " for a friend is coming from Louisiana,
a college friend."

" When will he be here ? "

" Very soon. I wish he were here already ! He is
gaiety personified . . . and so good-looking ! He
has a wonderful tenor voice, too, and I was thinking
of making a proposal to you. You told me you had
studied music at St-Denis ? "

" Oh, yes. I sing fairly well. They said I had a
good contralto. What I most regretted when I left

St-Denis, after my three college friends, Régina, Lydia and Fragola, whose affection meant to me what this friend of yours means to you, was having to give up my music. I thought if I had been able to work at it, I might have been fairly good. . . ."

" I won't offer to give you lessons," replied Colomban. " I'm not conceited enough for that ; but I was well taught by an old German Professor, M. Müller, and we could study together."

Colomban stopped, frightened. He had never dared to suggest such a thing before ; but the expected coming of his friend, Camille Rozan, had made another man of him. Carmélite, however, accepted with gratitude ; the offer of a fortune would not have been more agreeable to her than this proposition from her young neighbour and she was going to thank him when she saw coming up the stairs the young Dominican who had watched by her dead mother. She withdrew to her room. Colomban showed embarrassment as the monk looked at him with surprise and reproach.

In the next five minutes Dominique saw more deeply into the heart of his friend than had that friend himself. He had induced Colomban to tell him all the charming details of the night before. When he realized that he was in love the Breton was almost frightened, but the monk smiled.

" You need love, my friend," said he. " A noble passion such as this can only give you strength and regenerate you."

" Then, instead of blaming me, you . . .?"

" I should blame you if you hid your love from

me," replied the monk gravely, "for hidden love is
usually guilty. Reason leads to peace, it is true, but
the heart is our very life. Peace at your age, Colomban, would be a dangerous idleness, and sooner than
consume my strength in such idleness, sooner than
waste the valuable force that stirs within me, I would,
like Samson, pull down the columns of the Temple
even though I must perish in the ruins ! "

"Yet you, Brother, may not love," said Colomban.
The young monk smiled sadly.

"I may not love with earthly love for God has
taken me for Himself, but in denying me personal
love he has given me a stronger passion—love for all !
You love a woman, I—humanity ! "

At this moment a fresh young voice was heard calling "Colomban ! "

"That's Camille ! " cried Colomban; he had not
heard the voice for three years and yet he recognized
it and eagerly opening the door received Camille
Rozan with open arms. Never did a blind man receive Misfortune in so fraternal an embrace, thinking
to greet a friend.

When Colomban was at school, his patience led
some of his schoolfellows to call him a fool and they
took a delight in teasing him. One day a young
Creole from Louisiana mounted on the back of another boy and pulled the Breton's hair savagely.
Without a sign either of emotion or anger, Colomban
turned, seized the Creole by his collar and carried
him to the trapeze from which swung a knotted rope.
This he tied round his tormentor's waist and sent him
spinning through the air, his head and legs dang-

ling. The other schoolboys, who had been laughing, begged in vain for the Creole's release. Watch in hand, Colomban stood waiting. The big boy on whose shoulders Camille had mounted rushed at Colomban and tried to knock him down, but though he was a head taller than the Breton, he found himself on the ground and Colomban sitting calmly astride his body, watch in hand! Only at the end of ten minutes, during which the rope continued to spin round the trapeze, would Colomban consent to release his victims. But the Creole had fainted and was long ill with brain fever. Strange to say, however, the event established a friendship between the two. It took the form of making Colomban the defender of the more delicate boy, who, lively and charming, won from the less brilliant Breton a large-hearted admiration, and the protection that he started by according him changed insensibly into a deep friendship. He received him now as a brother.

Had it not been for his age, distinction and elegant clothes, Camille Rozan might have been taken for a Paris *gamin;* he had the quick wit, the vivacity, the hearty laugh and the speech of a *gamin.* It was unnecessary to talk to him long to know what he was like; five minutes were sufficient to probe him to the bottom. His face, his talk, his manner, all revealed his character.

He was, however, charming. He had a beautiful little head well set on a slim *svelte* form, and looked delicate because he was supple and graceful. His eyes were long and brilliant, black with a dash of chestnut, real Creole eyes, velvety with very long lashes. His black hair seemed like an ebony frame for the clearly cut olive face. His well-proportioned nose was on a line with the forehead as in Greek statues. His mouth was small and fresh, his lips curved as if always ready to kiss. In short, though this charming tropic bird, this butterfly from the Equator, might wear cravats too brightly coloured and waistcoats a thought too ornate, still he had such an air of distinction that the oldest of old Marquises would have taken him for a scion of good family. Yet he had hardly entered his friend's rooms before he had wounded him three times.

On his arrival, Brother Dominique discreetly withdrew and Camille followed him with his eyes till the door closed behind him.

"Oho," said he then with humorous gravity. "A Roman would take that for an ill omen."

And as Colomban looked his surprise, he added :

"Have you forgotten the saying : 'When you see a crow to your left, return home.'"

"So you are always the same, Camille," returned Colomban sadly. "Your first word is a disenchantment for the friend who has waited for you three years? Do you not know that that crow as you call him. . . ."

"I should have said magpie," retorted Camille, laughing ; "he is black and white ! "

He clapped his hand gaily on Colomban's shoulder, not realizing either the pain his words had given or the pleasure his friend felt at his caress.

"The years have not altered you," said the grave Breton, affectionately but thoughtfully.

"No! and they have left me my good appetite. Tell me, where does one eat here?"

"I should have had a meal for you if I had known."

"You never got my letter, then?"

"Yes, but only an hour ago."

"I see," said Camille, "an additional reason for asking you, 'Where does one eat here?'"

"I look on you as a Robinson Crusoe, that is to say, a man used to privations."

"Colomban! No jokes of that sort, please. I am no hero of romance. I eat! For the third time, I ask: 'Where does one eat here?'"

"Here, my friend, arrangements are made with a good woman who . . ."

"I know that good woman and her food also— not for me on this occasion!"

"Well, there is Flicoteaux."

"Oh, the brave Flicoteaux, of the place de la Sorbonne. He is still there? Flicoteaux? and he has not yet grilled all the biftecks?" And Camille began calling out:

"Flicoteaux! a bifteck, with lots of potatoes!"

Then he seized his hat.

"Where are you going?" asked Colomban.

"I am not going, I am running! that is, I am flying to Flicoteaux. Will you fly with me?"

"No."

"Why no?"

"I must go to buy you a bed, a table—other things."

13

" That is it—furnish my little room while I furnish my little stomach ! "

And Camille disappeared.

The first days passed pleasantly enough in talk about old times and in a recital of Camille's travels. He had seen Greece, Italy, the East and America, and his conversation should have been full of interest for a man like Colomban, who valued knowledge, but Camille had travelled as a bird flies, and each new wind had blown from his wings the dust of the country he quitted. One thing, however, had struck him during his travels; neither the monuments, the beauties of art or nature, the customs nor the scenery. No ! He had been entranced with the many forms of beauty among the women of the various countries. He was a man of sensations rather than impressions, and though his pleasures affected his whole body, they were but skin deep. He took joy, luxury and love as one might take a bath and remain plunged therein for a shorter or longer time according to whether the bath was more or less agreeable. He would have given all the woods, the savannahs, the lakes, the virgin forests,—given Greece with her ruins and Jerusalem with her memories for a kiss from the first beautiful woman he met on his way.

" Tell me what you think of Athens ! " cried Colomban, desperately.

" Athens ? Oh,—Well, you know Montmartre ?— It's on a height like that, you know—only it over-looks the Piraeus."

Camille's wit, temperament and character were all exhibited in that appreciation of Athens.

" Camille, Camille ! " sighed Colomban, " I am beginning to despair of you. I'm afraid you'll never be a man."

" That fear is not shared by your laundress, old fellow," laughed Camille.

" My laundress ? " exclaimed the astonished Colomban.

" You never told me you used soap like that to wash with, you rascal ! Fancy our Sobersides with a laundress of eighteen, called for her beauty the Princess of Vanvres and the Queen of Carnival ! You betray the first duties of hospitality, monsieur, in hiding from your guest your choicest treasure."

" You may believe me or not, my friend," replied Colomban, naïvely, " but I scarcely know what my laundress looks like."

" Why, if Raphael had treated the Fornarina with the same contempt that you show the Princess of Vanvres—she tells me that she has washed for you during three years—we should not have had the Virgin in the Chair. What was the Fornarina? A laundress washing her linen in the Tiber. Listen and I'll tell you how we met.

" Here follows the history of the first meeting of Guillaume Félix Camille de Rozan, Creole of Louisiana, with her Highness Mlle Chante-Lilas, Princess of Vanvres, laundress of that principality. A novelist would tell you that it was on a sunny afternoon in May ; but that would be deceiving you, for it was pouring cats and dogs. While you were at the École de Droit, I had the pleasure of receiving your laundress, who arrived drenched, as thoroughly

as our school wine used to be. My first idea was
to buy another umbrella, for—admire my logic,
Colomban—even as two umbrellas are useless on
a fine day, so one is insufficient for two people
on a wet day when they are going different ways!
But that is a detail. The laundress took refuge in
your ark, the white dove! and, seeing from your
window that the inundation 'prevailed exceedingly,'
as the Bible says, she made no ado about accepting
my offer to sojourn with me for the time being. Now
what would you have done in my place, Colomban?
Tell me!"

"Babble on, *gamin!*" said the Breton, amused in
spite of himself at the chatter of this mocking bird.

"Oh, of course you would have let her soak, or
if you had offered her shelter, you would have turned
your back, thus depriving her of the light of your
countenance and yourself of the charm of her figure.
You'd have pretended that there are women who are
not women for you. But I'm only a savage, so I
behaved as an Indian would in his wigwam or an
Arab in his tent; I fulfilled the duties of hospitality.
The first was obviously to remove her fichu, from
which rivulets of water were running down her back;
had I not done so, the Princess of Vanvres would
have caught a violent cold and I should have bitterly
reproached myself. No, I had no *arrière pensée;* as
Hippolytus says, 'The day was not more pure than
my heart.' It was pure charity, I tell you, and the
proof is that as it was very cold in your room, I presented her with a silk handkerchief I found on your
chair. It was that white one, the best of all your

handkerchieves, and of course the Princess carried it off with her, thinking it was now hers. But that is another detail. Next I offered a chair. I must confess she nobly refused to be seated, not because she thought herself unworthy, being Princess of Vanvres, to sit before the humblest of her servants, but because she was afraid, being dripping wet, that she would spoil the velvet cover. At least I divined this by the way she ended, after a little manœuvring, by accepting a seat beside me on the sofa, which, being shrouded in a cotton cover, did not seem to run the same danger.

" Now what you will never understand, Colomban, you who deny the Lisettes, disdain the Frétillons and despise the Suzons of M. de Béranger, is that when one was born in the 86.40—92.55 longitude West and the 29—33 latitude North, one does not sit down with impunity beside a pretty girl, even though she be a laundress. There was established between her and me a—I don't know what—an equivalent to what our Professor of Physics at College designated an electric current. Of course you don't know, O Socrates, king of Sages, but those currents cause all sorts of delightful thoughts to spring up immediately. That is what led me to say :

" ' Princess of Vanvres, on my honour, you are wonderful ! '

" And no doubt it was a similar thought that led her to blush furiously, and, innocent as you are, I need not tell you that the more a woman blushes, the more beautiful she looks. My head was beginning to be turned when, by good luck, my eyes, turning with it, fell on the white handkerchief, which had replaced her fichu. That handkerchief, my friend, was you ! I feared to betray our friendship and stopped on the very edge of the precipice ! Now, however, you tell me that the Princess of Vanvres is a stranger to you. Very well ! I come from the land of precipices and do not fear them. The next chance that presents itself will see me gliding sweetly down ! "

Colomban wanted to make some observations on this peroration, but Camille instantly began to sing in his charming voice :

> " Lisette, my Lisette,
>   I know that you deceive,
>   Yet long live the grisette !
>   I drink, Lisette,
>   To my heart worn on your sleeve."

And the tones of that harmonious voice, so vibrant and magnetic, causing the secret fibres of the heart to throb, Colomban could never refrain from applauding.

*   *   *   *   *   *

One day when he came back from Paris, as he called it, the young Creole, whose character our readers now understand, thanks to the " history," began as follows :

" I've just met your lovely neighbour."

" Where ? " cried Colomban, surprised.

" I came in as she went out. She had a parcel in her hand, so I asked the *concierge* what was in it."

" What did you do that for ? "

" I wanted to know. She said, ' Shirts.' "

" Oh, for some shop, I suppose."

" For the hospitals and convents, my friend. I

asked the *concièrge* what she thought the girl made by that work, and she said a franc a shirt.''

" Impossible ! " cried Colomban, startled.

" It takes her a whole day to make a shirt. That's impossible ! A woman—a creature made of rose leaves, perfume and dewdrops, whose smile to the heart of man is as a ray of sun to nature—that creature to be condemned to such hard labour ! "

" That is true ! " said Colomban, distressed. " It is terrible ! "

" Why, she works every night as late as three o'clock ! "

" Did the *concièrge* tell you that ? "

" I, Camille de Rozan, saw it for myself. She never puts out her light till that hour. Oh, I don't sit up working, but I am often out late with Ludovic, and on returning I have often looked up at her window.''

" What can we do, Camille ? She would not accept an offer of help, no matter under what form I tried to disguise it.''

" She would accept work,'' said Camille.

" How can I get her work ? "

" One of my Colonial friends asked me to send him six dozen shirts and fixed the price at 25 francs a shirt : suppose we ask your neighbour to make them ? They say she works like a fairy and it would mean a profit of over eight francs a shirt for her.''

" She would not accept,'' said Colomban, sadly. " She would see in the offer a pious fraud. . . .''

" Nonsense. I'll show her estimates for the shirts

from the big shops; then she'll accept, for she will
see it is fair."

" Hearty thanks, my friend. I'll suggest it to her
this evening."

" She is musical, isn't she?" asked Camille.
" What is her voice?"

" Contralto."

" And you are a baritone. We must get you a
better piano. I'll buy you one. It will arrive to-
morrow."

" But, Camille   . . ."

" I was going to surprise you with it on your birthday, but as that isn't due yet, and it bores me to
play on that thing over there, I'll give it to you to-
morrow. It must be the birthday of your father or
uncle or one of your cousins.—Some member of
your family, surely!"

" Oh, Camille," cried the Breton, moved to tears.
" How good you are!"

*   *   *   *   *   *

From that day, happiness entered the house. The
three met nearly every evening in the young girl's
room, which Camille had repapered, where the piano
was now placed, so that Carmélite might be spared
as far as possible the cruel remembrance of her
mother's death there. Colomban had a good collection of German music, but in a few months they
had exhausted it, and Camille undertook to supply
the Philharmonic Society with a fresh library. He
hunted through all the music shops to find his
favourite Italian airs, which Colomban stigmatized
as works of base Latinity.

" Italian music is as gay and full of sun," declared Camille, " as the Mediterranean itself in the shade of the Rose-laurels."

The young girl devoured both German and Italian music feverishly, and in time became a musician of some knowledge and possessed of remarkable talent. One thing surprised Colomban. The careless traveller, who seemed to have visited Greece, Italy and Asia Minor without seeing anything, when he came to recount his travels to Carmélite, proved to have observed with the mind of a savant, painter or poet. Sometimes he told them of his researches in the ruins, sometimes of his walks by moonlight on the shores of the great lakes, or of his camping in the virgin forest or the arid desert. Then they saw a new Camille, full of colour, enthusiasm, passion and candour. What had worked this miracle? Colomban wondered, but the cause is not difficult to find. Have you seen a peacock alone? A sad sight; but if a peahen becomes visible, then he spreads his jewelled fan. Well, the jewels in Camille's stories were spread, glittering, before the eyes of the young girl. He might have lived for twenty years with Colomban and not paid friendship the tribute of displaying one of his precious gems but for the mysterious and unknown god who floats invisible over the head of a girl. Camille had not sufficient treasures either of beauty, wit or imagination. With two old friends it is as with husband and wife; they do not feel themselves obliged to show the best of themselves to one another, but when a third person appears, that very moment the conversation will become brilliant, even as if two mutes regained the power of speech.

For Carmélite, brought up severely at St. Denis and then nurse to her mother and witness of her death, sadness was woven into her life, and the serious Breton involuntarily continued on the same note. Camille, on the other hand, was entirely opposite in character; his vivacity made her uneasy, and she was always ready to scold him like a schoolboy. When she was at work, if Camille appeared unexpectedly, she never hesitated to tell him he was in the way; but she would not have dared to say such a thing to Colomban. Moreover, Colomban was never in her way. It followed that Carmélite herself mistook her own feelings. She fell, little by little, into thinking that the familiarity between her and Camille was a sign of great affection and took the respectful love she felt for Colomban for fear. Colomban, too, seemed to hold her back, but Camille led her on; she was loved by Colomban—but she was seduced by Camille.

One night, when Camille and Carmélite had been singing a duet with wonderful fire, Colomban, on returning to his own room, laid his hand on Camille's shoulder and said, gravely :

" Camille, you love Carmélite."

" I ? " cried Camille, colouring. " I swear . . ."

" Don't swear, but listen. You love Carmélite differently perhaps, but as deeply as I love her myself."

" But Carmélite . . ." began Camille.

" I have not questioned her; what is the good ? Listen to my proposal."

"No, no. It is for me to speak. I was on the point of loving Carmélite, but I was horrified at myself. It seemed like betraying our friendship. I will leave this very night; cross the sea and bury myself in England or Scotland. . . ." And Camille threw himself on to the sofa and burst into tears.

"I am grateful for the sacrifice you propose," said Colomban, gravely, "but it is too late. Even if I were egoist enough to accept, could I now tear from Carmélite's heart the love she has for you?"

"Beautiful Carmélite loves me? You are sure?" cried Camille eagerly, leaping to his feet. Colomban looked at him; his tears had dried as if in the warmth of the sun.

"Don't bother about me, Camille. I must be the one to go away. But you must promise me one thing. . . ."

"And that is?"

"That you will make Carmélite happy and respect her . . ."

"Before God! I swear it. Oh, Colomban, to think you must sacrifice yourself like this! But I was deceiving you when I said I would go away, for I should simply have killed myself."

"No, no," said Colomban. "It is I who will go and I shall not kill myself. I have a father. Yet I can understand that one might die for the woman one loves. . . ."

"I cannot understand how one can live without her!" cried Camille. But the words on the lips of the careless Creole had a very different significance from those that issued from the mouth of the grave Breton.

Colomban told Carmélite that his father absolutely needed him, the only untruth he ever uttered to her.

We pass over the scene that took place in which she was plaintive and he was inflexible, in which she hardly believed him.

The day of departure arrived, Camille saw his friend to the diligence and then returned to the house, where he found the young girl in tears, but more lovely than ever. At the sound of his steps, Carmélite raised her head, but only to see if Colomban had come back. Seeing Camille alone, she let her head drop again.

" Camille, why has Colomban gone ? " she asked.

" Believe me, he had a serious reason for going, dear Carmélite," replied the Creole.

" But what *was* that reason ? " insisted Carmélite. " If you refuse to tell me I shall take it that it is something humiliating to me ! "

Camille hesitated.

" Colomban has left," he at last replied, " because . . . well, if I *must* tell you, because I love you."

The adroit Creole had reason to hesitate before he said, " Because *I* love you." If, instead, he had said, " Because *HE* loves you," the proof of loyalty would have made reparation, then and there, for the egoism which had led him to accept Colomban's devotion through so many years without ever making a return. If Camille had said, " Because *he* loves you and I love you, too," he would have left Carmélite free to choose; she could have seen at a glance the unselfishness of the Breton who departed and the egoism of the Creole who remained. But he answered

Carmélite with a half truth, and so the cause of Colomban's departure struck her like a stroke of lightning.

"Leave me alone," she said. " I . . . I must weep and pray."

Camille kissed her hand and went back to his room which, to his astonishment, he found lit up. He was even more astonished to find a woman there —the Princess of Vanvres. She had been waiting to deliver the linen personally and had had to wait some time. In fact, it was now half-past ten —very late for returning alone to Vanvres ! Camille offered her Colomban's room. . . . The Princess demurred, but when told that there was a bolt on the door, she accepted !

Now was there a bolt or was there not ? Was it or was it not used ? Perhaps we may be able to guess from our account of what happened at the next meeting of the fascinating Creole and the seductive Chante-Lilas.

*   *   *   *   *   *

Carmélite that night slept little and wept much and the next morning she received Camille coldly. Camille seemed to have changed his character; he toned down his usual vivacity and became grave and serious. One can understand his object; he wished to efface from Carmélite's mind the last thought of Colomban by showing her all the Breton's solid qualities joined to greater affability. Carmélite believed this change was due to love of her and her vanity was flattered. The result was that each day Camille gained ground. The young Creole had the

brilliance of the humming bird and the suppleness
of the cobra. He never said, "Will you be my
wife," but was continually saying, "When you are
my wife. . . ." Then he would unfold dazzling
projects of travel before the girl, till Carmélite,
through his passionate eloquence, saw unroll before
her eyes a panorama of enchanted pictures of their
life together.

One day, she said, smiling :

" It is just a dream, Camille ! "

" No ! " cried he, pressing her to his heart. " It
is a reality ! "

Then, one night, they went down to the garden;
the same where, months before, Carmélite had
walked at night with Colomban. It was suffocatingly
hot and the two young people felt the influence of
this electric atmosphere, but in different ways, for
Camille was a son of the Tropics, Carmélite a
daughter of France. During the spring day which
had preceded the night that Carmélite and Colomban
had been together in the garden, thunder had
sounded and life had seemed suspended, but then
rain had fallen and death was averted from the plants
and flowers. Now, on this night of summer, those
plants begged the Heavens for mercy in vain; their
heads drooped as they let fall their petals one by
one before they died.

Even so the young girl bowed down under the
oppression of this night of fire and in place of a
revivifying dew it was the joys of love that kept her
from her sleep.

When she re-entered her room alone she saw

her rose-tree, drooping too before the storm. She cut off all the flowers and buds, laying them in a white veil, and as she shut them away in a drawer she murmured :

" Die, roses that Colomban once gave me ! "

Then, pouring water over the stripped rose-tree, she said sadly :

" And now bloom, roses of Camille ! "

*   *   *   *   *   *

His object gained, Camille became his natural self again, for of what use was hypocrisy now ? Yet he polished the too obvious angles of his character, trying to please the young girl whom he loved with passion. She believed herself absolute mistress of the young man who obeyed her every wish, even moving to another house in the Bas-Meudon when she dreaded the knowing smiles that began to appear on the faces of the scandal-loving neighbours. The new home was a little nest of Robin Redbreast, almost entirely hidden under leaves, moss and flowers, and here Camille furnished a room for her as the twin sister of the one she had had in the rue St-Jacques; the same white curtains and the same rose-coloured quilt, and in this room, to her joy, Carmélite found her rose-tree. The two lovers passed in this nest the whole of September in a delightful intimacy, the one only rising to think of the other and that other only sleeping to dream of her mate. They had forgotten Paris and all the world.

To re-appear where they were known together was an impudence beyond Carmélite's force. Yet why should they not go separately ? The answer to this was that it meant separation, and to separate for a

moment during those first radiant hours of love
seemed like parting for Eternity. They could easily
do without the things that one could only buy in
Paris—or so at first it seemed. Then, gradually, those things became more necessary—and at
last it was decided that Camille should go alone and
buy in Paris or bring back from the house in the
rue St. Jacques all they still needed for their little
house at the Bas-Meudon.

He went to the door and returned five times for a
fresh good-bye before he finally departed; Carmélite
followed him with her eyes as he waved kisses to her
till at last the corner of the street hid him from sight.
It had been decided that he should take the first
vehicle he saw and be back again at the Bas-Meudon
house by two or half-past at latest. Providence,
however, had other plans, and it happened that he
had not taken two hundred steps beyond the Bas-
Meudon when in a cloud of golden dust he saw two
young girls in white frocks curveting on the backs
of two donkeys. Man proposes, but the Devil dis-
poses ! Directly the young Creole saw them, he
doubled his pace, and as he walked more quickly
than the donkeys, he was very near when one of the
girls, happening to turn, stopped her mount and
signed to her companion to do the same. Then as
Camille came up with them, she let her reins slip
on to the donkey's shoulders, and at the risk of
falling off, threw her arms round the young man's
neck and gave him a hearty kiss.

"So there you are, you wretch ! I've been looking for you everywhere ! " she cried.

" You've been looking for me, Princess ? "

" Over mountains and valleys, and I've only come here now on your account ! "

" That's my case," retorted Camille. " I've come here on your account."

" Then, since we've found one another, we need not go on looking. Let me present my intimate friend, Mlle Paquerrette, Countess of the Battoir.[1] I need not explain that Paquerrette is the name she was baptised by and that . . ."

" That Countess du Battoir is her order of distinction. But what is her surname ? "

" Colombier."

" Never has the cooing of love resounded from a nest more fresh and rosy ! And now, where are you going ? "

" If you are really the gentleman you look, you will take us to some nice little place where we can devour some milk and have a good drink of cake. Oh, I'm so thirsty, I don't know what I'm saying."

" I'll run and find a place," said Camille and started off, but the Princess of Vanvres seized hold of his coat-tails.

" You don't make me see any green, young man ! " said she.

" What DO you mean, Princess of my heart ? " asked the Creole.

" She means she's afraid, if you go off, you won't come back again," explained Paquerrette, " and we are so thirsty ! "

" You think I'd leave you, Princess ? "

[1] The stick used by French laundresses to beat their linen.— EDITOR'S NOTE.

14

"We'll go together," replied the Princess. "But try and find my donkey first. I don't know where it's gone while we've been exchanging greetings."

The donkey had indeed disappeared and was nowhere to be seen. It took some time to find him, as they did at last, calmly reposing in the gutter. They invited him to get back on to the road, and with the sweet docility that few men can equal, he acceded to their request and graciously offered his back to the young girl. The Countess du Battoir then surrendered her own donkey to Camille and mounted herself behind Chante-Lilas, on which the joyous caravan set out in search of a farm, cabaret or mill. Alas, that is another thing that has disappeared. —In ten years' time our grandchildren will burst out laughing when we tell them that we used to grind our wheat in mills, and if the museum authorities haven't the sense to preserve one, our descendants will refuse to believe that there ever were such things. Yet our young people greatly enjoyed their search for a mill and found mills of all sizes, all colours and all sorts of names. There were the "moulin Joli," the "moulin Rouge," the "moulin Noir," the "moulin de la Galette," the "moulin de Beurre"; in short, mills for every taste.

Our three young people entered and asked to be served with hot rolls and cold milk. Camille and Paquerrette demolished theirs with enjoyment, but at the third mouthful the Princess cried:

"How silly we are to eat these rolls when I'm sure M. Camille de Rozan, like a proper American gentleman, is going to offer us dinner!"

" Anything you wish, Princess. But not here ! "

" Where, then ? "

" In Paris at Véfour's."

For thirty sous (there were coins of that value then) the boy at the mill undertook to take their donkeys back, and mounting into an empty carriage they drove to Véfour's. By the time the dessert was on the table, the coffee drunk and the liqueurs tasted, Paquerrette Colombier, who found her place beside the other two getting embarrassing, suddenly remembered that her old uncle was expecting her to call and left the American gentleman *tête-à-tête* with Chante-Lilas.

*   *   *   *   *   *

Beautiful Carmélite leaned her elbow on the window-sill and her head on her hand. She listened to the rare, distant sounds of the night, and twenty times had started when the cracking of a branch made her think she heard Camille's footsteps. What a difference between this autumn night, passed alone, waiting for Camille, and that spring night passed with Colomban under the lilac bushes, among the roses ! Yet barely five months had gone by. Still, it does not need five months to change the whole of one's life; one moment is enough . . . one night of storm !

At last, as she grew pale with anxiety, about one o'clock in the morning, the sound of a carriage was heard from the street. Carmélite dried her eyes and listened. Yes, it was stopping at the gate ! Why was it that one fibre of her heart gave her acute pain when all the rest were vibrating with joy ? She

wanted to run downstairs and reach his arms without delay; yet she could not pass the first step.
Camille, who ran upstairs to her, found her leaning
against the wall; he pressed her in his arms with all
his usual effusion; in just the same way he had
embraced the Princess of Vanvres that very morning. On the whole, though, his embrace of Carmélite was the warmer of the two;—he had to earn forgiveness for his absence.

" Forgive me, dear, but I swear that I could not
get back sooner."

" Don't swear, Camille," said Carmélite. " Why
should you deceive me? If you still love me, some
strong reason must have kept you. If you do not
love me, why should I care what kept you? "

" Not love you? " cried Camille. " Oh, Carmélite, how could I live without you? "

He led her to her room and knelt before her. Over
his head she gazed at her rose-tree. On it were but
a few decaying flowers—the last! One of them
began to drop and Carmélite watched its petals fall.
Camille was telling her how he had been delayed by
two friends from Martinique and how they had talked
of her.—She heard the sound of his voice,
but paid no heed to his words. Two o'clock struck
and she shivered.

" You are tired and so am I," she said. " Go to
your room and leave me. You can tell me all the
rest to-morrow."

" Oh, I see you are annoyed with me ! " cried he.

" I ? Why? Why should I be annoyed? " But
no sooner had he left the room than she ran to open
the window again.

" Oh ! " she cried. " I'm stifled ! Stifled ! "

This was the first cloud that passed over their heaven. Camille had told her he had not bought all the things they needed; as a matter of fact, he had bought nothing, so another journey to Paris was imperative. After this, his absences became more and more frequent;—indeed, so numerous that it was his presence in the little home that became the exception.

One morning, when he was away, there was a knock at the door. Carmélite went to the window, and gave a cry of surprise—almost of terror, as she grew white and red. It was Colomban !

Colomban had written to Camille regularly, but as the Creole had left St. Jacques, the letters lay there unopened. Moreover, as the thought of Colomban reminded him of his treachery to his old friend, he kept that thought out of his mind as much as possible. His silence had made Colomban uneasy, and as the soul of the Breton had gained new strength from the savage beauty of his native land, he believed himself cured and saw no reason why he should not go back to Paris. He reached the rue St. Jacques at seven in the morning, his heart beating and a feverish flush on his cheek.

" Why, M. Colomban," said the *concièrge*, " where are you going ? "

" Where am I going ? " repeated Colomban, astonished. " Why, to see Camille, of course ! "

" But M. Camille has left ! "

" Left ? . . . And Mlle Carmélite ? " he asked with an effort.

"She has left, too."

"Where have they gone?"

"I don't know, but the laundress, Mlle Chante-Lilas, can tell you."

"She can? Oh, I see," said Colomban, leaning against the wall to save himself from falling. "Give me the key of my room, then."

"Your room? But it is not your room any longer!"

"What?" cried the Breton, harshly.

"You've moved too."

"I? Are you mad?"

"No. You can go up if you want to but there's nothing there. M. Camille took all your furniture, saying you were going to live with them."

"With them?" repeated Colomban, and a flame seemed to pass in front of his eyes. "And you don't know where they have gone?"

"I think it was somewhere Meudon way," replied the *concièrge*.

It took Colomban an hour and a half to get to Meudon, and then he had to enquire at every house; at the last one it was suggested that the young couple might be at Bas-Meudon. He set out for Bas-Meudon and there the house was pointed out to him. He rang twice and at last the gardener's wife let him in, but she took him to the pavilion in the garden, where Camille had put his furniture. By Carmélite's orders she did not mention that her mistress was at home.

When left alone, Colomban glanced round the room and passed a hand over his forehead. He thought he must be the victim of an illusion, for this was his room from the rue St-Jacques transported as it stood into the middle of a charming garden ! There is nothing more sad than to see again with a broken heart and tearful eyes the objects one knew when one was happy.   And in this room Colomban waited for four hours.   At last he heard the sound of wheels stopping at the gate; then the bell rang violently.   Evidently Nanette told Camille that Colomban had arrived, for he now appeared in the garden.   Colomban gave a cry of delight and opened his arms, for nothing could change the joy which he felt at seeing his friend again.

" Come to my room," said Camille, and took him into the house.   Carmélite had heard through her window what Camille said; she rose from her seat, pale and resolute, and when Camille's hand was on the handle of her door, she opened it herself. Colomban started violently.

" Kiss her, Colomban," cried Camille, hiding the uneasiness he felt under that aspect of gaiety which was with him sometimes a mask and sometimes his real mood.   " Why, what's the matter with you both ?   You don't want me to leave the room ? "

The others were cruelly embarrassed.

" But what's the matter ? " cried Camille again. " Since when has a friend refused to kiss the wife of his friend ? "

" The wife ? " cried Colomban, joyfully.   " Your wife ? "

" Well—practically, I was only waiting for your return to arrange for the marriage."

" Ah ! . . ." said Colomban, coldly ; then added with a touch of menace—" Well, I'm here ! " With this, he opened the door and went with Camille back into the garden.

" Well, how do you like your pavilion ? " asked Camille.

" Charming," replied Colomban, " but I will never consent to stay here."

" Why not ? "

" Because I will not be your accomplice. You promised me—it was one of the conditions of my going—that you would respect Carmélite and you have broken your word. From this moment our friendship is severed. I will not remain here another moment."

So saying, Colomban turned to go, but Camille barred the way.

" Listen ! " he said. " It is as true as that you are my only friend that I love and adore Carmélite, and it is not my fault that I have not kept my word."

Colomban smiled contemptuously.

" Ask her ! " Camille continued. " You will believe her, I hope ? Ask her if I have ever tried not to seduce her but to tempt her even. I tell you, as true as my name is Camille Rozan, that on the date you yourself fix Carmélite becomes my wife."

" Is that really true ? " asked Colomban.

" On my honour ! "

" Then if that is so, I will stay. As for the date of the marriage, that is for you to fix, of course. But naturally it should be as soon as possible."

" I will write to my father this very day and beg

him to send me all the necessary papers, and in six weeks we can publish the banns."

"Are you sure your father will consent? He is rich and Carmélite has nothing."

"Her virtue will be her dowry in my father's eyes."

"An unlucky omen," thought Colomban, "for you have spent that dowry in advance!" Aloud he said: "Suppose your father should refuse his consent?"

"Then I will wait till I come of age. When I am twenty-five (and I am now twenty-four) I can marry without my father's consent."

But a quarter of an hour after, Camille appeared, the letter still unwritten.

"I can't write," he said, "but I've thought of a better plan. I'll go myself and ask my father for his consent."

The Breton fixed his eyes on Camille, but he met his friend's gaze without flinching.

"You understand?" he said. "In eight days of personal pleading I can obtain more than in three months' letter writing. And yet "—he sighed—" the idea isn't practicable."

"Why not?"

"I can't take Carmélite with me and I can't leave her here. A young girl, all alone, exposed to insult from the neighbours."

"Do you think I'd let Carmélite be insulted?" asked Colomban, frowning.

"Then you consent to watch over her? You'll stay here?"

"Yes. Didn't I live in the same house with her for three months before she knew you?"

"Yes, but before she knew me, she . . ."

"Are you alluding to my love for her? Do you think me capable of betraying a promise?"

"No, Colomban. You would die first and your greatness makes me feel very small."

Carmélite heard the news with a shudder, but she made no objection; she did not analyze her strange emotion, but felt intuitively all the baseness of Camille and all the greatness of Colomban. It was arranged that Colomban should accompany Camille to the diligence, which started at ten in the morning. The Breton did not close an eye that night, and at six he was on foot waiting for Camille to wake. At eight he entered his room.

"What's the time?" asked Camille.

"Eight o'clock," replied Colomban.

"Oh, then, where's the hurry? Let me have another hour's sleep."

Carmélite's door was open and the girl heard the lazy Creole's reply.

"Let him sleep, Colomban," said she, as he entered her room.

It looked as if she had not been to bed, for the clothes were not disturbed.

"You are tired, Carmélite," said Colomban, looking at her drawn expression anxiously.

"Yes. I read the greater part of the night."

"And the rest of the time you cried?"

"I? . . No!" she replied, looking feverishly at the Breton.

Colomban sighed; then, though he knew that all was ready, he went out, making the excuse that he wanted to see to the luggage. His heart was breaking and he longed for air and solitude.--At nine he returned, went into Camille's room and forced him to get up. The carriage that was to take the Creole away was at the gate, and when he got in, they all three exchanged a farewell embrace, but only Colomban and Carmélite were crying.—It is true that Camille said to Colomban that he left his soul in his friend's keeping.—When the two young men had gone, Carmélite went to her rose-tree.

"Oh, rose," said she, "you, like me, one hot summer's night, were proud of your white petals and showed their treasures, glorying in the sun that you took for a friend. You believed in the eternity of life as I believed in the eternity of love!"

She broke off the few late blossoms that crowned the tree, but instead of wrapping them in her white veil, as she had done aforetime, she threw them out to the wind, which bore them down into the muddy street.

From that hour she looked upon the house as her tomb and her garden as the rose-planted cemetery of the Carmélites whose name she bore. Colomban thought that her grief was caused by Camille's departure and tried to console her by speaking of his return. But she shook her head and the time passed without revealing to him the mysterious cause of her despair.

Towards the end of December the first letter arrived from Camille, and Colomban rejoiced when

he took it to Carmélite, who was at the piano, but,
without taking her hands from the keys, she simply
told him to read it. It contained a long account of
the discussions Camille had had, not with his father,
but with his aunts, great aunts and all the rest of the
family, all of whom showed opposition to his marriage. Towards the end of January a second letter
arrived, full of affection. The opposition continued,
but Camille had gained over some members of his
family. This letter was received by Carmélite with
the same indifference as before.

In this way a whole year went by, but instead of
dragging as a year's absence should do, it passed
with extraordinary rapidity, in perfect serenity for
Colomban, and for Carmélite in passionate admiration of her companion and constant remorse for the
past. On the anniversary of Camille's departure,
Colomban declared that he would soon be returning,
for he was now twenty-five and his father's consent
no longer needed to his marriage. Carmélite, however, simply shook her head.

"He will not return," she said.

"What makes you think that?"

"The life we led together those three months. It
is possible to be with a friend for twenty years without really knowing him, but there are certain revealing moments—revealing to a woman. Believe me,
my friend, I am for Camille the prize of conquest,
that is all."

"You love him no longer, Carmélite," said Colomban sadly.

"I have never loved him," replied she proudly.

" Before God I speak the truth, Colomban. I never loved Camille."

" And yet . . ." began he, hesitatingly.

" Yet I was vanquished, you would say ? Yes, but not by him. By some unknown power, greater than myself or him. He merely waited for his chance and that is what I despise in him."

" Oh, hush ! " cried Colomban, covering his eyes with his hand.

" No. It was not to Camille that I yielded . . ."

" But then to what ? "

" To a phantom of my imagination, a dream of my heart ! "

" Carmélite ! I don't understand," he stammered.

" Oh, Colomban," she replied. " It was a lovely night, a night like that on which we fetched the rose-tree from the tomb of the poor La Vallière ! " Rising quickly, she ran from the pavilion to her room, whilst Colomban almost blind by this, the first ray of light, murmured :

" Oh, my God ! If she did not love Camille she might have loved me ! "

After this the relations of the two young people, from being simple and familiar, became constrained. Carmélite felt that she had said too much, and Colomban was afraid he had not rightly understood. He believed that Camille would return, and the thought that he himself was growing to love Carmélite more and more horrified him. Days, weeks and months passed and one morning came a letter from Camille's brother, saying that he was dangerously ill. Car-

mélite received this news with the same indifference
as she had shown towards the other letters. Then,
at last, came a letter from Camille himself, bringing
the news that, owing to his son's illness, his father
had withdrawn his opposition to the marriage. This
letter, drawing inspiration from the exaltation of the
moment, was a *chef'd'œuvre* of amorous passion, and
when he handed it to Carmélite, Colomban's eyes
were full of tears.

" You see I was right," he said, but Carmélite
saw in the letter merely the influence of fever. In
any case, it made no difference; she might not have
the coldness of the executioner, but she had the
courage of the judge and in her heart had pronounced
an irrevocable sentence on the absent.

Soon there came another letter. Carmélite read it
and passed it to Colomban. He grew pale as he
read :

" *Dear Carmélite,*
" *I shall be back in Paris by the seventh of next
month. . . .*"

He closed his eyes and a tear forced its way
between their lids.

" What is the matter ? " asked Carmélite gently,
" and why does the return of your friend so affect
you ? "

" Oh, Carmélite, don't ask ! " he cried. " Oh, I
shall die ! "

" Because you love me? Is that it, Colomban ? "
pursued the girl, pitilessly.

" Love you ? " cried Colomban, with agonized
eyes. " Love you ! "

" Yes," said she, simply. " Why not ? I love you ! "

" Oh, hush ! Hush ! " he cried. " Oh, can you ever forgive me ? "

" What is there to forgive, since I love you—have always loved you ? "

" Carmélite ! Your words burn ! " With a tremendous effort he stepped back from her. " My sister, we are both to blame. Let us ask God to give us strength to expiate. . . . Strength and resignation ! "

" What do you call resignation ? " asked Carmélite. " Do you mean that I should marry Camille."

" You must."

" Marry him, loving you and knowing you love me ? "

" You must ! "

" Why ? To whom am I responsible in this world ? I am alone, thank God, and consequently the only judge of my conduct."

" You are wrong, Carmélite. You are responsible towards Society and God is your only judge."

" How can Society constrain me to cause the unhappiness of two men and myself ? Did God come to my rescue when I felt myself slipping on the edge of the abyss ? "

" That's blasphemy, Carmélite. You must not mistake our desires and instincts for rights and duties. Oh, I am not reproaching you," he cried, falling on his knees beside her.

" Colomban, you don't realize that had it not been for you I should have been dead by now. I formed the project the day that Camille left me, when I threw to the winds the flowers from my poor rose-tree. It is thanks to the love of life that you have given back to me that I am still alive."

" And now you wish me to perish with you ? "

" Is it perishing—would it be suffering—to die, suffer, perish together ? "

" Carmélite, for God's sake ! "

" There are only two courses to take, Colomban. Either we must leave this house and fly to the end of the world, forgetting and forgotten."

" And the other course ? " asked Colomban, thus implying that he rejected this suggestion.

" The other course," replied Carmélite, firmly, " is to die. If we cannot be together in life, then let us be united in death. I would rather suffer with you, Colomban, through Eternity than be his wife on earth."

" Oh, Carmélite, no, no ! Yet I love you madly —madly ! I'll do whatever you wish. Whatever you decide I will agree to ! "

" Colomban ! I speak as a nameless creature, alone in the world and ruined. But you are the last of a noble family. You have a great name and a father who loves you. Think of your father ! Tell me to-morrow what you have decided."

This scene took place on the eve of the *mardi gras* of 1827. The next day came with that monotonous regularity of hours which, whether grave or gay, must make the circle of the clock twice over. It was a foggy day; we saw the end of it in the first chapter of this book when we met Jean Davy, Ludovic and

Pétrus in the streets of Paris. When the day began the rain had been pouring, fine and penetrating; the air was icy, the skies grey, the pavements black. It was one of those winter days on which many of us feel ill, no matter what we do; when we are melancholy by ourselves and even more unhappy when in company; a day when we are powerless to shake off a wretchedness more dangerous than actual illness, when we sit down before the sense of helplessness. On such a day, the morning of Shrove Tuesday, the young couple met in Colomban's pavilion. They sat by the fire, silent and sad, exchanging brief words such as two condemned men might exchange while waiting for the executioner. Then at last Carmélite said bluntly :

" He will arrive to-morrow."

" To-morrow ! " repeated Colomban.

" And we have not decided what we shall do, my friend," said Carmélite.

" I have decided," replied Colomban. " I shall die ! "

" I shall die also."

Colomban grew pale.

" You mean it ? You will die without regret ? "

" I shall die gladly."

" God forgive us ! " cried Colomban.

" He has forgiven us already," said the girl.

" Then now let us separate for the last time before we meet for ever. I have a letter to write to my father and one to Dominique Sarranti."

" And I must write to Régina, Lydie and Fragola, my three school friends," said Carmélite.

15

The letters written, they were given to Nanette to post, for she had leave to go to Paris to attend a masquerade on Carnival night. The two young people were thus alone, and from that moment the world ceased to exist for them. They walked beneath the gaunt, leafless trees, which under a leaden sky were as spectres. They looked down at the dead leaves. Death seemed to surround them. Silently they sought each room in turn to say good-bye. When they reached Carmélite's room she opened the window.

" I was standing here," she said, " when Camille left. Then only did I comprehend the extent of my hatred towards him and of my love for you. From that day I broke with life and made my pact with death. But—forgive me this, Colomban !—I wished to die with you ! " Colomban pressed her to his heart.

Then, picking up the rose-tree, they went to the pavilion. They entered, Carmélite first. Then Colomban turned and locked the door. . . . They had transformed the room into a mortuary chapel, of which all the apertures were carefully closed. Carmélite had hidden the windows with white curtains, and on the mantelpiece, the tables and all the furniture were vases of flowers;—even the carpet was strewn with them. As if she were afraid this dual death might escape her, Carmélite rose repeatedly to get the charcoal, waiting ready in the next room, but each time Colomban stopped her; he wanted to keep her before his eyes till the last moment. About nine o'clock, she went to the piano and the lovers sang their swan song. Never had song so vibrated with the cry of sorrow and the hymn of joy ! At last the piano became mute, as if its soul had fled, and the girl's head sank on Colomban's shoulder. There was a long silence . . . then the clock struck.

" Eleven ! " said they, and Carmélite added : " It is time."

Colomban rose, lit two candles, handed one to Carmélite and went with the other to the door.

" Where are you going ? " asked she.

" I agree to your dying," said Colomban, " but I will not let you suffer."

He meant to light the stove in the next room that the first fumes might evaporate, so that they need only inhale the later, subtle vapour which penetrates to the brain and brings death without pain.

" Leave the door open," said she. " Let me see you ! "

Her hands had returned to the piano as young birds to their nest, and whilst they ran over the ivory keys, her eyes, fixed on Colomban, watched the flickering flames, which lit up with a flickering red light the forehead of the young man as he knelt to tend the fatal charcoal fire. There was no sign of emotion on their faces; theirs was the strength and calm of people detached from the affairs of this world; their bodies seemed already dead and their souls alone were communing.

The charcoal took about a quarter of an hour to kindle; then, when the first gross vapours had dis- persed, Colomban shut the window and carried the stove to the middle of the room. He was pale and staggered slightly, for he had inhaled those first fumes that he wished to spare Carmélite. They sat down on the sofa, and were looking into one another's eyes when midnight struck. Yet what did the march of time matter to them, facing Eternity?

The air changed slowly to carbonic acid; the candle flame lost its colour, but the flames of the charcoal danced like a will-o'-the-wisp, taking on all the colours of the rainbow. Drops of perspiration fell from the young girl's body and her face showed violet tints; with a supreme effort, Colomban took her in his arms and, staggering like a drunken man, bore her from the sofa to the bed; then he fell at her feet, but rose again with one last effort and took his place beside her.

In spite of the circle of iron that was now biting into her brain, she felt his arm about her.

"Yes, my fiancé, yes," she murmured; "I am here!" And then, for the first time, they kissed as lovers.

It was Colomban who was the first to lose consciousness. He stopped in the middle of a kiss, his throat constricted, his tongue inert. He just managed to gasp:

"Come!—Come!—Come!   .   .   ." before his head fell on the breast of the girl, who gave a feeble cry.

"Colomban!—I   am   coming!"—she   cried, pressed her lips for the last time to his forehead, and then her head reposed by his.

The clock struck one.

CHAPTER XVIII
AN URGENT LETTER

I⊤ was as the clock was striking one that our three
young friends were in the act of sitting down to
supper at Bordier's with Salvator their preserver.
You have not forgotten, dear reader, have you, that
Salvator and Jean Davy, when they quitted the rue
Aubry-le-Boucher, left their two companions, Pétrus
and Ludovic, asleep on the table under the care of
the waiter? Well, then, the first to awake was Ludovic, disturbed by the noise of a lively lot of pleasure-
seekers who were anxious, in their turn, to have
possession of that fourth-floor room, the conquest of
which had been like to cost our young men so dear.
The waiter, however, faithful to Salvator's com-
mands, would allow no one to enter.

Ludovic opened his eyes and listened. His first
impression was that he would have to stand another
siege, but this time the attacking party were laughing so heartily that he thought it might be agreeable
to be overcome by such lively adversaries. He therefore opened the door to them himself. Instantly a
troupe attired as pierrots, pierrettes, scallywags and
fishwives surged into the room with such a clamour
of shouts and laughter that Pétrus in his turn
bounded up, crying:

"Fire! Fire!"

Pétrus always had incendiary dreams.

In the height of the tumult, Ludovic felt two
pretty arms wreathe themselves round his neck while
a mouth, whose every breath fanned the fringe of the

mask that covered the upper part of his face, whispered through teeth the whitest and lips the rosiest that he had ever seen :

" So it is you, my beloved sawbones, who indulge in the luxury of a private room all to yourself ? "

" If you will take the trouble to look round, my dear pierrette, you will see that I am not alone."

" Oho," replied the pierrette, " there's Maestro Raphael ! Would you like me to pose for the leg of the woman in the burning citadel ? You were crying ' Fire ! Fire ! ' when we entered ! " She lifted her fancy dress and showed a leg such as painters look for and cardinals find.

" I know that leg, Princess ! " said Pétrus.

" Chante-Lilas ! " cried Ludovic simultaneously.

" Since I'm recognized, I take off my mask," said the pretty laundress. " Besides, it's unpleasant to drink with the face covered and I'm dying of thirst ! "

On which the whole company, which consisted of five or six laundresses from Vanvres and three or four gardening girls from Meudon, with their lovers, sang in chorus :

" Drink ! Drink ! Drink ! "

" Silence ! " cried Ludovic. " This is my room, so it's for me to do the honours. Waiter, six bottles of champagne for me ! "

" And six for me, waiter," said Pétrus.

" Ah ! That's good. And we'll show our gratitude by keeping a cheek for each of you," declared the Princess.

" Double or quits ? " said Pétrus, drawing out a fistful of coins.

"What's that, Signor Raphael?" demanded Chante-Lilas.

"I was betting Ludovic his cheek of yours against my cheek," explained Pétrus.

"Heads for the Double!" replied Ludovic, responding in the same language as his friend.

"Oh, you gamesters!" cried the princess. "We only want Camille here to be complete. He's the cream of the vintage."

"The cream of the vintage is here," said the waiter who had just entered with the champagne, of which he had cut the wires of two bottles on the stairs.

"I've won!" cried Ludovic, saluting Chante-Lilas on both cheeks. "I carry off the Sabine!"

Taking the Princess in his arms as if she had been a child, he bore her off to a table where he sat down with her on his knee.

      ●   ●   ●   ●   ●   ●

In an hour's time the dozen bottles of champagne had been drunk and another dozen had followed them—this time ordered by the joyous company—down the same channels.

"And now," said Chante-Lilas, "we have to get back to Vanvres. Nanette promised her mistress she would be back at eleven and she has a letter to give her. It's now three and luckily the letter is urgent!"

"The time is four in the morning not three, Princess," said Pétrus.

"And my Old Woman gets up at five! Come along, everybody! *En route!*"

"Bah!" said the Countess du Battoir. "The old

lady will have been celebrating like everyone else. She won't get up before six."

" Princess, when are you coming to Paris again ? " asked Ludovic.

" As if it mattered to you ! " retorted Chante-Lilas.

" It does matter, for I've no more clean linen."

" That's a mere trifle. You shall have it if you come and fetch it."

" Chante-Lilas, don't be silly. It has been a bad week for white shirts and I can't see my patients in a laced one."

" I said come and fetch it ! "

" If there's room for me in your carriage, Princess. . . ."

" You mean that ? "

" It is as I have the honour to inform your highness."

" Bravo ! We'll get a drink of milk at the ' moulin de Vanvres.' Are you coming, Signor Raphael ? "

" Sacrebleu ! It isn't lack of good will, but I've an early sitting."

" Put it off ! "

" Impossible ! I've promised ! "

" Sacred word of honour, eh ? Then the Fornarina must take a fond farewell of Raphael. Come along, my king of Sawbones ! "

She offered her arm to Ludovic who, having decided to bury the Carnival with all ceremony, paid his bill and that of Pétrus too, went down the stairs four at a time and climbed into the enormous furniture-van that had brought the party from Vanvres to Paris. Pétrus, who lived in the rue de l'Ouest, said good-bye to his friend and waved farewells to the rest of the party as they receded into the distance.

" But where are we going? " asked Ludovic. " Surely we are taking the road to Versailles, not Vanvres."

" If Raphael hadn't left us, king of the Saw-bones," replied Chante-Lilas, " he would have told you that all roads lead to Rome. You see Nanette, there. She's pretty, isn't she? "

" Very."

" Well, she only came on condition that we took her back to her door."

" But why? "

" Didn't I tell you she had an urgent letter? "

" But why didn't she deliver the letter first, before starting? "

" Because she had got to the end of the village before she met the postman and as we were waiting for her it would have made her half an hour late. And then the letter had been twenty-six days getting here, anyway, as it comes from the Colonies, so a few hours more or less . . ."

" Don't kill a man! " finished the Countess du Battoir.

" Even if they did, haven't we the doctor with us? Why, he's gone to sleep! "

" Oh," yawned Ludovic, " let me sit at your feet, Princess, and rest my head on your lap. You will save my life."

" If I'd known you only came along with us to fall

asleep, I'd have put you to bed in a greengrocer's cart! You'd have been just as well there as here!"

"Ah, Princess, you don't do yourself justice," murmured Ludovic, half asleep. "There is no lettuce with a heart as tender as yours!"

"What a fool a man is when he's sleepy," cried Chante-Lilas, with an accent of profound contempt.

Five o'clock was striking when they reached their destination. The laughter had ceased bit by bit; discomfort and cold due to the coming dawn weighed on the masquerading party, all half asleep; they all wanted to get back to their own rooms, to a fire and a warm bed. The van stopped before the house where lived Carmélite and Colomban and Nanette leaped down. She drew the key from her pocket and entered.

"Good," she said when she saw through the open garden door that a light was burning in Colomban's room; "the man is still up, so he shall have his letter at once. Good night, everyone!" Then she shut the door.

Loud snores answered her from the interior of the vehicle which continued its way to Vanvres. But it had scarcely gone fifty yards when someone was heard crying:

"Help! Help! M. Ludovic!"

The van stopped.

"What's the matter?" asked Ludovic, waking up.

"I don't know. Someone's calling you," said Chante-Lilas. "I think I recognize Nanette's voice. Something must have happened."

Ludovic sprang down and saw Nanette running towards him, crying :

" Help! Help! "

CHAPTER XIX
SUICIDE

HE ran to meet her.

" Quick, M. Ludovic. Come, all of you! They are dead! "

" Who are dead? " asked Ludovic.

" Mlle Carmélite and M. Colomban."

" Colomban? Not Colomban de Penhoël? "

" Yes, yes. Oh, mon Dieu, how dreadful! So young, so bonny, and so kind! "

Ludovic rushed to the house and finding the door open, quickly gained the pavilion. The window opened by Colomban and carelessly shut, had been re-opened by Nanette, who, receiving no answer to her call, had tried to climb in through it to knock at the door. Getting no reply she had opened it but had started back again, almost fainting : a terrible gust of carbonic acid had enveloped her with its fatal cloud. She had instantly guessed what had happened and thinking the van could not have gone far had run to stop it. Ludovic got into the pavilion through the window and also tried to enter the room, but he, too, had been overcome. As the others rushed up he was filling his lungs with fresh air from the garden.

" Smash the windows, and break open the doors," he cried. " They have been asphyxiated! " They tried to open the sashes but they were fastened; a few good kicks, however, broke down the doors. But all who tried to crowd into the room recoiled.

" Get vinegar and salt water and knock up the chemist, if there is one in the village, and get some ammoniated salts. Nanette, light a fire somewhere and have warm blankets ready."

Then, as the miner descends into the depths or the sailor dives into the sea, Ludovic threw himself into the room. The gay masker had vanished to make way for the man of science; the doctor was ready to make use of all his trained resources. He felt his way to the window for the candle had gone out, as had the fire on the hearth and the charcoal stove gave now neither flame nor fumes. The curtains hanging over the windows hindered his finding the hasp, so he wrapped his hand in his handkerchief and broke two panes with his fist. A draught of fresh air came through at once and it was time; Ludovic was reeling. But he seized the curtains and tore them down; this done he managed to open the windows. The carbonic acid began to disperse, driven before the air which now came in through three openings.

" Come in," said Ludovic. " There is no danger now. Come in and give me some light." They lit the second candle and everything became visible. . . . The two young people were lying on the bed, in one another's arms, as if they had just fallen asleep.

" Is there anyone here—a doctor or barber or anyone, who can help me? " asked Ludovic.

" There's M. Pilloy, formerly surgeon-major. A clever man," said someone.

" Go and find him ! Shout till he wakes up ; bring him as quickly as possible." Then, going to the bed, he added sadly : " I am afraid it is too late."

The lips of the young couple were black and when Ludovic raised their eyelids, Carmélite's eye was glassy and Colomban's dull and bloodshot. Not a breath came from either.

" Too late ! " sighed Ludovic, despairingly. " But we must do what we can. Take charge of the young girl, Mesdames. I will see to the man."

" What are we to do ? " asked Chante-Lilas.

" Do what I tell you. Take her first to the window and try and light a big fire, a big wood fire. Heat flannels and blankets and take off their shoes. I'll try and open a vein in his foot. But it's too late ! " With this despairing cry he carried Colomban to the window.

" Here is vinegar and salt water," said Nanette.

" Pour the vinegar into a plate and wet handkerchiefs with it. Rub their temples. You understand, Chante-Lilas ? "

" Yes, yes," said she.

" Cut a quill, like this, do you see? Open the teeth if you can and blow air into their lungs."

They obeyed him as soldiers obey a general in a battle. Carmélite's teeth were clenched, but with the aid of a paper knife Chante-Lilas succeeded in introducing the quill.

" Now blow down it," said Ludovic. " I can't get mine in. His jaws are of iron. Have you taken off his shoes and stockings? "

" Yes," said the men.

"Then rub his temples with the vinegar and dash cold water into his face. Open his teeth somehow even if you have to break them. I will try to bleed him in the foot."

Ludovic opened his case and took out his lancet. He made two incisions but without result. No blood came.

"Open his waistcoat. Tear off his cravat—everything!"

"Here are hot flannels!" cried someone.

"Give them to Chante-Lilas and rub her chest. You know how, Chante-Lilas? As hard as you can. Ah, here is a knife." He managed to slip it between Colomban's teeth; then as he could not get a quill into the narrow opening, he laid his lips on the Breton's and tried to force air into his lungs. The throat was constricted and no air could pass beyond the pharynx.

"Too late!" sighed Ludovic. "We must try the jugular!" He took up his lancet again and with an admirable certainty of touch, found the vein in the neck. But no blood came.

"Here are salts and alkaline," said the messenger, giving two bottles to Ludovic.

"Take the salts, Chante-Lilas and hold them under her nose. I'll keep the alkaline. Do you think any air has got to her lungs?"

"I think a little."

"Then courage! Rub her temples with vinegar and make her inhale those salts." Meanwhile he was soaking a napkin in the alkalized water and with it he enveloped Colomban's head. But the body remained still; not a breath came from his breast nor could air penetrate to his lungs.

"Oh!" cried Chante-Lilas, "I believe her lips are a little paler!"

"Courage! That's a good sign. Just think how happy you would be if you could feel you had saved a life!"

"I think she sighed."

"Lift her eyelid and look at the eye. Is it still as dull as ever?"

"No, no. Not quite!"

"M. Pilloy isn't at home," said the messenger returning from the surgeon-major's house.

"Where is he?"

"At M. Gèrard's. He's very ill. He lives at Vanvres. Shall I go there?"

"No good. It's too far."

"M. Ludovic, she breathed!" cried Chante-Lilas.

"Are you sure?"

"I was rubbing her chest with a flannel and I felt it move.—Oh, she's put her hand to her head!"

"Then we shall save one of them, at least. Take her out of this room, quickly. She must not see her dead friend when she comes round."

"Take her to her own room," cried Nanette.

"Open all the windows and keep up a good fire. Quick!" As the women carried Carmélite away the day was just beginning to break. "You know what to do, Chante-Lilas? Keep up just the same treatment as before."

"And if she asks what has become of her lover?"

" She probably won't be able to speak for an hour and it will be two or three hours before she is properly conscious. And by then . . . either Colomban or myself will be with her." Then, turning to Colomban, he murmured : " Too late ! Poor, poor Colomban or, rather, poor Carmélite ! " He returned to the body with the sublime tenacity of the doctor who pursues life into the very arms of death.

CHAPTER XX

ROUND THE BED OF CARMÉLITE AND NEAR THAT OF
COLOMBAN

AT nine o'clock in the morning, the carriage containing M. Jackal, Salvator and Jean Davy stopped at the door of the house where the terrible events we have just related had been happening. Three other carriages were already at the door, a hackney coach, a small barouche and a large carriage with a coat of arms on its panels.

" They are all three here," murmured Salvator.

M. Jackal exchanged a few words with a man dressed in black who was standing at the door; the man then mounted a horse and departed at a gallop.

" I'm thinking of your schoolmaster," said M. Jackal to Salvator and Jean Davy.

Salvator gave a mute acknowledgment and went in. He had scarcely entered when a dog that was lying on the first floor landing bounded downstairs and put his paws on his shoulders.

" Yes, old fellow. Yes, Roland, I know she's there. Show us the way."

The dog rushed up first and stopped at Carmélite's

door. M. Jackal, as one having the right to go everywhere, opened the door and entered, followed by Salvator and Jean Davy.

A picture full of poetry met their eyes. Round the bed where Carmélite, still unconscious, but out of danger, was lying, three young girls knelt and prayed. They were equally young and beautiful and all dressed in the same costume as Carmélite herself —that of the boarders of St. Denis. It consisted of a frock of fine black serge, with full skirt and high bodice on which was a white pleated collar; the sleeves were ample and fell over the hands like the sleeves of Nuns; a broad ribband, passed round the shoulders, encircled the waist, forming at the back an angle, the base of which was at the waist and the summit at the shoulders. This girdle, as broad as one's hand, was woven of six different colours; green, violet, golden, blue, white and shell pink. It was, in short, half worldly, half religious; a woman of the world would not have dressed so severely and a Nun would not have worn that rainbow-coloured band. This is the costume the pupils at St-Denis assume when they enter what is called the *" classe de perfectionnement."*

Jean Davy recognized Fragola at once and glanced towards Salvator who put a finger on his lip to enjoin silence. Then, suddenly, the two friends recoiled for they thought the corpse moved and they did not know that Carmélite's life had been saved by Ludovic.

" Oh," said M. Jackal with the indifference of a man used to such sights, " so she is not dead ? "

16

" No, *monsieur*," replied the tallest of the three girls, who by her beauty and stature seemed to take the lead. Jean Davy turned. He recognized the voice; it was that of Mlle Régina de Lamothe-Houdan.

" And the young man? " asked M. Jackal.

" We still have hope," replied Régina. " There is a young doctor with him and so long as he doesn't give up, all is not lost."

At this moment the door opened and to the great surprise of Jean Davy and Salvator, Ludovic came in. He had thrown aside his Carnival costume, having sent a mounted messenger to bring him his usual black clothes.

" Well? " they all cried.

Ludovic shook his head.

" The priest is with him," he said. " There is nothing more that I can do." Then, looking at Carmélite, whose eyes, though open, seemed to see nothing. " Poor child! Leave her in her ignorance. She will come back to life only too soon."

" Gentlemen," said M. Jackal to Salvator and Jean Davy. " It is not merely accident that we are here. I think we had better leave the patient to her friends and the doctor, draw up our report as quickly as possible and set off for Versailles."

Jean Davy and Salvator bowed assent. Fragola whispered a few words in Salvator's ear and he nodded; then the commissionaire and the poet left as they had entered, preceded by M. Jackal. Downstairs all was ready for him to write his report. The door of the corridor was open and through the windows of the pavilion lighted candles could be seen.

" Won't you come and sprinkle a few drops of Holy Water over that poor fellow and say a prayer for his soul ? " said Salvator to the poet who made a sign of assent, and while M. Jackal, seeking inspiration, buried his nose in snuff, they went to the pavilion.

Colomban was lying on his bed; the sheet drawn above his head, showed beneath its folds the rigidity given by the hand of death to the human body. A Dominican monk was sitting by the bed, his book open on his knees, but his head was thrown back and from his eyes fell silent tears as he recited the prayers for the dead. When he saw the two young men enter with bowed heads, he rose; he glanced from one to the other, but it was evident that the two faces were unknown to him.

Salvator, on the other hand, when he saw the Dominican, gave a cry of joy, tempered, however, with respect. At the sound the monk turned; but the fresh glance he threw at Salvator told him no more than the first, and except for the slight expression of surprise which was instantly suppressed, he remained motionless. Salvator, however, advanced towards him.

" Father," he said, " without knowing it you saved my life, and although I never saw you, never met you before, I have vowed a profound gratitude. . . . Your hand, Father ! "

The monk offered him his hand and in spite of the attempt he made to withdraw it again, the young man kissed it.

"And now, listen, Father," said Salvator. "I don't know whether you will ever have need of me, but on the most sacred thing imaginable . . . on the body of this man who has so lately drawn his last breath, I swear that the life I owe you is at your command!"

"I accept, sir," replied the monk gravely, "though I do not know how or when I can have rendered you the service you speak of. All men are brothers and sent into this world to help one another; when I need you I will remember. Your name and address?"

Salvator went to Colomban's desk and wrote down his name and address, presenting the paper to the monk, who folded it and put it in his prayer book; then he re-seated himself and continued his prayers. The two young men took the branch of palm steeped in Holy Water and sprinkled the sheet covering the dead body; then both knelt at the foot of the bed in silent prayer.

Whilst they prayed a man entered, whose livery showed that he was a servant in a rich *bourgeois* family.

"Please, sir, I think it must be you I'm looking for," he said to the monk.

"What do you want, my friend?" asked Dominique.

"My master is dying, sir, and as the Curé of Vanvres is away he begs you to be good enough to allow him to make confession."

"But I am a stranger to the parish; this young man was my friend and I came here because of a letter he wrote to me, which, unfortunately, I received too late."

" Please, sir, I know it is just because you are a stranger that my master wishes for you. He is in extremis I fear. When he asked M. Pilloy, the surgeon, to tell him the truth, he said he had no time to lose, that I know."

The monk sighed as he looked at the corpse, the outline of which showed clearly under the sheet.

" Please, please, sir," pleaded the servant, " my master told me to beg you, in the name of God whose minister you are, to come to him as quickly as possible ! "

" Father," said Salvator, " I think consolation for the living should come before duty to the dead."

" I will stay here," said Jean Davy.

" Monsieur," insisted the servant. " What am I to say to my master ? "

" Tell him that I am coming. What is his name ? "

" M. Gérard."

" And where does he live ? "

" Oh, sir, anyone will tell you that. He is the benefactor of the whole countryside." So saying, the servant hastily went out.

" You will promise to remain here till my return, *monsieur?* "

" You will find me where you left me, Father," replied Jean Davy. " At the foot of the bed."

" And if you have any service to ask of me," added Salvator, " I would do my best to accomplish it."

" I accept your offer, sir. Colomban charged me to see that his body was laid with that of her whom he loved; Providence has decreed that there shall be but one corpse instead of two and so I cannot fulfil his wish. But this body should be taken from the sight of poor Carmélite as soon as possible; I therefore decided that I would start at four to-day for Brittany. There lives a father who has a right to the body of his son and to all the consolation I can bring."

" At four o'clock, Father, the dead body, in an oak coffin shall await you in a coach, all formalities fulfilled. You will only have to take your seat and start."

" I have only enough to pay for my own journey. How can I . . ."

"That need not concern you, Father. The expenses of the journey shall be paid on your return."

The monk approached the bed, raised the sheet, kissed Colomban upon the brow and departed.

Five minutes after, M. Jackal came in. He advanced towards the young men, planted himself with legs wide apart and hands in pockets; then addressing himself particularly to Jean Davy, he asked of that young man:

" You are a poet? "

" They say so."

" As a poet, of course you believe in Providence, don't you? "

" Yes, sir; I have the courage to confess that I do."

" It needs courage, indeed! " M. Jackal took out his snuff-box and wrathfully inhaled two or three pinches. Then, drawing from his pocket a letter which he showed to Jean Davy without letting him take it, he added : " You see this letter ? It arrived this evening and as you see with ' Very Urgent ' on it. The postman gave it to Nanette at the other end of the village; she took it to Paris; yet if it had been read last night by those to whom it is addressed, we should have had two happy people instead of one dead and the other in despair. Read it ! "

He gave the letter to Jean Davy who unfolded it and read as follows :

" *My dear Colomban and Carmélite,*
　　" *Won't you be happy when you see this letter from your friend Camille Rozan instead of seeing the man himself? I hear you cry: ' Oh, dear Camille ! ' Now listen, my friends. This is what one of my compatriots writes to me. I had told him of my proposed marriage with Carmélite:*
　　" ' *My dear Rozan, your two friends are living together like two turtle doves and never part. They not only love, they adore one another ! I fancy your return would trouble them vastly, so show yourself as great as Alexander, who ceded to Apelles his mistress Campaspe. I won't say, " Give Carmélite up to Colomban," but I do say, " Don't part two hearts that heaven intended for one another." '*
　　" *That is what my compatriot wrote to me, Colomban, and there is one thing I knew already . . . that you loved Carmélite. I now know that Carmélite loves you. Then there is a third thing that you said and that I believe: namely, that you would die rather than betray the oath you took to watch over Carmélite like a brother. I don't want you to die, my poor Colomban, and that is why I give you back your word, and Carmélite too. So be happy, Colomban, and if your sacrifice has been a burden, receive in compensation the greatest thing that I can offer, for it is only now, when about to separate from her for ever, that I realize how deeply I love Carmélite. That is why, as it was necessary to set a barrier between her and me that could not be overcome, I was married yesterday and I am writing to you now from the nuptial chamber. Farewell, dear Colomban ! Farewell, too, dear*

Carmélite! I wish you all the happiness you deserve, confessing in all humility my own weakness; I might even say my cowardice, if I were not sure that this news will overwhelm you both with joy. But especially Carmélite.

"*Your friend,*
"*Camille Rozan.*"

"Well," said M. Jackal, taking back his letter. "What do you say to that, M. Jean Davy?"

"It's heart-breaking!" replied the young man.

"And you still believe in Providence?"

"I do."

"Providence, M. Davy," said M. Jackal, ramming snuff up his nose, "Providence is a well-managed Police. And now let us go to Versailles to see if we can find the fiancée of that schoolmaster of yours."

And now if the reader should ask us by chance the question Jean Davy whispered to Salvator when, faithful to his promise, he remained behind to watch over Colomban's body while the commissionaire of the rue aux Fers and the commissioner from the rue de Jérusalem set out for Versailles—if, I say, my readers should ask: "How could M. Jackal know of events happening in the Bas-Meudon between midnight and five o'clock as early as half-past seven?" we must answer as follows:

There existed at that time an unique institution called the black cabinet. It was a room where a dozen or so clerks were secretly busy opening letters put into the post and reading those letters before they were read by the addressees. Nowadays, there is no black cabinet: the thing is done in the light of day.[1]

[1] In the days of the Second Empire when Dumas was writing.— EDITOR'S NOTE.

M. Jackal, because of the rumours of a triple conspiracy, Republican, Orleanist and Napoleonic, did
not disdain to do the work of a simple clerk in his
leisure hours; consequently he had passed the night
opening and reading other people's letters.   That
from Colomban to Dominique had fallen into his
hands; it was then half-past four or thereabouts.   He
had instantly sent a man on horseback post haste to
Bas-Meudon.   M. Jackal (who said Providence was
a well-managed police force) hoped that the man
would arrive in time; he did actually arrive a moment
after the room had been broken into and therefore
just too late.   In the midst of the confusion, no one
paid any attention to this man.   He saw a letter
addressed to Mlle Régina de Lamothe-Houdan, Mme
Lydia de Marande and Mlle Fragola Ponroy.   He
took it and sent it to M. Jackal who as he had read
the letter addressed to Dominique read the other also.
He then ordered his man to get a fresh horse and put
the other letter back where he had found it.   The
messenger had just done so when Salvator and Jean
Davy saw M. Jackal speak to a stranger on horseback; all he said to him was that he might now go to
bed and that the prefect of police should be told how
promptly and ably he had fulfilled his commission.

CHAPTER XXI

M. GÉRARD'S CONFESSION TO BROTHER DOMINIQUE

WE have seen how Brother Dominique, summoned
to the bedside of M. Gérard, went to that worthy
man whose imminent demise was plunging the whole
neighbourhood into despair.   The villagers met on

the way turned to accompany the priest to the house
and poured forth laudations of their patron's philan-
thropy. Why, said they, he often lends money without asking interest; nay, in some cases, without taking a receipt! His present condition was the result
of a good action, they explained, for M. Gérard had
contracted a severe chill from rescuing a child from
drowning—a chill which had given place to fever.
That very morning, his doctor, M. Pilloy, had said
that he would not answer for his patient and had tact-
fully warned poor M. Gérard that if he had any
arrangements to make he had no more than sufficient
time. On hearing this, the saintly man had swooned,
though surely death should have held no terrors for
him. On coming to himself he had called at once for
a priest and, as the Curé of Meudon was absent, they
had sent, at M. Gérard's request, for the stranger.

The Dominican, noble of heart, appreciated devoted loyalty and was profoundly touched by the grief
of these simple people. Eager to comfort and bless
he quickened his pace and soon reached the house,
which all pointed out to him.

" Oh, M. l'Abbé," cried the old women; " you are
going to hear the confession of a saint! You could
safely give M. Gérard absolution in advance! "

The Abbé Dominique thanked them all. Then he
entered and, passing quickly up the staircase, found
at the top the servant who had come to Meudon to
fetch him. The man had run all the way back to
announce that the consoler was coming, but the tid-
ings had seemed to redouble his master's agitation.
Indeed, his groans were so frightful that, instead of

staying with the nurse who remained imperturbable in her easy chair, the servant had gone out on to the landing to await the Dominican.

Opening the door, "*Monsieur,*" said the man to his master. "Here is he whom you expect."

The dying man shuddered convulsively and a moan escaped him. Then in a deep voice, he said :

"Show him in."

The priest entered the room, the details of which he took in with a keen glance. There, on the pillow, crumpled with the patient's restless fever, he saw the face of him whom the whole countryside called "good M. Gérard." That personage, seeing Dominique in his striking gown of black and white, gave a slight nod of greeting and called his nurse. The woman rose and approached the bed with the stagger of extreme sleepiness.

"How do you feel, sir?" she asked.

"Very bad, Marianne."

"Can I get you anything?"

"Something to drink and then leave us alone." The nurse gave him some drink, kept warm on a nightlight. He sipped it and fell back on his pillow, exhausted by the effort, but when the woman saw that the cup was still three-quarters full, she pushed it against his lips with that roughness so characteristic of her type.

"Thanks, Marianne," said M. Gérard, guiding her hand away, "but I want you to draw the curtains and leave us. The daylight troubles me."

The woman did as requested and the room was now in darkness, but for the nightlight. The young priest

had kept his eyes fixed on the sick man's face, surprised to find it so different from what he had
expected. Brother Dominique was exceptionally endowed with that gift of reading character quickly,
which is the special talent of priests and doctors, and
from all he had heard of M. Gérard he had pictured
him in harmony with such rare virtues, but the
patient's countenance had undeceived him. A movement he could not control resulted from his surprise
as he engraved every feature on his memory. M.
Gérard was fifty or fifty-five with a low, narrow forehead, although his baldness made it seem higher than
it was; his eyes were small and too deeply set, disappearing entirely at times behind lids reddened and
swollen, either from lack of sleep or past excesses;
heavy grey brows with harsh, longish hairs standing
out, met in a line over his nose, forming a penthouse
over his eyes; the nose was thin, and curved like a
hatchet; the mouth large with pale lips, so that the
face resembled that of a vulture. Allowing for the
ravages of disease, Dominique could but be struck by
the mean soul and cowardly spirit it betokened. It
had, moreover, an expression of abject terror. The
sight of a dying man, usually so touching, will lead
us by the golden thread of thought straight to God;
yet the aspect of this man, though so close to the
grave, instead of exciting sympathy aroused a feeling
of disgust. He moaned and shivered without speaking, so that at last Brother Dominique addressed
him.

" You sent for me, M. Gérard ? "

" Yes."

" I am ready to listen."

His interlocutor looked at him anxiously.

" You are very young."

" I did not ask to come," said Dominique, rising, but the man stretched out an emaciated hand and took hold of his gown.

" No, no! Sit down! I only meant that at your age, you cannot have seen enough of the seamy side of life to answer my questions. Now, tell me, do you believe in a future life?"

" If I did not," replied the priest, sternly, " should I wear this gown?"

" Yes, yes, I know.—But do you believe that confession is absolutely necessary for the remission of sins? If a man is really repentant, now . . ."

" Is he?—Or does he merely fancy he is? What guilty man can affirm that his remorse is exempt from fear? What dying man dare say: ' If God gave me back the days He is taking from me, I should employ them to repair the evil I have done ' ? "

" I dare! " cried the man eagerly. " Yes, yes, I can say that! "

" Then you have no need of me, sir," said the priest and rose for the second time, but, with a movement as rapid as thought, M. Gérard's skinny hand again seized the monk's robe.

" No, no! Stay, Father—I am cheating myself. —It is not repentance that urges me to speak, but terror! I need the forgiveness of Man before I dare face my God.—Now do stay with me, I beg of you! That is unless you could come back to-morrow? "

" No," said Dominique. " I have a sad duty to perform and in a few hours' time I shall have started for Brittany."

" Oh ! You are leaving Paris in a few hours' time ? For how long ? "

" That is as God wills. I go to console a father for the loss of his son."

" Then God sent you to me ! Answer me, you are really going ? It is certain ? "

" Unless God bring back the dead man to life, I shall go."

" And you are sure that is impossible ? "

Dominique felt his heart contract. The cowardly hesitation and terror M. Gérard showed caused him indescribable repulsion.

" He will be leaving and for some time. It is better so," murmured the sick man. Then with a supreme effort, he said : " Listen, Father. I will tell you all."

He now visibly collected all his strength. The wan light of the nightlight gave a note of fantastic mystery to the room and, seen in the shadow, the face seemed more livid, the expression meaner and more abject. He began to speak as if by rote, as follows :

" I should tell you that I became a widower at thirty and that my marriage had been so unhappy that I had resolved not to risk a second. My only relative was my elder brother Jacques, who was in Brazil. In 1817 I received a letter from him, telling me that he had made a large fortune—several millions of francs—that he would soon be returning to France for the sake of his health with his two children, and that he hoped I would meet him in Paris. Directly I received his letter I determined to go to him and said good-bye to my friends at Vic-Dessos . . .''

" At Vic-Dessos ?" cried the monk, lifting his head. " You lived at Vic-Dessos in the Ariège ? "

" I was born there. I only left the village to come to Paris and I wish to God I never had ! "

The monk fixed a strange and anxious look on the patient, who continued without noticing :

" When I reached Paris, my brother, far gone in consumption, who looked much as I do now, embraced me warmly and showed me his motherless children, for his wife had died on the voyage. They were charming; the boy, Victor, fair and rosy, like his mother, and the girl, Léonie, with magnificent hair, lashes and eyes of velvety black. She was four and the boy six and I still remember how frightened they were when they saw me and how they refused to kiss me. I was fond of my brother and worried to see him look so hopelessly ill; we consulted the best doctors in Paris and their advice was that he should live in the country, which was as much as to say that they could do nothing. I looked for a home for him and one day heard of a large country house at Viry."

" At Viry-sur-Orge ? " interrupted the priest, in the same tone in which he had said " At Vic-Dessos ? "

" Yes. Do you know the place? "

" I have heard of it, but I have never seen it," replied the priest in a slightly altered tone; but the invalid was too occupied with his own thoughts to pay attention.

" I need not describe the place; it was a Paradise. The woman who showed me over was about thirty, tall and strong and her Basque accent showed that she came from our part of the country. There was something masculine about her manner which repelled me at first, but, as we were compatriots, I promised to use my influence with my brother to buy the place and to keep her on. Her name was Orsola Poutaé. Our (that is my brother's) household consisted, then, of Orsola, Gertrude, the children's maid, a manservant and a gardener. There was, moreover, a large dog, called Brésil, whom the children loved and played with from morning to night. I should also include their tutor, M. Sarranti, an old friend of their father's and a man of great erudition and experience. He had a son, destined for the Church . . ."

"Forgive me," said Dominique, rising. "I cannot, nay, I must not, listen longer to your confession."

"Why not, Father?"

"Because," replied the monk, and his voice trembled . . . "because I know you and you do not know me. Your name is Gérard Tardieu, is it not? Not simply Gérard."

"Yes, but who are you?"

"I am Dominique Sarranti."

The sick man gave a frightened cry.

"Yes, I am the son of that Gaetano Sarranti whom you accused of theft and assassination and who is innocent, I swear!" Pushing back his chair with some violence, the monk again moved towards the door, but for the third time M. Gérard laid a hand upon his gown.

"Stay!" cried he with all the force he could muster. "It is Providence that sent you here. Stay and listen, for God is allowing me to repair the evil I have done before I die!"

Shuddering, the monk sank back into his chair and, raising his eyes to Heaven, murmured:

"Oh, God! What am I about to hear?"

"My brother's illness proved incurable," continued M. Gérard, in a voice frequently broken by sobs, "and after having lingered some months he died at Viry in February, 1818. The greater part of his fortune he had bequeathed to his children, but in the event of the death of the survivor of them during infancy, it was to be mine, though two hundred thousand francs were to be paid to Sarranti, who was charged with the children's education.—I must tell you that your father had confided to my care a hundred thousand crowns, moreover, which I had deposited with a notary at his request, that he might lay his hands on it again at a moment's notice should necessity arise. This money, you understand, he held in trust and I in turn held it in trust for him. . . . Oh, Father," gasped the sick man, "give me a spoonful of the cordial on the mantelpiece! I must find strength to continue!"

The cordial taken, he resumed in a voice frequently broken by sighs:

"I told you Orsola at first repelled me, but not because she was ugly. On the contrary, she was strikingly handsome.—One's eyes returned to her and then . . . they did not quit her again! I caught myself watching her as she passed; when she

17

was not there, I thought of her. . . . She was, did I tell you? a Basque, and her accent charmed me who knew it so well. One night, the chimney in my room caught fire and I had to call her to help me put it out.—From that moment, my fate was sealed and I belonged to her.—From that moment, began my life of crime. God drew away from me and left me to the Devil ! "

* * * * * *

" Orsola soon came to exercise such a fascination over me that, little by little, I lost my will-power. I came to obey her in everything, but, alas, so clever was she that she made me believe it was I who commanded and she who obeyed. She was a magician in the art of loving and knew how to make my bondage to her seem like empire over her; it was her supreme art to make me wish what she wished, giving my weakness the appearance of power.

" For two or three months after my brother's death, all appeared to go on as before; yet in reality, Orsola was using the time to bring about a prodigious piece of work, unrecognized by me until too late. Like all men from the Midi, I was naturally sober, but when Orsola offered me absinthe and kirsch, I could not refuse her; those two terrible poisons soon became my favourite drink and in the morning my eyes revealed but too plainly how I had passed a part of the night.

" One morning Orsola asked me an extraordinary question :

" ' You promised me long ago,' said she, ' to dismiss Gertrude. Why have you not done so? What is it about the woman that attracts you?'

" I was stupefied, for I recalled no such promise; I had no reason to dismiss Gertrude, an inoffensive woman who loved the children devotedly. I should have been ashamed to take them from her care and, for once, I met Orsola with a refusal. She returned to the attack again and again, but I felt I could not face the tears of the children, who loved their nurse, or the reproaches that M. Sarranti would have been sure to voice had I committed an action so palpably unjust. This time Orsola gave way. This happened on a day when our little household was diminished by the absence of Jean, the manservant, and of M. Sarranti, both away on business. The only people left in the house were the two children, Gertrude, Orsola and myself. This seemed to me at the time of no importance.

" That night, I drank more than usual. Orsola kept refilling my glass. . . . About eleven o'clock, I fancied I heard a cry.

" ' What is that?' I asked.

" ' I do not know,' replied she. ' Perhaps you had better go and see.'

" I tried to rise, but fell back into my chair. ' There!' said she, refilling my glass. ' Stay and drink that while I go and see what's the matter!'

" I do not know how long she was gone for I was in that stage of somnolence when one is indifferent to everything. It was the touch of a glass to my lips that awoke me to consciousness again. I opened my eyes and saw Orsola before me.

" ' Gertrude is ill,' said she.

" ' Gertrude . . . ill ? ' I stammered.

" ' Yes. She is complaining of pain and will not take what I gave her. You had better go yourself. Take her some *eau sucré*." She prepared some in a glass and gave it to me and, ashamed of my state, I made an effort and reached Gertrude's room.

" ' Drink this, my good girl,' I said, offering her the glass, which she took readily and drained to the last drop.

" ' Oh ! ' she cried. ' It has the same taste ! Oh, monsieur, a doctor. I've been poisoned ! '

" ' Poisoned ? ' I repeated, terrified.

" ' Oh, monsieur, for God's sake. . . . A doctor ! Fetch a doctor ! ' I left her room thoroughly frightened.

" ' Do you hear ? ' I said to Orsola. ' She thinks she has been poisoned ! '

" ' Run to Morsang and fetch the doctor ! ' cried she. ' Stay ! Wait ! Drink this last glass of wine; it is so cold to-night and you have two leagues to go.' She offered me a drink that, used as I was to strong liquor, seemed to burn as if I had swallowed vitriol. I went out, staggering, managed to cross the garden and go through the outer gate, but there the road seemed to slide from under my feet and I fell.

" The next day I found myself in bed and fancied I must have had some terrible nightmare. I rang for Orsola.

" ' Gertrude ? . . . ' I said to her. ' She isn't . . .'

" 'Dead,' she said without a tremor.

" 'Dead then. But not . . . poisoned ? '

" ' I should not be surprised,' she continued, calmly. ' But, as she took nothing except what we gave her, you and I, I should not suggest that it was poison, if I were you. They might think *we* had done it."

" ' But, but, Orsola, who could think such a thing ? What motive could we have for such a crime ? ' cried I, horrified.

" ' Oh, well I don't know. They might say we got rid of the nurse first to make it easier to get rid of the children, whose heir you are, you know ! ' "

" The wretch ! " murmured the monk.

" Wait, wait . . ." stammered M. Gérard, the perspiration rolling off his forehead. " I have not finished. . . . Don't interrupt me. . . . I am so weak ! " And Father Dominique listened, his heart wrung.

" No one suspected. M. Sarranti, on his return, tried to comfort me. He thought I was taking the death of the faithful girl too much to heart and he suggested engaging another nurse, but I was afraid of displeasing Orsola. Oh, Father, naturalists tell us of the power of fascination possessed by certain animals and among others, of the snake, who can make a bird fall from the very top of a tree into its open jaws; the Devil, Father, had gifted that woman with a like power. . . . After nights spent in drinking, I had but a confused idea of what I had said or done, and it seemed to me that she and I talked of nothing but the pleasure one could purchase with a fortune of two or three million francs. Yet, when I remembered those talks I always shuddered, for I could only own such a fortune through the death of my brother's children. What likelihood was there that God would recall to Himself those charming little ones, fresh as the flowers among which they played? I thought of Gertrude's sudden death and, seeking out M. Sarranti, begged him not to leave the children.

" ' I will never leave them,' answered he, ' unless circumstances should compel me to do so.'

" He frowned as he spoke as if he divined some sinister influence, but I added quickly, to reassure myself as well as him:

" ' I love them so ! '

" Yet, though I could foresee but a distant chance of such a hope being realized, I gradually became used to regarding the fortune as my own, and once I found myself saying to Orsola:

" ' When I am rich, I shall buy the land adjoining this.'

" But what could make me rich? *A lucky chance;* that is what Orsola called it; a lucky chance that made me heir."

At this point, M. Gérard's features were so convulsed that the monk felt it his duty to interrupt, though both curiosity and self-interest made him long to hear the rest. The man rested for a few moments and then re-assembled his strength for another effort, for now he seemed as anxious to finish his confession as at first he was reluctant to begin it. But he resumed in a voice so feeble that Dominique was obliged to bend his ear close to those faltering lips.

"I must tell you this," he panted. "The little girl, Léonie, though sweet-tempered, was very proud for her age and had been used in infancy to have twenty servants waiting on her will. Since the death of Gertrude, she had received little care from Orsola, who hated the child and treated her brutally. One day the children were throwing stones into the water for Brésil, their dog, to fetch, which he did with bounds and barks of joy. Orsola called out to them to stop, telling them the noise made her head ache, but they took no notice.

" 'Take care, Léonie!' cried Orsola, 'or I shall come down and thrash you!'

" 'Will you?' retorted the high-spirited child. 'Just try!'

" 'You defy me?' cried Orsola, and, rushing across the garden, she reached out a hand to seize the child who had waited for her without deigning to run away, but, as the woman laid hands on Léonie, the dog sprang at her and seized her arm in his teeth. She came back to the house and showed me the wound.

" 'Now,' said she; 'now, perhaps, you will punish your niece and shoot that horrible dog.'

"I might have done as she wished, but M. Sarranti interposed with such firmness that I dared not. Orsola, moreover, gave up the idea of vengeance with a docility which surprised and frightened me for I was beginning to know her and above all to realize that she was not the woman to forgive. Indeed, an event shortly happened which gave her the chance to accomplish the sinister project she had cherished for so long."

The sick man paused and fought for breath. Brother Dominique, afraid that the confession would never end, administered a second spoonful of the cordial.

" It was, as I remember, the month of August, 1820. For the last three weeks, M. Sarranti had changed his usual habits in a way that was causing talk in the village. People came to see him at all hours of the night and with these people he would disappear for several days at a time. Others would arrive from Paris in the early morning hours and he would shut himself up with them, taking no notice of meal times. Orsola had often listened at his door, trying to find out the cause of these secret conferences, but without success, though the frequent mention of Louis XVIII and the Emperor Napoleon enabled her to guess that some plot was hatching against the existing Government, with the purpose of re-establishing the Empire. Orsola told me of this discovery with diabolic joy for she detested your father, and no doubt she would have denounced him at once to the police if she had not seen something in the matter which might be used to assist her own evil purpose. She therefore awaited the moment to act as the jaguar, crouched on a branch, awaits the moment to spring.

" Where was I ? I am thinking. . . . Yes, yes, it was on the eighteenth of August that M. Sarranti asked me to get for him the sum of money he had left in my care. When I returned with it from the notary he sent word that he wished to speak to me. I was about to go downstairs to him, when Orsola advised me to ask him to come to my room. Then, just as M. Sarranti entered, she glided into a cupboard from which she could hear all that passed. I ought to have taken him to another room, but I was too afraid of what Orsola would say to me if I crossed her and so, when he asked if we were alone, I did not hesitate to say that we were. Do you know what your father wished to tell me?"

"I know nothing, monsieur," replied Dominique. "When my father left France I was at the Seminary and he had no time to bid me good-bye. I received a letter from Lahore but it merely reassured me about his health and enclosed a sum of money that I needed."

"Then, if I live to do it, I must tell you. Let me rest first."

After a painful pause he continued as if reading from a book. "Your father told me this:

"'You know my name and country,' he said. 'I am a Corsican. Born at Ajaccio the same year as the Emperor, I have devoted my life to him. I followed him to Elba after the abdication at Fontainebleau and to St. Helena after the battle of mont St. Jean. One day the world will know the torment to which the kings condemned the man who had held them in the hollow of his hand. History will mete out to those gaolers and executioners their punishment! From the very beginning of 1817 I busied myself with plans for his escape and, without telling the illustrious prisoner, I had made arrangements with

an American ship which brought us dispatches from
the ex-king Joseph, who had withdrawn to Boston,
but the Emperor completely disapproved and even
denounced me himself to the Governor.

" ' " Send this fellow back to France ! " he cried.
" He wishes me to escape from this earthly Paradise ! '¹
His request that one of his faithful servants should be
sent back to France was the one thing they willingly
accorded him and my departure was fixed for the next
day. Believing myself in disgrace with my Emperor,
I was in despair, when I received an order to appear
before him. General Montholon introduced me into
his bedroom and no sooner was I alone with the
august captive than I cast myself down at his feet,
begging him to forgive me and not send me away !
He smiled and taking me by the ear :

" ' " Fool ! " said he. " Get up ! I can't forgive
you because there's nothing to forgive, except a too
great devotion and one doesn't forgive that, you silly !
One remembers it."

" ' Then, for God's sake, Sire, do not send me
away ! ' "

" ' " Sarranti," he replied, looking at me fixedly,
" I have need of you in France. Listen, for what I
am going to say is very important. I have still some
partisans in France. . . ."

" ' The entire people, Sire ! ' I cried. ' Why not
return and remount your throne ? You returned
from Elba.'

" ' " One does not write two pages alike in a life
like mine," he replied, shaking his head. " Besides
I believe it will be better for the world's future if I

die here and if the people's Emperor has his Gol-
gotha like Jesus Christ. . . . My death will have
its beauty, Sarranti, and I would not spoil it."

" ' Then what am I to do and why will you not
permit me to stay, like another Simon of Cyrene and
help you to bear your Cross ? '

" ' " No. I need a safe man in France, a man who
will tell those of my brave lieutenants who have not
prostituted their swords to the Bourbons—the
Clausels, Bachelus, Gérards, Foys, Lamarques—to
think of me no longer."

" ' Sire ! But why ? '

" ' " Because, like the ancient Roman Emperors,
already deified, I watch from my flaming Heaven.
But find them and tell them this from me : ' *Think
no more of the Emperor except as one who loves you
and bids you take courage; think, instead, of his son
whom they may bring up to hate or at least to despise
him, but do not compromise his childhood with any
plot unless you are certain that it must succeed. Remember what they did to Astyanax and Britannicus
when they, too, showed that they might prove dangerous!' Tell them, Sarranti, that this is my will—
my last testament—that I have abdicated, but in
favour of my son!* "

" ' I will tell them, Sire.'

" ' " Listen, Sarranti. My son is living in the
same château in which I twice stayed, one league
from Vienna. I was there after Austerlitz and again
after Wagram and the second time I stayed three
months. He is in the right wing, the one I chose for
my own lodging. . . . Who knows? His bed-

room may be my old room. You must find out."

" ' I will, Sire.'

" ' " I will tell you why. Tired of having to traverse the antichambers, full to overflowing with
courtiers and petitioners, I had a secret door made,
not by the palace architect, but by my own clever
officers, and through that I went to walk in the
gardens, in the early morning or late at night
through that secret door and down a hidden stair.
You understand, Sarranti? Perhaps my son could
flee by way of that secret door and rejoin his friends
waiting in the park and so, with them, attain the
frontier! See! Here is a plan of the château that I
made last night. Look, this is the right wing; here
the bedroom and here the hidden spring you have
to press. I have signed the plan. Hide it carefully
from the English spies. It will serve as your creden-
tials to our friends."

" ' Rest assured, Sire, that they will have to kill
me if they wish to take it from me.'

" ' Try to live and keep the paper safe; that is the
better way. Wait! There is something else.'

" ' With that, he took a coffer from under his bed
and gave me three hundred thousand francs for the
good of the cause. It was not much, he said, but he
himself had had but two thousand louis for the
expenses of his first campaign in Italy. Then he
added:

" ' If you should be obliged to fly.—Listen
and remember, Sarranti!—I would prefer that
you took refuge in India. There you would find
one of my most faithful friends, General Lebastard

de Prémont, with the Maharajah of Lahore and Cashmire. I sent him out in 1812 to see if he could not provoke another revolt, arranging for the Maharajah Runjet-Singh the rôle of a more fortunate Tippoo-Sahib. Trouble came and I turned my thoughts from India but, though he entered the service of the Maharajah, he is none the less faithful to me. Share with him whatever may remain of the sum I now confide to your care, for he is not rich and he has left a little girl in France for whose education I was to arrange had I remained Emperor. You now understand, my dear Sarranti,' he concluded, ' why I dismissed you, why I had you sent to Europe and that at once—do you hear, traitor? Now then, you and I, shall we not henceforth have nothing to do with each other?' And he held out his hand which I kissed.

" ' The next day I left the island and came to France, where of course, like all who come from St. Helena, I was subjected to strict surveillance. That is why, having told your brother the whole story, I placed the money in your care. For four years I have been awaiting my opportunity and now at last the plan is fixed to take place to-morrow. . . . I cannot tell you the names of the conspirators because that is not my secret, but many of those bearing the most illustrious names of the Empire will attempt to-morrow the downfall of the Bourbons. If we succeed, we shall be the masters. If we fail, the scaffold waits for us. Don't be afraid that you will be compromised. That is impossible; but if you wish to aid me, let me take Jean with me. He is a faithful fellow and if he will have two horses ready saddled to-morrow, each with fifty thousand crowns in the saddlebag, then, if we fail, he and I will ride to Brest where friends will hide us and from Brest I can embark for India and join General Lebastard de Prémont in Lahore.'

"'Now, M. Gérard, you hold my life in your hands as did your brother who knew all. Do not be in a hurry to reply. I have papers to burn in my own room and will return in a quarter of an hour for your answer.'

"Father, he had no sooner left the room than Orsola glided from the cupboard, and to my surprise, told me to do as he wished. I was to get back the receipt I had given him for the money then and leave the rest to her! I did as she ordered me and M. Sarranti departed having given me the receipt and told me that I could count on his eternal gratitude! Dare I narrate the rest?"

The monk kept silent. The nightlight at that moment flickered and went out. Presently the feeble voice went on again:

"That night, when supping with Orsola, I promised her Father—I dare not tell you what! But it was decided that the morning of August the nineteenth, 1820, should see us millionaires.

"The next day, I waited in terrible suspense, but it was not till four in the afternoon that I heard the sound of galloping. Your father, his horse flaked with foam, was riding into the courtyard.

"'Betrayed! Denounced!' he cried. 'I must fly at once. Is everything ready?'

"'Yes,' said Orsola, 'everything.'

" As for me, I could not speak. A mist of blood seemed floating before my eyes, as M. Sarranti sprang from the saddle and seized my hand.

" ' Betrayed ! ' he repeated. ' Some wretch has betrayed us ! '

" Orsola had called for Jean who now brought the horses, ready saddled. I had just strength to point to them and say :

" ' Fly instantly ! '

" He pressed my hand, mounted, and rode off with Jean towards Orléans.

" ' Good ! ' murmured Orsola in my ear. ' Now, as the gardener goes home every night at eight, we shall be all alone ! '

" ' Alone ? ' I repeated mechanically. ' Alone ? . . . '

" ' Yes,' replied she, ' since we took the precaution of ridding ourselves of Gertrude.'

" That word ' we,' making me an accomplice in the crime, filled me with chill fear. . . . Now was the time to fight against this fatal influence . . . but I could not. She offered me drink. . . . God knows what was in the cup ! All I remember is a voice that ceaselessly whispered and still whispers in my ear :

" ' You manage the boy; I'll see to the little girl.'

" And I, as if possessed, replied :

" ' Yes. . . . Yes. . . .''

" ' We must make it seem as if M. Sarranti had done the thing. . . .''

" ' Yes . . . yes . . . M. Sarranti . . .' I repeated as she drew me into the room where I kept my money. She locked my private drawer, and broke open the lock again with a chisel.

" ' You understand ? ' said she. ' He stole the money your notary returned to you and then fled. As for the children, they came into the room while he was forcing the lock and he had to dispose of them. You understand ? '

" ' Yes, yes. But suppose he comes back and denies it ? '

" ' How dare he come back when, if he did, he would be condemned to death as a conspirator ? Besides we shall be millionaires and one can do much with a million."

" ' But, but how shall we be millionaires ? '

" ' You are going to manage the boy and I shall see to the little girl. Come ! '

" I remember I resisted, intuitively, but she dragged me down to the courtyard where the children were sitting, watching the setting sun.

" ' How strange ! ' said I. ' The sky seems filled with blood ! '

" When they saw us, they came running, hand in hand.

" ' Is it time to come in, Uncle ? '

" ' No, dears,' replied Orsola. ' You can play a little while longer.'

" ' Oh, can I ever forget it ? ' cried the miserable man.—' Drunk as I was I saw them standing there, beautiful as angels; the boy so fair and rosy and the little girl, grave and dark, fixing me with her intelligent glance as if she asked me why I staggered as I walked. Then eight o'clock struck and I heard the gardener closing the gate. He was going home. I looked round for Orsola. She was not there! I breathed freely again. I wanted to take the children in my arms and fly with them . . . Would that I had done so! Then Orsola came back, with my gun.'

" ' Oh, Uncle,' cried little Victor. 'Are you going shooting? Do take me with you ! '

" I trembled.

" ' Take your gun, you coward,' whispered Orsola and I obeyed.

" ' Oh, Uncle, I'll be so good! I won't make a sound. Do let me come ! "

" I looked at the little boy.

" ' You wish to come with me ? '

" ' Oh, yes, yes ! I'll be so good ! '

" ' If Victor is going, I want to go too,' declared Léonie.

" ' No, no ! ' cried I quickly. ' One is enough. . . .'

" ' You hear, mademoiselle ? ' said Orsola. ' Come with me. We'll go to bed.'

" ' But I don't want to go to bed,' protested the little girl. ' I want to wait till my brother comes back. Then we can both go to bed together.'

" ' Tell this child, once and for all, that she is to do as I say ! '

" ' Go with Orsola, Léonie,' said I.

" ' And I'm to come with you, am I not, Uncle ? ' cried Victor, happily. He gave me his hand but I could not bear it in mine—that trustful little hand ! I pushed it away.

" ' Come with me ! ' cried Orsola, pulling Léonie away, but the child kept turning her head towards us and crying:

" ' Come back quickly, Uncle ! Victor, come back soon ! '

" I, too, turned my head and saw the little girl disappear into the château. Then I, in my turn, went on into the park with Victor some ten paces in front of me. The night was dark and the gloom under the great trees was extreme. My forehead was bathed in perspiration and my heart beat so that I had to keep stopping. . . . Both barrels of my gun were loaded. Orsola knew this when she gave it to me. —The child, as I have said, was walking in front and I had only to bring the gun to my shoulder and fire.—I placed it in position several times and put my finger on the trigger—but each time I lowered it again, murmuring:

" ' I can't ! I can't ! '

" But little Victor turned before I had lowered the gun and he saw what I was doing.

" ' Why, Uncle,' he said, ' I thought you told us never to point a gun at anyone, even in fun ! '

" ' Yes, yes, my boy. So I did. I was only joking but it was silly.'

" ' Of course I know you were only joking,' replied he. ' Why should you want to kill me ? You loved father so much, didn't you ? ' I gave a cry. A fire seemed to flash through my brain and I feared I was going mad.

" ' Yes, yes, Victor,' I stammered, putting my gun behind me. ' I did love your father ! Let us go back to the house. We won't shoot to-day.'—Then I took his hand and hurried him back to the house, hoping to be in time to prevent the murder of his sister. Unfortunately we had to pass the small lake, for to reach the house one had either to go round this lake, which meant a delay of ten minutes, or to row across.

"'Oh, Uncle, let's take the boat! It will be fun!' said the child, jumping into the boat. I stumbled in after him. The water was deep and calm as a mirror. I seized the oars and began to row rapidly, for I had only one thought: to reach the house in time to prevent the crime. . . . We were almost in the middle of the lake when I heard a terrible cry in which I recognized the voice of Léonie! Brésil started barking furiously. No doubt though chained to his kennel, he, too, had heard that cry. Then came another cry and then another! I looked at Victor who had turned very pale.

"'Uncle! My sister is being killed!' Then he called, as loud as he could: 'Léonie!'

"'Silence, boy!' I cried, but he called again:

"'Léonie! Léonie!'

"Clenching my fist, I moved towards him and the expression of my face so terrified him that he seemed about to throw himself into the lake, though he could not swim. Instead he fell on his knees with clasped hands.

"'Uncle! Don't kill me!' he cried. 'I love you I do, indeed I do, Uncle! I've never harmed anyone!' I seized him by his collar. 'Oh, Uncle, have pity! Help! Help! Save me!'

"He stopped calling, for my hand was round his little throat like an iron ring. My head swam. . . . I scarcely knew what I was doing. . . . He made a great effort to get away, but with my eyes shut, so that I should not see, I lifted him above my head and threw him with all my force into the lake. The water splashed up . . . opened . . . and closed over him!

" I once more seized hold of the oars, but at that moment, the child appeared again, struggling in the water. . . . Oh, how can I tell you, Father?" The dying man broke down and sobbed. . . . "I was drunk.—I was furious.—I was mad! I raised the oar and . . ."

"Oh!" cried Brother Dominique, rising, as if he could not bear to listen longer.

"The poor child sank again and this time, to rise no more. The moon had hidden behind a cloud and when it reappeared, it shone on the livid brow of an assassin!"

The monk fell on his knees and prayed. There was a ghastly silence of long duration in that room of horror, a silence broken at last by the murderer. With a groan, he gasped:

"Father, Father, I am dying . . . but, there are still things that I must tell for the sake of your father's honour and the salvation of my soul! Give me the salts and then perhaps I can finish."

The monk rose, got a light, lit a fresh wick, passed his arm round the sick man's shoulders and held a bottle of salts for him to inhale. It would have been difficult to say which of the two men the light found the more livid. There was a long, long silence this time, before M. Gérard gathered strength enough to continue.

" I leaped out of the boat and ran towards the house. Léonie's cries and the dog's barking—all had ceased ! I called ' Orsola ! Orsola ! ' timidly at first and then with all my strength . . . but there was no reply. I thought of calling ' Léonie ! '— but I dared not ! It had seemed to me that the cries came from the basement and as the moon had again gone behind a cloud, I went down the stairs in the dark, feeling my way. . . . There was a small fire in the kitchen and I could see that all was in order there.—Nor was there any sign in the scullery. I remembered then a small cellar behind the scullery and tried to push open the door, but something was in the way. Again I called Orsola and again there was no reply. Then I noticed by the light of the moon, now visible once more, that the glass roof of the cellar was broken. . . . My foot struck against something and I stooped; my hands touched a body, lying on the ground and I found that the floor was wet with blood. I felt the still form over in the darkness; it was not that of a child.—I ran back to the kitchen to get a candle with which I returned to the body. It was that of Orsola; the blood was her blood, welling from a horrible wound in the throat. A long kitchen knife was lying near and seemed to have slipped from her hand.

" I thought at first that I must have gone mad or that I was suffering from some terrible hallucination !—But no, it was true ! There was the dead

body lying in its blood and it was the body of Orsola!
Then I remembered the child's cries and the frantic
barking of the dog. I went to look at the broken
glass and understood. Orsola must have dragged the
child to the cellar and seized the knife. The child's
cries had brought the dog to the rescue of his little
playmate; with a violent effort, he had managed to
break his chain, after which he crashed through the
glass and fell down into the cellar, there to fly straight
at Orsola's throat. Thus she had been forced to drop
the knife and let the child slip from her grasp. But
where had they gone—Léonie and the dog? I
must find them at any cost! The sight of Orsola's
body had filled me with fury and I rushed through
the cellar door, which was open; no doubt Léonie had
fled that way. I hurried after her; if I found her,
fear for my own safety would compel me to kill her,
since I had killed her brother."

The monk rose shuddering.

" But, Father," protested the feeble voice, " such
is the fatal consequence of crime; the assassin is in
the iron hand of destiny and, having once committed
murder is forced to continue his murderous course.
. . . I was mad with rage, drunk with blood! As
I rushed down the main path through the park, I
lifted my gun to my shoulder at every sound, calling
Brésil and shouting:

" ' Léonie, are you there? '

" But there was no reply. The park was silent as
a tomb and empty as the void!

" At last I found myself beside the lake and
stopped, horrified; then turned off with a cry in the

opposite direction. . . . Yet I saw nothing. For nearly an hour I ran from path to path, from bush to bush; but there was no sign; all was still. I even thought of firing off my gun, merely to break that terrifying silence, silence own brother of death! Finally, harrassed, exhausted, having lost all hope of finding either the child or the dog, I retraced my steps and found myself again near the lake. That cold, motionless water appalled me; I saw the boat by the bank, among the reeds and lying on the grass was the oar—I could not bear it!—Returning to the house, I went up to my room, where the windows were wide open; they looked out onto the lake.—Everywhere, I saw that hateful lake! I went to the window to close the shutters and as I bent forward I saw an animal, his nose to the ground, as if following a scent; it was Brésil. What was he seeking?

" He ran right round the lake; then, stopping at the place where Victor and I had got into the boat, he lifted his head, sniffed, looked about, gave a long-drawn howl and plunged down into the water. It was horrible! He followed the exact course of the boat, just as if he saw the ripples it had made. When he reached the spot where I had thrown the child into the water, he turned about for a moment and then dived again. The water circled round the spot where he disappeared. Twice his head came to the surface and I heard him take a deep breath; the third time he rose with something in his mouth . . . something formless . . . that he brought, swimming, to the bank. He leaped onto the grass, dragging this object after him, with a mighty effort. It was the dead body of little Victor."

" Oh, Lord Jesus ! " murmured the priest.

A convulsion seized the wretch. His face was terrible to see.

" Ah ! you understand what my feelings were . . ." he went on at last. " It was as if the Day of Judgment had come and the grave were giving up its dead ! I shouted with rage, seized my gun and ran down stairs, leaping steps at a time. Why did I not fall down and break my neck ? I do not know ! Now there was a clump of trees between me and the bank of the lake, and I kept behind this so as to approach the dog without being seen by him. When at last I reached within thirty feet of him I found he was dragging the corpse away from the house. I remembered that there was a hole in the wall, through which, no doubt, Léonie had escaped and now the dog was trying to drag the body that way. If I had not happened to see him, the wretched creature would have disclosed the whole affair !

" Directly I emerged from the clump of trees he saw me and, dropping the body, turned howling towards me, with open jaws and eyes that shone in the night like points of fire. I heard his great teeth clamp, but while he hesitated whether to take up the body again or spring at me, I adjusted my gun carefully and fired. . . . He fell, but gathered himself together and rushed for the wood with bloodcurdling yelps and howls of agony. I hurried after him, hoping to despatch him with a second bullet. I saw blood on the grass, and I followed this trail in the open, by the light of the moon, but in the wood I lost it. However, I pushed on to the hole in the wall and just there I found a fragment of Léonie's collar caught on an eglantine bush. What had become of her? If I tried to find out, someone, coming to the château, might see Victor's body lying on the grass. . . . The thought appalled me. The first and most important thing was to hide that body.

" It was then that I first began to think of my own safety. Carefully detaching the morsel of collar from the twig I returned to the lake. As I ran I was thinking, ' Suppose it has vanished again ! ' But luckily it was still there. Luckily! How horrible that sounds ! "

" Horrible truly," murmured the monk.

" I had to find a spade. I had suffered too much anxiety when I left the body before to let it stay where it was again, so I lifted it and carried it to the shed where the gardener kept his tools. I took a spade. But I could not bury the child there. I had to find a lonely spot. Once more I crossed the grass, accompanied step by step by a hideous man carrying under his arm the dead body of a child. That man was myself or rather my shadow cast by the moon-light. To realize this caused me inexpressible agony and it seemed an eternity before I reached the shelter of the wood; my legs tottered and bent beneath me and I gasped for breath. Suddenly I stopped. I wanted to go on but could not. Something was holding me back! I thought I should die of fear! . . . At last, with a supreme effort, I glanced behind me to find that the child's golden hair had caught in a broken branch. . . . It took but a second to realize what was detaining me but during that second I saw before me the knife of the guillotine! With a frightful cry which I can still hear, I shook the body free. A lock of hair remained fastened to the branch but I went on my way.

"At last I thought I had found the right place; a small bit of sward between the bushes. By working hard for an hour or more I could do the dreadful task, so I set to work; but what an hour it was!

It was about two when half dead I began to dig the little grave; in the month of August that is the time when nature begins to stir; when the birds twitter in the branches and the small game rustle the bushes. At the slightest sound I swung round, thinking I heard a footstep, while the perspiration poured from my forehead and my breath came whistling with terror from my lungs. Dawn was near!

"At last the gruesome work was finished and I laid the child's body in the little grave, covering it with earth which I carefully smoothed with my foot. Then I took some turf from another place and put this over the earth till not a trace remained of my work. It was high time! I had scarcely finished when the sun came out from behind the clouds and on an oak above my head a blackbird burst into song. I wept. O the relief of the blinding tears!

"Yes, sun and daylight brought with them those haunting phantoms, remembrance and reflection. With the horror of the condemned criminal I saw the sun rise when the door of his cell opens to admit

the gaoler announcing the moment of execution. I
was too overwhelmed to think out any plan, but I
realized that the death of Orsola threw over the events
of the night a veil of added mystery, especially as I
was known to have adored her. No one could suspect
me of having compassed her death. The flight of
Léonie was the most alarming circumstance, but if
she spoke, she could only accuse Orsola, and Orsola
was dead. Some strength returning, I tottered back
to my room, put it in order, washed, changed my
clothes, swallowed some food and managed to set off
to the mayor. To him I told the tale Orsola and
I had prepared; I said that the two children had
disappeared and that this coincided with the flight of
M. Sarranti and the theft of a hundred thousand
crowns. I spoke of the lock of my bureau having been
forced and did not hesitate to accuse Sarranti of the
robbery, nay, of the murder. . . ."

"My dear, dear father!" murmured Dominique.

"Yes, yes, but since Heaven is punishing me and
since I am myself restoring his good name . . .
surely you will grant me forgiveness, Father. For
how can you expect God to forgive me if you will
not?"

"Continue," said the monk sternly.

But the miserable supplicant could not then speak.
At last, he feebly murmured:

"I explained the matter in this way. I said I had
come home very late the night before, and gone
straight to bed. That I had awakened at daylight,
risen, found the drawer of my bureau forced open,
gone to Orsola's room and found it empty as were

the rooms of the two children. I said that I had then searched the house and at last, in the cellar, had found the body of Orsola bathed in blood. It was easy to see her throat had been torn out. I found the dog on the grass, his chain broken and, in a fit of impulsive horror, had fired at him and he had fled, wounded.

" The mayor believed my story, putting down my state of extreme fatigue and my hesitations to the shock I had suffered; he even tried to comfort me and kindly returned with me to the house. Of course I was careful to say that the direction of M. Sarranti's flight was unknown to me for you will understand that I wished him to get safely out of France. I then shut myself up in my room, begging the worthy mayor to respect my grief. The news of the conspiracy reached him that same day. The fact that M. Sarranti was a fanatical agent of the Buonapartists led the government to charge him with theft and murder without hesitation. Indeed, the police would have been disappointed had he been proved not guilty. They looked on it as good luck to be able to make such an accusation against a man from St. Helena, an intimate friend, moreover, of the Emperor. I was therefore, not afraid. Had your father been arrested, innocent as he was, he would assuredly have not escaped the scaffold."

The priest rose. He was as white as the sheets on the villain's bed. The thought of his father falling a victim to a false accusation with all the appearance of guilt, tortured him to the point of madness.

" I knew he was innocent ! " he cried in a thundering voice. "And yet I might have had to see him die without hope of saving him! . . . Oh, —you . . . you . . ."

He stopped, but the sinner only bowed his head. He wished the outraged son to spend his grief in words that there might then remain in his heart only the pity of the priest.

"In spite of your confession," continued the monk, "made as it is to me alone, this terrible suspicion must rest eternally on the head of my noble father."

"But I am going to die," stammered the abject wretch.

"Then after your death I may reveal what you have said?"

"Reveal everything! Is not that why I blessed God for sending you to me?"

"Oh, my father!" sighed the monk, "my poor father! Surely you feel, monsieur, that if he had known of the suspicion attaching to him he would have returned to protest his innocence even at the risk of his life."

"It is true, yes, it is true! Well, when I am dead, you can write to him, but for pity's sake do not add to the terror and despair of my last few hours! Let me confess.—During the whole of the seven years that have passed since the crime was committed.—Oh, this is terrible!—this is the worst of all!—I have never felt remorse pure and simple, never wept save when the blackbird sang that morning. No, it was not remorse that disturbed my sleep; it was the fear of justice; it is the dread of punishment that has made my life a torment.

How often in my sleep have I not appeared before a tribunal! How often, in spite of my tears, prayers and denials, have I heard myself pronounced guilty of murder! How often have I felt the scissors strike cold on the nape of my neck, cutting my hair as the fatal tumbril stood without the prison door! How often have I seen, above the heads of the watching crowd, the shining knife of the guillotine!"

"Poor wretch!" murmured the priest, looking pityingly at this living image of terror.

"Oh, thanks! That is why I left Viry and came to live in Vanvres. That is why I took to good works."

The priest turned quickly at these words.

"Yes, yes, Father; benevolence has been a cloak to cover my bloody hands! Who would dare to accuse me now, encircled by those whom I have bound to me by ties of gratitude?"

"Who? Miserable man. You ask who?" answered Dominique, lifting his hand in a noble gesture. "He who is coming is God!"

"Ah! yes, I know. . . . I know. . . . I, who am dying. . . . But I have two powerful intercessors.—My terror and your innocence."

The wretched man did not dare to plead repentance.

"And now I have only a few words to add; that is, if I can—I am drawing my last breaths. The disappearance of Léonie was not the least of my anxieties, as you may suppose, but though I tried in every way to trace her, I never heard of her again. I travelled for some time—then returned to France and settled here. And now I have sacrificed my good name after death to M. Sarranti. If you can obtain his pardon as conspirator I undertake to disprove the accusation of the murder."

" But will they believe the testimony of a son in favour of his father? "

" I seem to have foreseen all. Feel under my pillow. There! Take the key. . . . You have it? Good. Well, open the second drawer of that bureau, you will find a paper with three seals."

Dominique rose, opened the drawer and took out the paper.

" I have it," ejaculated he.

" Read the endorsement aloud, I beg."

" This is my last confession before God and man, to be made public, if necessary, after my death.
                              " Gérard Tardieu."

" Yes, yes. I confirm it. That document contains the history I have told you. Never could I have done so had I not written and got it by heart. It is all in my own hand. I release you when I am no more from your priest's oath of secrecy."

With a movement of intuitive triumph, the monk pressed the paper to his breast.

*   *   *   *   *   *

"And now, Father, will you not speak a few words of hope? " the supplicant dared to gasp.

" My brother," replied the Dominican with solemnity, " it may need a more powerful intercession than mine to procure your forgiveness from Our Lord, but as a man, a son and a priest, I pardon you. May God ratify the absolution I pray that He may grant you! In the name of the Father, the Son and of the Holy Ghost! "

As he spoke, he placed his thin white hands on the dying man's head.

The gentle, holy touch moved even *that* sinner.

"What must I do?" he entreated.

"Pray!" rejoined the monk.

And he left the room and the house, supplicating in his noble heart that he might be permitted by God to take away with him all that was wretched, low and base in the man about to die. Left alone, that creature fell back on his pillow and there lay as motionless as if his soul had already departed.

The confession had taken six hours to make.

I have read the written version of which the fore-going is almost a transcript. It frightened me.

CHAPTER XXII
JUSTIN AGAIN

LET us leave Brother Dominique, who, re-assured as to the life and honour of his father, was full of hope, to traverse rapidly the short distance between Vanvres and Bas-Meudon, where he found the hearse bearing the body of Colomban on the point of starting—let us leave him for a time and return to Justin, whom we last saw spurring his horse along the road to Versailles.

To those of our readers to whom the schoolmaster may not seem to deserve the interest he inspired in Salvator, Jean Davy and ourselves, let us confess that resignation, which at first sight might be taken for lack of energy, is to our mind, on the contrary,

one of the highest forms of power. The material
activity of the body must not be confounded with
the active movement of the brain. Those men who
believe themselves energetic, walking, running,
doing their two leagues a day on horseback or on
foot, may move more but accomplish less than the
man who, from his quiet study, after ten years of
apparent repose, sends forth the completed thought
that is to revolutionize the world. We must add
that when the schoolmaster, apparently so apathetic,
found himself face to face with an emergency, he
came forth, armed *cap-à-pie,* ready to fight to the
death. He was bowed down, apparently, by the
weight of his family responsibilities, but once relieved of his filial duties, he would soon have been
seen adding his corner stone to the social edifice, the
erection of which we are all born to aid, and which
we may venture to call Universal Harmony. Anyone
who had seen Justin, urging on Jean Davy's horse,
with the art of an experienced horseman, at top
speed along the roads, would have affirmed that here
was a man of strong arm and wrist of steel, control-
ling a steed that may well be said to have flown.

After galloping for a whole hour, with his anxious
thoughts coursing as madly through his brain as his
horse along the roads, Justin pulled up, panting,
before the school door. He had taken just over an
hour to ride the five leagues, and it was half-past
eight when he dismounted and rang Mme Desmarets'
bell. The inmates had been up some time; but Mme
Desmarets herself was still in her room, not yet fully
dressed. Justin sent word that he must see her at

19

once. Astonished by so early a visit, she asked him to wait for a quarter of an hour while she finished dressing, but he answered that his business admitted of no delay and requested that she would see him instantly. Worried at this insistance, she slipped on a dressing-gown and opened her door to go down to the sitting-room, but she found Justin standing on the landing. He made the astonished woman go back into her room and carefully closed the door. At sight of him she cried out. The light from the window fell full upon him, and she was horrified both by his deadly pallor and resolute look.

" *Mon Dieu!* What can have happened?" cried she.

" Something very serious, madame," he replied.

" To you or to Mina?"

" To both!"

" *Mon Dieu!* Shall I call her or would you rather go to her?"

" She is not here."

" Not here? Then where is she?"

" I do not know. She was abducted last night."

" Abducted! But I took her to her room myself and left her there with Mlle Suzanne de Valgeneuse!"

" She is not there now."

Justin took from his pocket the little pencilled note that Babolin had given him.

" Read this, madame."

Mme Desmarets recognized the young girl's writing, and seemed on the point of fainting. Justin sprang forward and helped her to a chair.

" We must not give way, madame, till we are sure that this disaster is irremediable."

" But what can we do? " asked the schoolmistress.

" We must wait, and while we wait we must see that no one enters either Mina's room or the garden."

" But for whom are we to wait, *monsieur?* "

" For the Chief of Police, who will be here in an hour's time."

" You are bringing the police inspector-in-chief here? " cried Mme Desmarets, more horrified than ever. " My school will be ruined ! "

" What else can I do? " asked Justin, shocked at this egoism.

" *Monsieur*, I beg you to do all in your power to avoid such a scandal ! "

" The scandal, to my mind, madame," replied Justin, coldly, " is that a woman to whose care Mina was confided should venture to beg me not to speak of the matter ! "

" But all the mothers will take their daughters away ! Remember the affection I had for Mina and do not ruin me ! "

Justin, revolted by this woman's selfishness in harping on the misfortune to her school in face of a grief like his, sternly replied :

" Remember the confidence I had in you and do not beg any such thing."

The reply was so just that Mme Desmarets seemed overwhelmed by it. She glanced at Justin's set face and realized that she could expect no consideration, so she seemed to resign herself to the inevitable.

"I will do as you wish, *monsieur*," said she, "without further protest." Then after a slight silence, she added: "May I ask you a few questions? What do you think is the cause of Mina's disappearance?"

"I do not know, but Justice will discover."

"You are sure she did not go voluntarily?"

"What? You, who have had her under your care for six months—you dare to ask such a question?" cried Justin, enraged at this insult to his little fiancée.

"I only meant . . . you are sure she loved you?"

"You read her letter. She calls to me for help."

"Then you think she was abducted by force? But, *monsieur*, it is not possible. The walls are high and the windows safely fastened. Mina would have called out."

"There are ladders for every wall, madame, chisels to open windows and gags for a young girl's mouth."

"Have you been into her room?"

"No, madame."

"But that should have been your first step! Come at once!"

"No—please! . . . Do not go into that room, I beg!"

"But how else can you be sure she is not there?"

"This letter . . ."

"But suppose, for some reason, someone had sent you a forged letter. Suppose Mina has not gone but is still in her room."

Justin felt his head reel; the whole thing was so inexplicable to him that this hope, absurd as it was, took hold of him, and so, contrary to Salvator's instructions, he decided to go with Mme Desmarets to the door of the young girl's room. When they got there, the schoolmistress knocked softly while Justin tried to still the beating of his heart. She knocked again, more loudly—then again—but it was in vain. No one replied. She then tried to open the door, but it was locked on the inside. Mme Desmarets wanted to send for a locksmith, but Justin, reverting at the sinister silence to his original despair, remembered Salvator's advice and strongly opposed this.

" Then let us go into the garden and try if we can see into the room through the window," suggested the schoolmistress.

" I am sorry, madame, but no one is to be allowed to go into the garden."

" But, *monsieur*, this is my house ! "

" You are mistaken, madame. When the law once intervenes she is mistress everywhere, and in the name of the law I forbid you to enter the garden ! "

For greater surety, he locked the garden door and put the key in his pocket. Mme Desmarets longed to protest—to send for the police herself and have Justin turned out—but she realized that, gentle by nature, he would not be acting as he was if he had not authority behind him. He was now leaning quietly against the wall.

" How long, pray, are you going to stand sentinel

at that door, may I ask?" demanded the school-mistress.

"Until the people I am expecting arrive."

"And when will that be, pray?"

"Not so soon as I could wish. They have to come from Paris."

"Then you will allow me to leave you for a while?"

Justin bowed assent and Mme Desmarets went back to her room, where she dressed quickly; then, open-ing her window, she watched the Paris road. In about half an hour's time she saw a carriage bowling rapidly along it. It stopped at her door and two men got out; they were Salvator and M. Jackal. They were about to ring when the door was opened by Justin, who had heard the noise of the carriage wheels. Salvator, seeing how white and agitated he was, pressed his hand cordially:

"Courage, my friend! Believe me, there are worse troubles even than yours!"

He was thinking of Carmélite's despair when she came to herself and learned that Colomban was dead.

CHAPTER XXIII
THE DOMICILIARY VISIT

HAVING learned from Salvator that Justin was Mina's fiancé, M. Jackal accorded him a deep bow and asked if anyone had been into the bedroom or the garden.

"No one, sir. Here is the key of the garden door."

"And that of Mlle Mina's room?"

"It is locked from inside."

"Ah!" said M. Jackal, and, taking a pinch of snuff, he added : "Let us see!"

Guided by Justin, he entered the little ante-room between hall and garden, in which were the stairs leading to Mina's bedroom.

"Where is the mistress of the house?" asked he, looking round.

"I am here, sir," replied Mme Desmarets, coming into the room.

"Did you know of Mlle Mina's disappearance before M. Justin told you?" asked M. Jackal.

"No, sir, and I am not sure even yet that she has disappeared!" Mme Desmarets' voice shook with emotion. "I have not yet been into her room!"

"We are going into that room; don't worry," said M. Jackal.

His spectacles on his forehead, he examined Mme Desmarets, as usual, beneath them. Then he shook his head, the spectacles falling into place, while Salvator and Justin waited impatiently for him to continue the examination.

"Won't you come to the drawing-room?" asked Mme Desmarets. "It would be more comfortable than this place."

"Thanks," said M. Jackal, casting another glance round the ante-room, which showed him that he had intuitively chosen a strategic position. "And now, madame, remember the responsibility that rests on a schoolmistress one of whose pupils is missing, and think well before you reply to my questions."

"Oh, sir, I could not feel it more than I do," she replied, drying her eyes. "And as for reflecting before I reply, that is not necessary, as I shall only tell the truth."

" When do your boarders go to bed? "

" At eight in winter, sir."

" And the under-mistresses? "

" At nine."

" Do any wait up after the others? "

" Only one, who gets to bed about eleven or half-past."

" And where does she sleep? "

" On the first floor. But her room looks out on to the dormitory and street, while Mina's looks on to the garden."

" And where is your own room? "

" On the first floor, next the drawing-room, and looking on to the street."

" Then none of your windows look on to the garden? When did you go to sleep last night? "

" About eleven o'clock."

" Ah! " said M. Jackal. " And now let us go over the house. Come with me, M. Salvator. M. Justin, you had better remain here with Mme Desmarets." As they went down the steps, he added : " That woman has nothing to do with it."

" How do you deduce that? "

" From her tears. The guilty tremble on being confronted; they don't cry."

M. Jackal now examined the house, which stood in an angle between the street and a paved, deserted alley. Down this alley M. Jackal darted like a weasel. To the left was the wall of the garden, and above it could be seen the trees. M. Jackal examined the bottom of the wall with deep attention; then looked down the alley, nodding his head.

" A nasty spot at night ! " said he. " These alleys are the very places for elopements and burglaries."

About twenty-five feet further he stooped and picked up a small piece of mortar that had fallen from the wall—then a second—then a third. He examined them a moment and wrapped them carefully in his handkerchief. Then, picking up a bit of broken tile, he threw it over the wall.

" Is that where they got over ? " asked Salvator.

" We'll see. Let us go back."

They found Justin and Mme Desmarets where they had left them.

" Have you learnt anything ? For heaven's sake, tell me ! " cried Justin. " Have you found a clue ? "

" You are a musician, young man, and know the saying : ' Don't outpace the violin.' I am the violin. Follow me but do not rush ahead. The garden key, please ! "

Giving him the key, they went into the corridor, where Justin pointed out Mina's bedroom door.

" Good, good, but one thing at a time. We will take that after."

M. Jackal opened the garden door, but stopped on the threshold, glancing keenly over the ground he meant to examine in detail.

" Good ! Now we must be careful and walk gingerly. Follow me, please, in this order : M. Salvator after me, then M. Justin and Mme Desmarets last. That's it. Now tread in my footsteps."

He then went towards the part of the wall which

he had examined from outside, but instead of cutting straight across to it, he followed the little path that ran along the wall, thus skirting the angle between house and wall. First, however, he threw a glance over his glasses at the window of Mina's room. The shutters were closed.

"Hum!" said he and started for the wall. The path, of yellow gravel, showed nothing out of the common, but, some twenty-five feet from the corner, M. Jackal stopped and, smiling silently, picked up the bit of tile he had thrown over and showing Salvator a mark in the flower-bed, said:

"Here we are!"

All looked where he pointed.

"So you think that is where they took the poor child over the wall?" said Salvator.

"Without a doubt," replied M. Jackal.

"Oh, good heavens! An abduction! From my seminary!" moaned Mme Desmarets.

"Oh, sir, for God's sake, make certain!" cried Justin.

"Certain? Look for yourself."

While poor Justin peered, M. Jackal, feeling that he was on the right track, took another pinch of snuff, examining the ground closely from under his glasses and Mme Desmarets from over them.

"But what do you see there?" asked Justin impatiently.

"These two holes in the ground, with a straight line between, as you can see for yourself."

"Don't you see they are the marks of a ladder?" said Salvator to Justin.

" But that transversal line ? "

" Tell him," said M. Jackal to Salvator.

" That is the last rung of the ladder, pressed an inch into the ground, owing to the dampness of the soil."

" Now we have to find out how many people it needs to drive a ladder thus far into the ground."

" Can't we examine the footprints ? " asked Salvator.

" Oh, they are confused, and besides two of them may have walked in one another's footsteps. We know of several fine fellows who always take that precaution. But it is simple enough." Turning to the schoolmistress, to whom what was being said was so much Sanskrit or Arabic, he asked : " Madame, is there a ladder in this establishment ? "

" The gardener has one. It is probably in the stable. Down there—that little thatched place."

" Don't move. I'll get it myself."

M. Jackal then took a leap of some metre and a half across the numerous traces on the gravel path and in the surrounding beds, to which, however, he refused to pay attention till their turn had come ! He was soon back with the ladder and placed its legs in the two holes.

" Good ! " said he. " There's one piece of evidence already. We probably have the very ladder they used. It is exactly the same size."

" But are not all ladders the same size ? " asked Salvator.

" This is broader than ordinary ladders. The

gardener has an apprentice . . . a son perhaps, eh, Mme Desmarets ? "

" He has a little boy of twelve, sir."

" Ah ! And he gets the boy to help him while teaching him his work, I expect. So he bought a broader ladder so that the boy could use it with him."

" Oh, please, sir, get back to Mina ! " cried Justin.

" We are getting back to her, my friend, but we are going a circular path."

" We are losing time ! "

" My dear sir, in affairs of this sort, time is of no consequence. Either your fiancée has been taken out of France and in that case she is already too far for us to catch up with her ; or her abductor reckons on hiding her in the neighbourhood of Paris, and in that case, we shall know where she is before three days are over."

" Pray God you are right, M. Jackal. But you said you could find out how many people had to do with the abduction."

" I am doing that now." M. Jackal placed the ladder against the wall, about a metre from the place where were the marks in the ground; then he climbed five or six rungs, stopping on each to see how deeply the legs had sunk into the ground. They had sunk at most some three inches. From his place on the ladder, he dominated the garden and saw a man in shirt-sleeves at the threshold of the garden door.

" Hullo, my friend, who are you ? " he cried.

" Pierre, Mme Desmarets' gardener, *monsieur*."

" Mme Desmarets, will you kindly go and see if
that is so and bring him the way we came ourselves ? "

Mme Desmarets went to do as requested.

" I tell you, M. Salvator, that woman had nothing
to do with the abduction," said M. Jackal.

Then as the schoolmistress returned with the
astonished gardener : " Now, my friend Pierre, were
you at work in this garden yesterday ? " enquired
the Chief of Police.

" No, sir. It was Shrove Tuesday."

" And the day before   .   .   ."

" Was the day before Shrove Tuesday, and I
always rest on that day. The day before that, of
course, was Sunday, and   .   .   ."

" So you haven't been at work here for three
days ? "

" Monsieur ! In Shrovetide ? I do not wish to be
damned ! "

" Then for the last three days your ladder has
been in the stable ? "

" My ladder is not in the stable. You are standing on it."

" This is a man of intelligence," said M. Jackal,
" but I will answer for it, he doesn't practise abduction ! And now, my friend," he added to the staring
gardener, " will you kindly come up here beside
me ? "

Pierre, after glancing at Mme Desmarets for con-
firmation of these instructions, did as ordered.

" And now," said M. Jackal to Salvator, " how
deeply have we sunk into the ground ? "

" Not as far as the bottom rung," replied he.

" Get down, my friend," said M. Jackal to the gardener, " and take Mme Desmarets in your arms."

" Sir ! " stammered the lady, while Pierre stared.

" Pick her up in your arms," repeated M. Jackal.

" Please, sir, I wouldn't dare ! " replied the gardener.

" And I forbid you to do anything of the sort ! " cried Mme Desmarets.

M. Jackal leaped down from the ladder.

" Go up to where I was standing,'' said he to the gardener, and when this was done, M. Jackal approached Mme Desmarets, slipped one arm under her shoulders and the other under her knees and lifted her from the ground before she had begun to understand what he was about.

" *Monsieur! Monsieur!* What are you doing ? " she cried.

" Imagine that I am your lover and about to abduct you, madame."

" What an idea ! " cried Pierre from his perch.

" *Monsieur!* " cried the schoolmistress simultaneously.

" It is only an idea—a supposition," M. Jackal explained, and mounted the ladder with the lady in his arms.

" Now it's going into the ground ! " cried Salvator. " But not quite so far as the first rung."

" Put your foot on the second rung."

" That's it ! " cried Salvator, doing so. " Now it is sunk exactly as far as the other."

" Good," said M. Jackal. " Then we will all come down again."

He was the first to descend and set Mme Desmarets on her feet. Drawing the ladder from the soil, he pointed to marks exactly similar to the other marks. " I imagine, M. Justin, that Mme Desmarets is a little heavier than Mlle Mina. I am probably lighter than the man who abducted her. So one compensates for the other."

" Then you conclude? "

" That Mlle Mina was abducted by three men, two of whom carried her up the ladder, while the third held it steady by putting his foot on it. And now we must try and find out who those three men were."

" Oh, I see," said Pierre. " So one of the little missies has been abducted, has she? "

M. Jackal pushed down his glasses to gaze at his ease at the speaker, and after a prolonged scrutiny, he said :

" Mme Desmarets, never dismiss that man. He is a perfect treasure! "

Then to Pierre, he added : " My friend, you may take your ladder back to the stable. We have done with it."

CHAPTER XXIV

THE FOOTPRINTS

WHILST Pierre went off to the stable, M. Jackal, his spectacles once more pushed on to his forehead and his nose buried in snuff, examined the footmarks. He drew a small knife from his pocket, half penknife, half pruning-knife; opened one of its eight or ten blades, and cut a little twig, with which he began to measure the footprints.

"Here are marks from the wall to the window and from the window to the wall, both going and coming," said he. "The abductors were perfectly well informed as to the habits of the household, and did not feel obliged to take many precautions, and yet . . ." He seemed embarrassed. "And yet here are shoes of exactly the same size. Once in the garden, did one man only do the job, the others standing waiting?"

"The shoes were of the same length and breadth," said Salvator, "but they do not appear to be for the same foot."

"Aha! How do you know that?"

"By the nails in the sole which are differently arranged."

"Why, that is true! Every other step one finds a left shoe with the nails placed in a triangle. One of our men is a Freemason."

Salvator flushed slightly, but M. Jackal did not seem to notice—or did not wish to notice!

"Moreover," Salvator continued, "one of the men limped with the right foot. You can see that the sole of that foot is less worn than the other."

"That is true, too. Are you a detective?"

"No," said Salvator, "but 1 am or I have been a sportsman."

"Hush! Here is a third clue. Aha, a singular footstep, bearing no resemblance to the flat feet we have been examining. This foot belonged to a man of the world, an aristocrat, a grand seigneur, or an abbé."

" Grand seigneur, M. Jackal ! "

" And why do you insist on the grand seigneur ? I would just as soon find an abbé mixed up in this affair," was the comment of the Voltairean M. Jackal.

" I am afraid you will have to deprive yourself of that pleasure. We are no longer in the times of M. Gondy, when abbés rode horseback. The man who left this trace was a horseman. Look ! On the heel of that boot you can see the tiny marks of the spurs."

" You are right ! " cried M. Jackal. " Really, M. Salvator, you are nearly as good as a detective ! Now help me to follow the footsteps to the window."

" That will not be difficult," said Salvator, and indeed the marks of shoes and boots took them right to the window.

Justin followed them, intercepting their glances, devouring their words. The poor fellow was like a miser robbed of the treasure which he has gloated over for ten years and, having lost all hope of finding it himself, sees friends, cleverer than himself, track down the thieves. As for Mme Desmarets, she was completely overwhelmed and watched mechanically, haggard of eye and powerless to move.

" Which of you was it who tried to open the room door ? "

" I did, monsieur," they both replied at the same time.

" You found it locked and bolted ? "

" It was Mina's custom to lock herself in every night," explained Mme Desmarets.

20

" Then they entered by the window," said M. Jackal.

" Hm ! The shutters seem to me firmly fastened," put in Salvator.

" Oh, it isn't difficult to swing a shutter to," said M. Jackal, and tried to push them open. " Aha ! " he cried, " they also are fastened inside and barred as well."

" That is a little more difficult, eh ? " smiled Salvator.

" You are sure the door was locked and bolted from within ? "

" The door was fastened to its frame both at the lock and above it," replied Justin.

" Ho ! The shutters barred and the door bolted from within ! They must have been a clever lot ! "

He shook the shutters again. " I only know two men who could have got out of a bolted door or a shuttered window and if one of them weren't at Brest and the other at Toulon, I should say it was either Robichon or Gibassier who had managed this affair."

" Then there is a way of getting out of a bolted door ? " asked Salvator.

" My dear fellow, there is a way of getting out when there is no door at all, as was proved by one of my predecessors, M. Latude ; but luckily, it is not a thing everyone can accomplish."

He took snuff again and said : " And now let us go back into the house."

Without bothering about the rules of courtesy, he went in first, and stopping at Mina's door, he added :

" I suppose you have a second key ? "

"What is the good when the door is bolted?" began Mme Desmarets, but his testy voice sent her to fetch the key.

M. Jackal placed it in the keyhole and tried to turn it.

"The other key is inside," he said, "but it is not double locked." As if to himself, he added : "That proves that the door was locked from outside."

"But the bolt!" cried Salvator. "How could the abductors bolt it from outside?"

"I'll show you in a minute, young man. It's an invention of Gibassier, which got him off with five years at the galleys instead of ten; it was a second offence, but they could not prove burglary. Fetch a locksmith."

The locksmith at last came with his tools, and when he opened the door, everyone wanted to rush into the room, but M. Jackal stopped them, with widespread arms.

"Gently! Gently! The first glance is everything. Our quest is hanging by a thread!"

He smiled as he spoke as if the words contained a hidden joke. Then, entering alone, he examined the keyhole and bolt. His first glance not being satisfactory, he took off his glasses, the one thing that prevented his eyes assuming lynx-like sharpness; then a smile of triumph lit up his face and with finger and thumb he seized an almost invisible object and raised it triumphantly in the air.

"I told you our quest hung by a thread! Well, here is the thread!"

The onlookers then saw a fragment of silk thread,

some fifteen centimetres long, caught between the iron of the bolt and the wood of the door.

" Is that how they shut the door ? " asked Salvator.

" Yes, only the thread was some half metre long. This bit broke off and they did not bother about it."

" Well," said the locksmith, open-eyed, " I thought I knew all the ways of opening and closing doors, but I seem a mere baby at the work ! "

" You see how it is done," said M. Jackal. " You slip a doubled thread round the knob of the bolt, silk being better than cotton because it is stronger. The thread must be long enough for both ends to be outside when the door is shut. You then shut your door and pull at your thread. The thread pulls the bolt and the thing is done. Only sometimes the thread breaks, or tangles, or remains in the bolt, and then M. Jackal comes along and says : ' If that devil of a Gibassier was not rowing in the galleys, I should wager it was he ! ' "

" M. Jackal ! " cried Justin, who was not at all interested in this explanation, however important it might be from the scientific point of view, " may we not go into the room ? "

" Yes, now you may," said the detective, and they all surged in. " Aha ! Footsteps again, from the door to the bed and from the bed to the window." Then with a glance at the bed and the table that stood beside it, he added : " She went to bed and read some letters."

" My letters ! " cried Justin. " Dear little Mina ! "

" Then she put out her candle. All was well so far."

" How do you know that she put out the candle herself ? " asked Salvator.

" Why, look ! The wick has bent over with the puff of breath, and that puff was given, to judge by the curve, from the bed. Now about those footsteps, M. Salvator. Just cast your hunter's eye over them."

" Oh," said Salvator, bending down. " Here is something new. A woman's foot."

" What did I tell you ? Find the woman ! Well, was I not right ? Yes, that is the footstep of a reso-lute woman, treading not only on the great toe, but planting down the flat of the sole and the heel."

" We may add that the woman is a coquette," said Salvator, " for she kept to the paths in the garden, for fear of soiling her little boots; you see the mark of yellow gravel but no sign of mud."

" M. Salvator, what a pity you chose your present profession ! I'll make you my aide-de-camp when-ever you like. Now don't move ! "

He went out into the garden, along the gravel path, to the foot of the ladder, and returned.

" That's it ! The woman came from the house, walked along the path, stopped at the foot of the ladder, and returned the same way that she came. And now I'll tell you how the thing was done; I could not be more certain if I had seen it happen."

All turned to listen.

" Mlle Mina came in at the usual hour, sad, but calm, and went to bed. The bed is just used, as you see. She read certain letters and cried over them. Here is her handkerchief, all rolled up into a ball, like the handkerchief of a person who has been crying." Justin seized it and pressed it to his lips.

" She went to bed," continued M. Jackal, " she sat up reading and she wept, but as one cannot keep on doing that, she felt sleepy and blew out the candle. Did she sleep or not? It does not matter. But, once the candle was out, someone knocked at the door."

" Who, sir? " asked Mme Desmarets.

" Ah, you want to know more than I know myself, my dear madame. Perhaps I may tell you later. Anyway, it was the woman . . ."

" The woman? " murmured Mme Desmarets.

" Under the name of woman I mean not the individual but the sex. The woman knocked at the door; Mina rose and opened it."

" Do you think Mina would open the door without knowing who it was? " asked Mme Desmarets.

" Who says she did not know? "

" She would not have opened to an enemy—or a stranger."

" No. But suppose it was a friend? Do I need to tell you, Mme Desmarets, that at school we may have friends who are dangerous enemies? She opened the door to her friend. Behind that friend was the young man in riding boots and spurs, the man whose bootnails are set in a triangle. . . . How did little Mina go to bed? "

" I don't understand! "

" I mean what did she wear at night? "

" In the winter time, a vest and long nightgown."

" Good. They stuffed a handkerchief into her mouth, and wrapped her in a shawl or coverlet.

Here are her shoes and stockings and on that chair are her petticoat and gown. They then carried her off through the window."

He pointed to a tear in the curtain, where the hand which had clung desperately to it had torn away a fragment.

" She was then passed over the wall, after which the accomplice who remained here took back the ladder to the stable. Then she came in, shut the window and shutters, slipped the silk thread round the knob of the bolt, pulled the door to, drew out the thread and went tranquilly to her own bed."

" But she must have been seen leaving or returning to the dormitory ! "

" Have you no other boarders with their own room, like Mlle Mina ? "

" Only one."

" Then she is the one. My dear M. Salvator, we have found the woman ! "

" You think it is Mina's friend who was the cause of this abduction ? "

" I said accomplice, not cause, and I don't think . . . I state facts."

" Suzanne ! " cried Mme Desmarets.

" Believe me, madame," said Justin, " that is the truth."

" But, sir, how can you think such a thing ? "

" I felt an antipathy for that girl the first time I saw her. It was like a presentiment ! Directly this gentleman spoke of a woman I thought of Mlle Suzanne; I did not dare accuse her, but I suspected

her. In the name of heaven, M. Jackal, have her in
and confound her ! ''

'' No, no,'' replied the detective, '' let us go to
her. Madame, will you kindly take us to her room ? ''

Mme Desmarets seemed to have lost all power of
resistance to M. Jackal, and submissively led the
way. Suzanne's room was on the first floor, at the
end of the passage.

'' Knock, madame,'' whispered M. Jackal.

Mme Desmarets did so, but there was no reply.

'' She may be in the recreation ground. It is
eleven o'clock,'' said the schoolmistress. '' Shall I
call her ? ''

'' No. First, let us see her room.''

'' The key is not in the door.''

'' But you have a second key to all these rooms.
Go and get it and not a word to anyone you may
happen to meet ! ''

When the key was fetched and the door opened,
he said :

'' Wait for me in the passage. Only Mme Desmarets is to come in.'' Then, when he was in the
room, he asked : '' Where does she keep her
shoes ? '' On being shown, he took a little pair of
laced shoes from the shelf and looked at the soles;
they still showed traces of the yellow gravel. '' Do
the boarders walk in the garden ? '' he asked.

'' No, *monsieur*. As it looks on to a side alley,
they are strictly forbidden to go there.''

'' Good,'' said M. Jackal, putting back the shoes.
'' I know what I wanted to know. And now, where
is Mlle Suzanne ? ''

" Probably in the recreation ground."

" And what room overlooks that ? "

" The drawing-room."

" Then let us go to the drawing-room."

He then left the room, leaving Mme Desmarets the task of relocking the door.

" Well ? " cried Salvator and Justin together.

" Well," replied M. Jackal, taking a colossal pinch of snuff, " I think we have found the woman ! "

CHAPTER XXV

THE FAMILY OF VALGENEUSE

THE drawing-room looked on to the recreation ground, where all the pupils were taking advantage of the sunlight, wan as it was, to display their flower-like grace.   One girl, taller than the rest, was walking apart.   Through the window, M. Jackal took in the scene at a glance, and the solitary figure arrested his attention.

" Is not that Mlle Suzanne under the lime trees ? " he asked.   " Will you kindly beckon to her to come in ? "

" I do not know whether she will come."

" You don't know whether she will come ?   Why not ? "

" She is very proud."

" Signal to her, please, madame, and if she does not come, I will go to her."

Mme Desmarets went out on to the steps and waved her hand to Suzanne, who did not appear to see the gesture.

" If she's blind, she is not deaf ! " said M. Jackal.
" Call her, please."

" Suzanne ! " called Mme Desmarets, and Suzanne
turned her head. " Will you kindly come this way.
There is someone here who wants to speak to you."

Mlle Suzanne then approached, but very slowly
and with a disdainful air. This gave M. Jackal and
Salvator time to examine her from behind the curtains. Justin, of course, already knew her.

" It's strange," said Salvator, " but I fancy I know
that face."

" What do you think of it ? " asked M. Jackal,
who was watching with no less attention from over
his glasses.

" I would swear that girl has an evil nature."

" Swearing is wrong," said M. Jackal. " But for
all that, I agree with you. Her mouth is too thin
and close, her eyes, fine but hard. Besides, look
how wicked she looks under the stress of anxiety ! "

" You were asking for me, madame ? " said
Suzanne, as she came up the steps. " I fancy you
did me the honour to call me ? " she added with an
intonation which made the words mean " You did
yourself the honour."

" Yes, my child. There is someone here who
wishes to speak to you."

Suzanne, passing in front of the schoolmistress,
entered the room. When she saw Justin with two
strangers she could not suppress a slight start,
though her expression remained inscrutable. Mme
Desmarets was visibly embarrassed by the angry look
in her pupil's eye, but indicating M. Jackal, she said

quietly : "This gentleman wishes to ask you a few questions."

"Indeed? But I do not know this gentleman!"

"He represents the authorities," said Mme Desmarets, quickly.

"The authorities? What have they to do with me?"

"Please, please, Mlle Suzanne! It is about Mina."

"We want some information about Mlle Mina," interposed M. Jackal.

"I can tell you no more than this gentleman," said Suzanne, nodding haughtily towards Justin. "I mean—that he found her in a cornfield one evening, took her home and was about to marry her when news came from Rouen of some mysterious and unknown father that stopped the marriage . . ."

M. Jackal was watching the girl, whom he judged destined to every evil passion, with a curiosity that was fast turning to admiration.

"No, mademoiselle," said he. "That is not what we wanted to know."

"Why not question Mina herself? I have told you all I know."

"Unfortunately we cannot do that because Mlle Mina has been abducted."

"Has she really? Poor Mina!" replied the young girl in a tone of mockery which forced an angry cry from Justin and caused Salvator to frown. M. Jackal, also visibly jarred by the answer, made them a sign to control themselves.

"I thought that as you were her intimate friend,

you might have been able to tell us something about her disappearance."

"You are quite wrong, sir. I can tell you nothing of my *friend's* disappearance, for I know nothing. Indeed, I did not even know she had disappeared."

"But, mademoiselle, think of the despair of her fiancé, and the grief of his mother and sister, who looked on Mlle Mina as one of the family."

"Oh, of course, I sympathize deeply, but what can I do? I parted with her at half-past eight last night, when she went to her room, and I have not seen her since. And now, if that is all you want of me . . ."

"This scornful tone comes very ill from a young lady of your age, mademoiselle," said M. Jackal sternly, opening his coat and showing his scarf of office, "especially when assumed towards the representative of the law."

"Why did you not say at once that you were a commissioner of police?" insolently retorted Suzanne. "I would then have answered with all the consideration to which the force is, of course, entitled!"

"Let us waste no more time, please. Kindly tell me your full name, means and station."

"Oh, so this is an official interrogatory?"

"It is."

"My name is Suzanne de Valgeneuse, and I am the daughter of the Marquis Denis René de Valgeneuse, peer of France, and the niece of M. Louis Clément de Valgeneuse, the Cardinal, sister of Count Lorédan de Valgeneuse, Lieutenant in the

Guards. I am heiress to some half million francs a year.—I think that answers your question, monsieur."

This reply, spoken with royal disdain, had a very different effect on the three men. Justin shuddered, understanding how impotent was he, the humble schoolmaster of the obscure quarter of St. Jacques, against this family of haughty aristocrats, who had so deeply injured him.

" Suzanne de Valgeneuse ? " cried Salvator, as he stared at the girl, with a surprised and menacing gaze.

" Mlle Suzanne de Valgeneuse ! " repeated M. Jackal, recoiling as if he had trodden inadvertently upon a snake. Then, slowly buttoning his coat, he seemed to reflect, the result of his reflections being that he bowed respectfully and added : " Pardon, mademoiselle ; I did not know."

" I knew you did not, but, now you do know, see that you do not forget."

" I am extremely sorry that I have displeased you. It was merely due to the distasteful duties my work imposes on me."

" I take it you have no more to say ? "

" Nothing, mademoiselle, except to repeat that I am extremely sorry I caused you inconvenience, and hope sincerely that you will not harbour resentment."

" I shall do my best to forget you, monsieur," said Suzanne.

And without a further glance she marched to the

door, passing M. Jackal, who drew back with another deep bow.

Justin longed to strangle her, for it was more obvious than ever that she was actively concerned in the abduction of his sweetheart, but Salvator went up to him and seized his hand.

" Patience ! " he said. " Make no sign ! "

" But all is lost ! "

" Nothing is lost when 1 tell you to hope ! I know these Valgeneuses, and I tell you nothing is lost. But do not forget the name, Gibassier."

Then turning to M. Jackal : " I think we can do no more here, *monsieur?* "

" Well . . . er . . . er . . ." stammered M. Jackal, embarrassed and putting his spectacles straight over his eyes : " I really do not think we can learn more than we already know."

" We know enough ! " replied Salvator.

M. Jackal pretended not to hear. He approached instead the mistress of the house, who was over-whelmed at the turn the affair had taken.

" Madame, I have the honour to offer my re-spectful salutations. In a lower tone, he added : " Assure Mlle Suzanne that I was obliged to act as I did, and that I beg her to regard my visit as if it had not taken place. You understand ? "

He then left, signing to Salvator and Justin to follow him. Salvator, as we have seen, hoping, no doubt, to re-unite Justin and Mina without the aid of the Chief of Police, showed little concern at this metamorphosis, but it was not so with Justin, who but a moment ago had been told by M. Jackal him-

self that they were on the track of his poor little
sweetheart. He spoke out.

" Pardon, M. Jackal, but I think that, after saying
' Find the woman,' you told us you had found the
woman, and then added that she was Mlle Suzanne."

" You must be mistaken, M. Justin."

" I appeal to M. Salvator."

M. Jackal threw a glance at Salvator as if to say,
" You understand. Do help me ! " Salvator did
understand, but he did not approve and so he was
inexorable.

" My dear M. Jackal," said he, " I must confess
that, unless my memory is entirely at fault, you did
say, word for word, what M. Justin asserts, namely,
that Mlle Suzanne was an accomplice in the abduction."

" Pooh ! It's a mistake to say anything till it is
proved. If I said accomplice, I was wrong."

" But you were the first who accused her ! " cried
Justin.

" Accused is not the word ; I may have suspected
her, but . . ."

" Then do you suspect her no longer ? "

" Suspect her ? Dear innocent child ! God forbid ! "

" What about those thin lips, that hard eye, that
evil aspect ? " asked Salvator drily.

" Oh, she was too far off to see properly. Of
course, when I saw her close to. Then I saw her
charming lips, beautiful eyes and most gracious
expression of countenance.—But you had better
come and see me, M. Justin. Say, at eight

o'clock to-night, at the prefecture of police. I may have some good news for you. I will put all the men I can on to the job."

" Go back home, Justin," said Salvator, with a warm pressure of the hand, " and I will undertake to tell you, within twenty-four hours, what you have to hope . . . or to fear ! " Then, as M. Jackal was about to close the door of the carriage on himself, he cried : " What are you doing ? You brought me here and you must take me back again. Besides," he added, getting into the carriage, " I want to talk to you about those Valgeneuses."

" Back to Paris ! " ordered M. Jackal, though he would evidently have preferred to travel alone. The carriage departed swiftly, and Justin slowly returned home, a prey to despair, for he placed little reliance in Salvator's promise.

CHAPTER XXVI

OF WHICH THE READER IS BEGGED NOT TO SKIP A LINE

M. JACKAL ensconced himself in one corner of the carriage as did Salvator in the other. In spite of what he said when he got in, Salvator seemed disinclined to interrupt M. Jackal's meditations; yet he kept an eye upon him. M. Jackal had to meet that sarcastic glance every time he looked up and at last seemed to decide that it would be less embarrassing to enter into explanations. He alternately raised and lowered his glasses, fortified himself with several pinches of snuff and eventually turned to the commissionaire.

" Did not you say that you wanted to make some

reference to the Valgeneuse family, my dear M. Salvator?"

"I wanted to ask you what made you change your mind so quickly with regard to that little . . . shall I say the word, M. Jackal?"

"Hsh! We are alone now, we two, and you are a sensible man and not in love. . . ."

"How do you know that?"

"Not in love with the girl who has been abducted, at any rate. So you can look at the matter dispassionately and with understanding."

"I perfectly understood, M. Jackal."

"Ah, good, good. . . . Er. . . . What did you understand?"

"That you were frightened."

"I should think I was!" sighed M. Jackal, with at least the courage of his own cowardice. "When that girl told me her name, my blood ran cold!"

"Yet I thought the first article in the Code was: 'All men are equal.'"

"My dear M. Salvator, they put that in all Codes, just as they say in royal manifestos: 'Charles, by the grace of God, king of France and Navarre.' Louis XVI used the same formula and they cut off his head. Can you detect the 'grace of God' in the event that took place on the *place de la Révolution* at four o'clock in the afternoon of the twenty-first of January, 1793?"

"So that, simply for having accused that girl—whom you judge to be capable, some day, of a really great crime—of having been the accomplice of an abduction, you see yourself disgraced, imprisoned

21

. . . who knows? Perhaps strangled in prison as were Toussaint Louverture and Pichegru?"

"Please do not joke. On my word of honour, I did see myself . . . just as you say."

"These Valgeneuses must be a powerful family?"

"Oh, my dear sir, the marquis has the king's ear, the Cardinal the Pope's ear and the Lieutenant . . ."

"The Devil's ear!" concluded Salvator, drily. "I see. Besides, he is affiliated, is he not, with a certain powerful Society?"

M. Jackal cast a strange glance at him.

"I thought so! Then the Marquis is one of the protectors of St-Acheul, if I am not mistaken, and carried one of the supports of the daïs at the last procession?"

M. Jackal nodded.

"Strange! And I thought the Jesuits were a mere delusion of the *Constitutionel!*"[1]

At this remark M. Jackal merely grunted, but the grunt seemed to imply that he thought the poor dear youth naïf to a degree.

"So you believed it would be dangerous to annoy these people, eh, M. Jackal?"

"You know the story of the Pot of Earthenware and the Pot of Iron?"

"But surely the Head of the family died some five or six years ago," continued Salvator. "Had he no children that the entire fortune passed to his brother?"

"Well, he was never married."

[1] A newspaper which bitterly attacked the Jesuits.—EDITOR'S NOTE.

"Of course, I remember. Was there not some story of a natural son, who was to be adopted or recognized but who was not?"

"How do you know that?" asked M. Jackal, casting a sidelong glance at him.

"Oh, well, people of my class get to know all sorts of things! I have taken letters to a certain M. Conrad de Valgeneuse who lived in the rue du Bac; why, in the very same house in which the Marquis lives nowadays."

"Yes, yes," said M. Jackal. "That is so."

"I suppose it's a mysterious story, eh?"

"Not for everyone," replied M. Jackal, looking very pleased with himself.

"I see," said Salvator, laughing; "not for those who have found ' the woman,' eh?"

"Oddly enough," confessed the police officer, "there was no woman in that case."

"Indeed? Well, you see, I knew the young man when he was rich and carefree and so I should rather like to know what became of him."

"Naturally and, as it happens, I can tell you all about it—or nearly all."

"Nearly all? That sounds like a mental reservation. Have *you* ever carried a support of the daïs in the procession of St. Acheul?"

"Good Heavens, no!" cried M. Jackal. "I am afraid of the Jesuits, and for fear of their revenge, extend them a certain measure of protection and even of obedience, but I do not like them! I only said ' nearly all,' because, you know, we cannot always tell all we know, we gentlemen of the police."

"Perhaps even, there may be cases in which you do not know quite everything?" suggested Salvator with the sarcastic smile that was characteristic of him.

"I will tell you what I do know," said M. Jackal, looking at him over the top of his glasses. "Then YOU can tell ME what I do not know!"

"It's a bargain."

"Then here you are! The Head of the family, the Marquis Charles-Emanuel de Valgeneuse, peer of France and owner of an immense fortune that he inherited from an Uncle on the maternal side, was never married, but there was a fine young fellow known simply as M. Conrad whom the friends of the family, and finally even strangers, used to call M. Conrad de Valgeneuse."

"Was not that his name?"

"Not altogether, but though he was an illegitimate child, the Marquis saw everything through his eyes."

"But if he loved his son to that extent, why did he leave all his money to his brother, nephew and niece, leaving the boy to die in poverty?"

"Simply because his father loved him too well —so well that his very love was the cause of the boy's ruin. There are two ways of providing for an illegitimate child; the first is to declare openly that one is the father from the moment of registering its birth or if that cannot be done, by signing a simple Act of Recognition before a notary. But, in that case, though you can give the child your name you can only leave it one-fifth of your fortune. The other way is to wait till you are fifty years old and then send for a notary and adopt the child, but the Law will not allow you to adopt it till you are fifty. You can then give the child not only your name but your entire fortune. M. de Valgeneuse preferred this method and consequently he sent for his notary on his fiftieth birthday and shut himself up in his study with him to prepare the Act of Adoption. At the very moment when he took up the pen to sign it, he was struck down by apoplexy."

" At the moment of taking up the pen—or of laying it down after having signed the document?" asked Salvator.

This time M. Jackal took off his spectacles altogether and looked Salvator full in the eyes.

" If you know that, M. Salvator, you know more than I do, for that was the question; had he or had he not signed? The Marquis himself could not tell us for, though he lived for three days more he never regained consciousness."

" Strictly between ourselves, M. Jackal, which do you think was the case?"

" I think," replied M. Jackal, evading the question, " that the family were somewhat hard on poor M. Conrad."

" Hard? Bah! If that Act was not signed—nay, if the notary declared that it was not—why should they trouble about the fellow?"

" But everyone knew that he was the son of the Marquis Emanuel," ventured M. Jackal.

" Yes, but if they admitted it they would have to give the fellow at least a fifth part of the fortune and even that was something like two millions. Surely it was better to inherit everything . . . the seat in the House of Lords, the title, and the fortune and turn the rascal out. That is what they did, is it not? They just packed him off?"

" He went with the utmost dignity, as a matter of fact, leaving his horses and carriages in the stables, his money in the bureau, and taking with him— even his enemies admit that—merely two thousand francs that he felt was his own as he had gained the sum the previous night at écarté."

" A young fellow used to spending the sums M. Conrad must have spent would not be able to make two thousand francs go far."

" There you are wrong, my dear sir. We keep an eye on these penniless young scions of good family. He lived for fifteen months on that two thousand francs, trying to earn his own living in every possible way, as music master, dancing master, teacher of English and German—for he was a very clever youth—but nothing succeeded with him. He could not get employment of any sort and so one day, seeing no honest means of livelihood, he decided to end things, bought a pistol off Lepage; it was recognized by the shopman; took a last turn in the Bois, said a prayer in the Church of St. Roch and returning to his modest room . . ."

" Yes? What then?" asked Salvator.

" Why, then he did as Colomban and Carmélite did; wrote a long letter. Not to his friends, for he had none since his ruin, but to the Police Inspector of the District; in that letter he told of all his struggles and his intention of committing suicide. Then he got into bed, read the few pages of the 'Nouvelle Heloïse ' on suicide and blew out his brains."

" Really ?   You are a perfect newsbag."

" Suicides are my speciality and I drew up the *procés-verbal.*"

" Then he owes the last consideration ever shown him and the declaration of his death to you ? "

" It was not difficult to prove the death.   Both barrels had been discharged and half the face blown to pieces, the rest of it being badly burnt.   Proof of death depended on the letter more than on recognition of the body which was impossible under the circumstances."

" I presume the Valgeneuses were informed of the catastrophe ? "

" I told them myself, showing them a copy of the *procés-verbal.*"

" Were they much affected ? "

" Oh, profoundly. . . . Pleasurably, of course."

" I see.   They were uneasy while he remained alive."

" Yes.   They asked me to see to everything with the utmost care and gave me a sum of five hundred francs to do the thing well."

" Generous relatives ! " said Salvator.

" And asked me to see the body properly buried.   I went myself with the remains to *Père Lachaise* and saw the coffin sunk in the ground.   I had the word ' Conrad ' engraved on the tombstone and I then visited the Marquis to tell him he might rest easy as he would not see his nephew again till the Day of Resurrection."

" And in that belief the family are enjoying tran-
quillity of mind."

" Why not ? What have they to fear ? "

" Well, strange things do sometimes happen. But
here we are at Bas-Meudon. Will you kindly stop
the carriage ? " M. Jackal pulled the cord, the carriage stopped and Salvator got down.

" Pardon," said M. Jackal, " but you did not
entirely answer my question."

" Which question ? "

" As to what is to be feared about Conrad."

" Ah ! Well, it might happen, M. Jackal, that
Conrad is not dead, in which case one would not have
to wait for the Day of Resurrection for a meeting between him and the Marquis of Valgeneuse. Good-
bye, my dear M. Jackal."

Shutting the carriage door, Salvator left the detective so astonished that he had himself to bid the
coachman drive to the rue de Jérusalem.

CHAPTER XXVII

M. GÉRARD REGRETS HIS CONFESSION

WHILE M. Jackal was taking copious pinches of
snuff to try and clear his mind after the enigma that
Salvator had presented to him, our hero went back to
the house of Death to rejoin Jean Davy. Dominique
had started for Penhoël an hour ago with the body of
Colomban, and poor Carmélite was just awakening
to the consciousness of the terrible news which her
three faithful friends were gently breaking to her.

Ludovic, for his part, having left rigorous instructions and promised to return next day, set out for his own home in the rue Notre-Dame-des-Champs. His head heavy with want of sleep, he had decided to walk and he was passing through Vanvres when he saw some fifty people kneeling outside M. Gérard's house, praying that a miracle might restore him to life and health.

" Is he dead? " asked Ludovic, remembering that Dominique had been sent for.

" No, but the Curé is administering extreme unction."

" How old is he? " asked Ludovic.

" About fifty, sir."

" Only fifty? That's young to die, especially for one so regretted as he will be. Could I see him? I am a doctor."

" From Paris, sir? Oh, please go up at once! "

In the sick room, Ludovic found two men. Going up to one of them he said :

" I beg your pardon, but are you not M. Pilloy? "

" Who told you my name, young man? " asked the doctor, a man of twice Ludovic's age, with heavy grey moustaches.

" I heard it coupled with such high praise, sir. I should not have ventured to come in but the good people outside practically insisted on my doing so. I do hope you will forgive me."

" Nothing to forgive, young man. Two heads are better than one. But I am afraid, in this case, all the consultations in the world will prove of no avail. He is done for! "

Low as was the doctor's tone, the invalid heard it and gave a lamentable sigh.

"Hush!" said Ludovic. "Hearing is the last sense to leave us and he heard you. What is the matter with him?"

"The usual thing," shrugged Pilloy.

Ludovic smiled. He knew he was dealing with a disciple of Broussais who was applying his master's doctrines inexpertly.

"You mean gastritis?"

"Of course. Impossible to doubt it. Look for yourself."

Ludovic looked at the yellow skin and listened to the rattle of the breath. Then he examined the eye, and was surprised at its vitality. The face was that of a dying man, but the eyes gave signs of unexpected life.

"Show me your tongue," he said.

It was whiteish-yellow and thick, but it was not pointed nor had it the red edges of gastric tongues. Doubtful before, Ludovic now felt certain of his facts; his next act was to place his hand on the patient's chest and press slowly but heavily. Though his breathing seemed more difficult under the pressure, M. Gérard gave no sign of pain. Ludovic smiled. This was not gastritis; it was evident the patient had been treated for the wrong complaint. But what was his malady? Ludovic picked up the handkerchief lying by the patient's hand and saw on it traces of blood. Once more he uncovered the emaciated chest and this time he laid his ear upon it, to the stupefaction of the older surgeon who was unacquainted with this new mode of auscultation. Ludovic turned to M. Pilloy almost with an air of triumph and asked how long the malady had lasted. When the surgeon had replied to all his questions, and had recounted the origin of the illness, namely the immersion in the lake for the purpose of rescuing a child, Ludovic said gravely:

" Many thanks for your courtesy, sir. I now know what I wanted to know, and can diagnose the case."

" That was not difficult. I told you it was gastritis."

" Yes, but I differ from you. Shall we go into the next room? I fear we are tiring the invalid."

" Do not go! Please, *monsieur!*" cried M. Gérard, collecting all his energies to make this appeal.

" I am not going, my friend," replied M. Pilloy, who thought the words were addressed to him. " I promised not to leave you and I shall keep my word."

As the two doctors were leaving the room, they met the nurse coming back to it and Ludovic said to her, earnestly:

" We shall be back in five minutes. No matter what the patient asks for, give him nothing whatever."

Marianne turned to M. Pilloy in surprise and the old doctor shrugged.

" *Monsieur* thinks he will be able to cure our patient," he said banteringly, and looked to see Ludovic deny it, but to his great surprise, Ludovic did not reply. He simply stood aside to let the older man precede him into the next room.

" Will you kindly tell me why you have brought me here ? " demanded M. Pilloy.

" Because a discussion would have tired the patient."

" But, in any case, the man is at death's door ! "

" I venture to differ, sir. I think the illness is due to a different cause from that you assign to it."

" You say that M. Gérard . . ."

" Is not suffering from gastritis, but from pneumonia," said Ludovic, coldly.

" You call that pneumonia ? "

" Certainly."

" And you say you could save him ? "

" I cannot be sure, but I hope so. That is, if you give me permission to treat one of your patients."

" You ask permission to save my best friend ? God grant you can do it ! For my part, I doubt if the poor fellow will see to-morrow's sun."

" I will do my best. What treatment have you pursued so far ? "

" I've bled him twice and applied leeches to the stomach and kept him on a thin diet."

Ludovic smiled; the treatment amused him; but before he could reply, several of the waiting peasants pushed into the room.

" Is he better ? " they cried. " Can you save him ? "

The old doctor thought they were addressing him, but if tides are uncertain and women changeable, there is one thing more mutable still and that is the opinion of a crowd. One of the intruders said roughly :

" We weren't talking to you ! "

Then, turning to Ludovic: " Well, how do you find him ? No hope, eh ? "

" While there is life there is always hope," replied Ludovic. " Have confidence, not in medicine but in nature. He is not dead yet and I shall do my best to save him."

On hearing this the listeners broke into such noisy demonstrations of joy that Marianne opened the door of the sick room.

" What is the matter ? " groaned the invalid. " Can't they let me die in peace ? "

" Oh, *monsieur*," cried the woman. " It's not a question of dying any longer."

" What ? I shall not die ? "

The reaction of feeling caused the patient to fall back on his pillow.

" He is dying ! " cried the nurse.

Ludovic seized the sick man's pulse.

" It's nothing," he said. " Only syncope. Have this prescription made up at once. I must get back to Paris, but give him a half teaspoonful of this every half-hour and I will come back in three hours' time to see how he is."

He then took his departure.

M. Pilloy also left, but chagrin and curiosity to see the effect of Ludovic's potion brought him back in two hours and a half. When he took his place at the bedside, however, the invalid looked on him with a certain repugnance, and when he tried to question the sick man he got no reply. He then turned to the nurse.

"Well, Marianne, how are we going on?"

"Very badly, sir. I gave the poor gentleman the medicine and it made him sick."

"Sick? . . . Well, I am glad of one thing. If it kills him, the responsibility will not rest on my shoulders!"

Half an hour later, Ludovic entered the room. He came in just as M. Pilloy, seeing the invalid instantly bring up the half-spoonful of medicine that he had just taken, cried pitilessly:

"That settles it. He is a dead man!"

Taking no notice, Ludovic, after looking attentively at the patient, felt his pulse. Then, lifting his head with an expression of satisfaction, he said:

"Good! His pulse is stronger."

"And so you think him better? My dear young man, he has been vomiting!"

"Good. That medicine I gave him was an emetic. If he has been vomiting, he is saved."

"You mean to say you answer for his recovery?"

"I will answer for it, monsieur, with my head."

The old doctor seized his hat and left the room, like a mathematician whom someone has tried to convince that two and two make five. Ludovic, however, wrote another prescription and gave it to the nurse. "I have taken over the responsibility of this case, nurse," said he. "You know what that means? See that my instructions are executed to the letter and take no orders from anyone else, and we shall save M. Gérard."

The invalid gave a joyful exclamation, and, seizing the young doctor's hand, raised it to his lips before Ludovic could stop him. . . . Then starting violently, his face took an expression of sudden and absolute terror.

Falling back, appalled, on his pillows, " The monk ! " he cried. " The monk ! "

FINIS

Printed in Great Britain by Ebenezer Baylis & Son, Ltd., The Trinity Press, Worcester.

THE
INTERNATIONAL LIBRARY
Edited by F. L. LAWSON-JOHNSTON, B.A.

Crown 8vo.   Dark Blue Embossed Cloth.   Gold design.
With Frontispieces and Coloured Jackets.   **2s. 6d. net.**

ANTON CHEKHOV   The Grasshopper.
                          The Shooting Party.
Translated and with Introductions by A. E. Chamot.
GUY DE MAUPASSANT   Selected Stories.
Translated by J. Lewis May. Introduction by Holbrook Jackson.
GIOVANNI BOCCACCIO   The Decameron.
ALESSANDRO MANZONI   The Betrothed.
With an Introduction by Rafael Sabatini.
ALEXANDRE DUMAS   The Prussian Terror,
                          Love and Liberty,
                          The Neapolitan Lovers
Translated and with Introductions by R. S. Garnett.
EUGENE SUE   The Mysteries of Paris
FORTUNE DU BOISGOBEY   The Convict Colonel.
                          The Angel of the
                          Chimes.
BERNARDIN DE ST. PIERRE Paul and Virginia.
With a Memoir of the Author by Sarah Jones.
ALFRED DE VIGNY   The Spider and the Fly
Translated by Madge Pemberton.
BENJAMIN CONSTANT   Adolphe.
Translated and with an Introduction by J. Lewis May.
DIMITRY GREGOROVITSH   The Fishermen.
Translated and with an Introduction by Dr. A. S. Rappoport.
RENE MILAN   The Undying Race.
Translated by Henry Havelock, with a Preface by the Author.
CERVANTES, and Others Little Novels of Spain.
Edited and with an Introduction by F. L. Lawson-Johnston.
MARGARET, QUEEN OF
NAVARRE   The Heptameron.
MENDOZA and Others   Picaresque Tales from
                          the Spanish.
Edited and with an Introduction by F. L. Lawson-Johnston.

LONDON : STANLEY PAUL & Co., LTD., 8 Endsleigh Gardens, W.C.1.

www.ingramcontent.com/pod-product-compliance
Lightning Source LLC
Chambersburg PA
CBHW050549260626
47157CB00002B/486